The Shuttered Room and  dows opening onto the we Lovecraft world. These ta Lovecraft's working life – f Arkham-Dunwich horrors the Cthulhu Mythos.

The Shuttered Room and other tales of horror are the last, rare stories of a master craftsman of terror, left unfinished on Lovecraft's death and completed by his friend and fellow fantasy writer, August Derleth.

H. P. Lovecraft and August Derleth

The Shuttered Room

and other tales of horror

A Panther Book

Granada Publishing Limited
Published in 1970 by Panther Books Ltd
Park Street, St. Albans, Hertfordshire
Reprinted 1973

These stories appeared as part of the compilation
The Shadow out of Time and other tales of horror
first published in Great Britain by
Victor Gollancz Limited 1968
Compilation copyright © Victor Gollancz Limited 1968.
The Survivor, copyright 1954 by *Weird Tales*, for
Weird Tales, July 1954; copyright 1957 by August Derleth.
The Gable Window, copyright 1957 by Candar Publishing
Company, Inc. (as *The Murky Glass*), for *Saturn*,
May 1957; copyright 1957 by August Derleth.
Wentworth's Day, *The Peabody Heritage*, *The Ancestor*,
The Shadow out of Space, *The Lamp of Alhazred*, copyright
1957 by August Derleth. *The Fishermen of Falcon Point*,
copyright 1959 by August Derleth. *The Dark Brotherhood*,
copyright 1966 by August Derleth. *The Shuttered Room*,
copyright 1959 by August Derleth.
Made and printed in Great Britain by
C. Nicholls & Company Ltd
The Philips Park Press, Manchester
Set in Intertype Plantin

Contents

The Survivor

'Certain houses, like certain persons, manage somehow to proclaim at once their character for evil. Perhaps it is the aroma of evil deeds committed under a particular roof, long after the actual doers have passed away, that makes the gooseflesh come and the hair rise. Something of the original passion of the evil-doer, and of the horror felt by his victim, enters the heart of the innocent watcher, and he becomes suddenly conscious of tingling nerves, creeping skin, and a chilling of the blood . . .'

— ALGERNON BLACKWOOD

I had never intended to speak or write again of the Charriere house, once I had fled Providence on that shocking night of discovery – there are memories which every man would seek to suppress, to disbelieve, to wipe out of existence – but I am forced to set down now the narrative of my brief acquaintance with the house on Benefit Street, and my precipitate flight therefrom, lest some innocent person be subjected to indignity by the police in an effort to explain the horrible discovery the police have made at last – that same ghastly horror it was my lot to look upon before any other human eye – and what I saw was surely far more terrible than what remained to be seen after all these years, the house having reverted to the city, as I had known it would.

While it is true that an antiquarian might be expected to know considerably less about some ancient avenues of human research than about old houses, it is surely conceivable that one who was steeped in the processes of research among the habitations of the human race might occasionally encounter a more abstruse mystery than the date of an ell or the source of a gambrel roof and find it possible to come to certain conclusions about it, no matter how incredible, how horrible or frightening or even – yes, damnable! In those quarters where antiquarians gather, the name of Alijah Atwood is not entirely unknown; modesty forbids me to say more, but it is surely permissible to point out that anyone sufficiently interested to look up refer-

ences will find more than a few paragraphs about me in those
directories devoted to information for the antiquary.

I came to Providence, Rhode Island, in 1930, intending to
make only a brief visit and then go on to New Orleans. But I
saw the Charriere house on Benefit Street, and was drawn to it
as only an antiquarian would be drawn to any unusual house
isolated in a New England street of a period not its own, a
house clearly of some age, and with an indefinable aura that
both attracted and repelled.

What was said about the Charriere house – that it was haunted – was no more than what was said about many an old,
abandoned dwelling in the old world as well as in the new, and
even, if I can depend on the solemn articles in the *Journal of
American Folklore,* about the primitive dwellings of American
Indians, Australian bush-people, the Polynesians, and many
others. Of ghosts I do not wish to write; suffice it to say that
there have been within the circle of my experience certain mani-
festations which have lent themselves to no scientific explanation, though I am rational enough to believe that there is such
explanation to be found, once man chances upon the proper
interpretation through the correct scientific approach.

In that sense, surely the Charriere house was not haunted.
No spectre passed among its rooms rattling its chain, no voice
moaned at midnight, no sepulchral figure appeared at the wit-
ching hour to warn of approaching doom. But that there was an
aura about the house – one of evil? of terror? of hideous, eldritch things? – none could deny; and had I been born a less
insensitive clod, I have no doubt that the house would have
driven me forth raving out of mind. Its aura was less tangible
than others I have known, but it suggested that the house concealed unspeakable secrets, long hidden from human perception. Above all else, it conveyed an overpowering sense of age –
of centuries not alone of its own being, but far, far in the past,
when the world was young, which was curious indeed, for the
house, however old, was less than three centuries of age.

I saw it first as an antiquarian, delighted to discover set in a row of staid New England houses a house which was manifestly of a seventeenth-century Quebec style, and thus so different from its neighbours as to attract immediately the eye of any passer-by. I had made many visits to Quebec, as well as to other old cities of the North American continent, but on this first visit to Providence, I had not come primarily in search of ancient dwellings, but to call upon a fellow antiquarian of note, and it was on my way to his home on Barnes Street that I passed the Charriere house, observed that it was not tenanted, and resolved to lease it for my own. Even so, I might not have done so, had it not been for the curious reluctance of my friend to speak of the house, and, indeed, his seeming unwillingness that I go near the place. Perhaps I do him an injustice in retrospect, for he, poor fellow, was even then on his deathbed, though neither of us knew it; so it was at his bedside I sat, and not in his study, and it was there that I asked about the house, describing it unmistakably, for, of course, I did not then know its name or anything about it.

A man named Charriere had owned it – a French surgeon, who had come down from Quebec. But who had built it, Gamwell did not know; it was Charriere he had known. 'A tall, rough-skinned man – I saw little of him, but no one saw more. He had retired from practice,' said Gamwell. He had lived there – and presumably older members of his family, though Gamwell could not say as to this – for as long as Gamwell had known the house. Dr. Charriere had lived a reclusive life, and had died, according to notice duly published in the Providence *Journal*, in 1927, three years ago. Indeed, the date of Dr. Charriere's death was the only date that Gamwell could give me; all else was shrouded in vagueness. The house had not been rented more than once; there had been a brief occupation by a professional man and his family, but they had left it after a month, complaining of its dampness and the smells of the old house; since then it had stood empty, but it could not be torn down, for Dr. Charriere had left in his will a considerable sum of money to keep the property off the tax delinquent list for a long enough time – some said twenty years – to guarantee that the house would be standing there if and when heirs of the surgeon appeared to lay claim to it, the doctor having written vaguely of a nephew in French Indo-China, on military service. All attempts to find the nephew had proved futile, and now the house was being permitted to stand until the period specified in the will of Dr. Charriere had expired.

'I think of leasing it,' I told Gamwell.

Ill though he was, my fellow antiquarian raised himself up on one elbow in protest. 'A passing whim, Atwood – let it pass. I have heard, disquieting things of the house.'

'What things?' I asked him bluntly.

But of these things he would not speak; he only shook his head feebly and closed his eyes.

'I hope to examine it tomorrow,' I went on.

'It offers nothing you could not find in Quebec, believe me,' said Gamwell.

But, as I have set forth, his curious opposition served only to augment my desire to examine the house at close range. I did not mean to spend a lifetime there, but only to lease it for a half year or so, and make it a base of operations, while I went about the countryside around the city as well as the lanes and byways of Providence in search of the antiquities of that region. Gamwell did surrender at last the name of the firm of lawyers in whose hands the Charriere will had been placed, and when I made application to them, and overcame their own lack of enthusiasm, I became master of the old Charriere house for a period of not more than six months, and less, if I so chose.

I took possession of the house at once, though I was somewhat nonplussed to discover that, while running water had been put in, electricity had not. I found among the furnishings of the house – these had been left in each room, exactly as at the death of Dr. Charriere – a half dozen lamps of various shapes and ages, some of them apparently dating back a century or more, with which to light my way. I had expected to find the house cobwebbed and dusty, but I was surprised to learn that this was not the case, though I had not understood that the lawyers – the firm of Baker & Greenbaugh – had undertaken to care for the house during the half century it was to stand, short of someone's appearing to lay claim to it as the sole survivor of Dr. Charriere and his line.

The house was all I had hoped for. It was heavily timbered, and in some of the rooms paper had begun to peel from the plaster, while in others the plaster itself had never been covered with paper, and shone yellow with age on the wall. Its rooms were irregular – appearing to be either quite large or very small. It was of two storeys, but the upper floor had not been much used. The lower or ground floor, however, abounded in evidence of its one-time occupant, the surgeon, for one room of it had manifestly served him as a laboratory of some kind, and an adjoining room as a study, for both had the look of having been but recently abandoned in the midst of some inquiry or research, quite as if the occupation of the house by its brief tenant – *post-mortem* Charriere – had not touched upon these rooms. And perhaps it had not, for the house was large enough to permit of habitation without disturbing them, both laboratory and study being at the back of the house, opening out upon a garden, now much overgrown with shrubs and trees, a garden of some size, since the house occupied a frontage of over three lots in width, and in depth reached to a high stone wall which was but a lot removed from the street in its rear.

Dr. Charriere had evidently been in the midst of some work when his hour had struck, and I confess its nature intrigued me at once, for it was plainly no ordinary one. The inquiry was not alone a study of man, for there were strange, almost cabalistic drawings, resembling physiological charts, of various kinds of saurians, though the most prominent among them were of the order *Loricata* and the genera *Crocodylus* and *Osteolaemus*, though there were also recognizable drawings of *Gavialis*, *Tomistoma*, *Gaiman*, and *Alligator*, with a lesser number being speculative sketches of earlier members of this reptilian order reaching back to the Jurassic period. Yet even this fascinating glimpse of the surgeon's odd vein of inquiry would not have stimulated any really genuine delving into his affairs had it not been for the antiquarian mystery of the house.

The Charriere house impressed me at once as having been the product of its age, save for the later introduction of waterworks. I had all along assumed that Dr. Charriere himself had built it; Gamwell had nowhere in our somewhat elliptical conversation given me to understand otherwise; nor had he, for that matter, mentioned the surgeon's age at his death. Presuming it to be a well-rounded eighty years, then it was certainly not he who had built the house, for internal evidence spoke clearly of its origin in the vicinity of the year 1700! – or over two centuries before Dr. Charriere's death. It seemed to me, therefore, that the house only bore the name of its most recent long-time tenant, and not that of its builder; it was the pursuit of this problem which brought me to several disturbing facts which bore no relationship, seemingly, to credible facts.

For one thing, the year of Dr. Charriere's birth was nowhere in evidence. I sought out his grave – it was, strangely, on his own property; he had obtained permission to be buried in his garden, not far from a gracious old well which stood, roofed over, with bucket and all still as it had stood, doubtless, for almost as long as the house had been standing – with a view to examining the headstone for the date of his birth, but, to my disappointment and chagrin, his stone bore only his name – Jean-Francois Charriere – his calling: Surgeon – his places of residence or professional occupation – Bayonne; Paris, Pondicherry; Quebec: Providence – and the year of his death: 1927. No more. This was enough only to further me on my quest, and forthwith I started to make inquiry by letter of acquaintances in various places where research might be done.

Within a fortnight the results of my inquiries were at hand. But, far from being in any way satisfied, I was more perplexed than ever. I had made my first inquiry of a correspondent in Bayonne, presuming that, since this was first mentioned on the stone, Charriere might have been born in that vicinity. I had next inquired in Paris, then of a friend in London, who might have access to information in British archives pertaining to India, and then in Quebec. What did I glean from all this correspondence but a riddling sequence of dates? A Jean-François

Charriere had indeed been born in Bayonne – but in the year 1636! The name was not unknown in Paris, either, for a seventeen-year-old lad of that name had studied under the Royalist exile, Richard Wiseman, in 1653 and for three years thereafter. At Pondicherry – and later, too, on the Caronmandall Coast of India – one Dr. Jean-François Charriere, surgeon in the French army, had been on duty from 1674 onward. And in Quebec, the earlier record of Dr. Charriere was in 1691; he had practised in that city for six years, and had then left the city for an unknown destination.

I was left, patently, with but one conclusion: that the said Dr. Jean-Françios Charriere, born in Bayonne 1636, last known to have been in Quebec the very year of the erection of the Charriere house on Benefit Street was a forbear of the same name as the late surgeon who had last occupied the house. But if so, there was an absolute lacuna between that time in 1697 and the lifetime of the last occupant of the house, for there was nowhere any account of the family of that earlier Jean-François Charriere; if there had been a Madame Charriere, if there had been children – as assuredly there must have been for the line to continue to the present century – there was no record of them. It was not impossible that the elderly gentleman who had come down from Quebec might have been of single status upon his arrival in Providence, and might have married thereafter. He would then have been sixty-one years of age. Yet a search of the appropriate registry failed to reveal any record of such a marriage, and I was left more bewildered than ever, though, as an antiquarian, I was fully aware of the difficulties of discovering facts and I was not at that time too discouraged to continue my inquiries.

I took a new line, and approached the firm of Baker & Greenbaugh for information about the late Dr. Charriere. Here an even more curious rebuff awaited me, for when I inquired about the appearance of the French surgeon, both the lawyers were forced to admit that they had never laid eyes on him. All their instructions had come by letter, together with cheques of generous figures; they had acted for Dr. Charriere approximately

six years before his death, and thereafter; before that time, they
had not been retained by Dr. Charriere.

I inquired then about his 'nephew,' since the existence of a
nephew implied, at least, that there had at one time been a sister
or brother to Charriere. But here, too, I was rebuffed; Gamwell
had misinformed me, for Charriere had not specifically identified him as a nephew, but only as 'the sole male survivor of my
line'; this survivor had only been presumed to have been a
nephew, and all search for him had come to naught, though
there was that in Dr. Charriere's will which implied that the
said 'sole male survivor' would not need to be sought, but would
make application to the firm of Baker & Greenbaugh either in
person or by letter in such terms as to be unmistakable. Mystery
there was, certainly; the lawyers did not deny it, but it was
understood, also, that they had been well rewarded for their
trust, too well to permit of any betrayal of it save in such casual
terms as they had related to me. After all, as one of the lawyers
sensibly pointed out, only three years had elapsed since the
death of Dr. Charriere, and there was still ample time for the
survivor to present himself.

Failing in this line of inquiry, I again called on my old friend,
Gamwell, who was still abed, and now noticeably weaker. His
attending physician, whom I encountered on the way out, now
for the first time intimated that old Gamwell might not rise
again, and cautioned me not to excite him, or to tire him with
too many questions. Nevertheless, I was determined to ferret
out what I could about Charriere, though I was not entirely
prepared for the keen scrutiny to which I was subjected by
Gamwell, quite as if he had expected that less than three weeks'
residence in the Charriere house should have altered my very
appearance.

After the amenities had been exchanged, I turned to the subject about which I had come; explaining that I had found the
house so interesting, I desired to know more of its late tenant.
Gamwell had mentioned seeing him.

'But that was years ago,' said Gamwell. 'He's been dead
three years. Let me see – 1907, I think.'

I was astounded. 'But that was twenty years before he died!' I protested.

Nevertheless, Gamwell insisted, that was the year.

And how had he looked? I pressed the question upon him.

Disappointingly, senility and illness had encroached upon the old man's once fine mind.

'Take a newt, grow him a little, teach him to walk on his hind legs, and dress him in elegant clothes,' Gamwell said. 'I give you Dr. Jean-François Charriere. Except that his skin was rough, almost horny. A cold man. He lived in another world.'

'How old was he?' I asked then. 'Eighty?'

'Eighty?' He was contemplative. 'When first I saw him – I was but twenty, then – he looked no older. And twenty years ago – my good Atwood – he had not changed a jot. He seemed eighty the first time. Was it the perspective of my youth? Perhaps. He seemed eighty in 1907. And died twenty years later.'

'A hundred, then.'

'It might well have been.'

But Gamwell, too, was dissatisfying. Once again there was nothing definite, nothing concrete, no single fact – only an impression, a memory, of someone, I felt, Gamwell had disliked for no reason he could name. Perhaps some professional jealousy he did not care to name biased his judgment.

I next sought the neighbours, but I found them for the most part younger people who had little memory of Dr. Charriere, except as someone whom they wished elsewhere, for he had an abominable traffic in lizards and the like, and none knew what diabolic experiments he performed in his laboratory. Only one among them was of advanced age; this was an old woman, a Mrs. Hepzibah Cobbett, who lived in a little two-storey house directly behind the Charriere garden wall, and I found her much enfeebled, in a wheel chair, guarded over by her daughter, a hawk-nosed woman whose cold blue eyes looked at me askance from behind her pince-nez. Yet the old woman spoke, starting to life at mention of Dr. Charriere's name, realizing that I lived in the house.

'Ye'll not live there long, mark my words. It's a devil's house,' she said with some spirit that degenerated rapidly into a senile cackling. 'Many's the time I've laid eyes on him. A tall man, bent like a sickle, with a wee tuft of beard like a goat's whisker on his chin. And what was it that crawled about at his feet I could not see? A long, black thing, too big for a snake – though 'twas snakes I thought of every time I set eyes on Dr. Charriere. And what was it screamed that night? And what barked at the well? – a fox, indeed, I know a fox and a dog, too. Like the yawping of a seal. I've seen things, I tell ye, but nobody'll believe a poor old woman with one foot in her grave. And ye – ye won't either, for none does.'

What was I to make of this? Perhaps the daughter was right when she said, as she showed me out, 'You must overlook mother's ramblings. She has an arteriosclerotic condition which occasionally makes her sound quite weak-minded.' But I did not think old Mrs. Cobbett weak-minded, for her eyes snapped and sparkled when she talked, quite as if she were enjoying a secret joke of proportions so vast that its very outlines escaped her keeper, the grim daughter who hovered ever near.

Disappointment seemed to await me at every turn. All avenues of information yielded little more together than any one had yielded. Newspaper files, library, records – all that was to be found was the date of the erection of the house: 1697, and the date of the death of Dr. Jean-François Charriere. If any other Charriere had died in the city's history, there was no mention of him. It was inconceivable that death had stricken all the other members of the Charriere family, predeceasing the late tenant of the house on Benefit Street, away from Providence, and yet it must have been so, for there was no other feasible explanation.

Yet there was one additional fact – a likeness of Dr. Charriere which I discovered in the house; though no name was appended to it where it hung in a remote and almost inaccessible corner of an upstairs room, the initials J. F. C. identified it beyond reasonable doubt. It was the likeness of a thin-faced ascetic, wearing a straggly goatee; his face was distinguished by high cheek-bones, sunken cheeks, and dark, blazing eyes. His aspect was gaunt and sepulchral.

Thus, in the absence of other avenues of information, I was driven once again to the papers and books left in Dr. Charriere's study and laboratory. Hitherto, I had been much away from the house, in the pursuit of my inquiry into Dr. Charriere's background; but now I was as much confined to the house as I had previously been away from it. Perhaps it was because of this confinement that I began to grow more keenly aware of the aura of the house – both in a psychic and a physical sense. That unhappy professional man and his family who had remained here but a month and then left because of the smells abounding had perhaps conditioned me to *smell* the house, and now, for the first time, I did indeed become sharply cognizant of various aromas and musks, some of them typical of old houses, but others completely alien to me. The dominant one, however, was identifiable; it was a musk I had encountered several times before – in zoos, swamps, along stagnant pools – almost a miasma which suggested most strongly the presence of reptiles. It was not impossible that reptiles had found their way through the city to the haven of the garden behind the Charriere house, but it was incredible that they should have persisted in such numbers as to taint the very air of the place. Yet, seek as I might, I could find no source of this reptilian musk, inside or out, though I fancied once that it emanated from the well, which was doubtless a result of an illusory conviction.

This musk persisted, and it was especially strong whenever rain fell, or a fog formed, or dew lay on the grass, as might have been expected, moisture heightening all odours. The house was moist, too; its short-lived tenantry had been explained in part by this, and in this, certainly, the renter had not been in error. I found it often unpleasant, but not disturbing – not half so disturbing as other aspects of the house.

Indeed, it was as if my invasion of the study and laboratory had stirred the old house to protest, for certain hallucinations began to occur with annoying regularity. There was, for one, the curious barking sound which seemed to emanate from the

garden late at night. And, for another, the illusion that an oddly
bent, reptilian figure haunted the darkness of the garden outside
the study windows. These and other illusions persisted – and
I, in turn, persisted in looking upon them as hallucinatory –
until that fateful night when, after hearing a distinct sound as
of someone bathing in the garden, I woke from my sleep convinced that I was not alone in the house, and, putting on my
dressing-robe and slippers, I lit a lamp and hurried to the
study.

What I saw there must certainly have been inspired by the
nature of my inquiry into the late Dr. Charriere's papers; that
it was a figment of a nightmare, I could not doubt at the moment, though I caught but a faint glimpse of the invader, for
there was an invader in the study, and he made off with certain
papers belonging to the Charriere estate, but as I saw him in
the brief glimpse I had of him in the wan yellow light of the
lamp held overhead and partially blinding me he seemed to
glisten, he shone blackly, and he seemed to be wearing a skin-
tight suit of some rough, black material. I saw him for only an
instant, before he leapt through the open window into the darkness of the garden; I would have followed then, had it not been
for the disquieting things I saw in the light of the lamp.

Where the invader had stood there were the irregular marks
of feet – of wet feet – and more, of feet which were oddly broad,
the toes of which were so long-nailed as to leave the marks of
those nails before each toe; and where he had bent above the
papers there was the same wetness; and over all there hung the
powerful reptilian musk I had begun to accept as an integral
part of the house, so powerful, indeed, that I almost reeled and
fainted.

But my interest in the papers transcended fear or curiosity.
At that time, the only rational explanation which occurred to
me was that one of the neighbours who had some animus against
the Charriere house and were constantly agitating to have it
torn down, must have come from swimming to invade the study.
Far-fetched, yes, certainly. But could any other explanation
readily account for what I saw? I am inclined to think not.

As for the papers, certain of them were undeniably gone. Fortunately, these were the very ones I had finished with; I had put them into a neat pile, though many were not consecutive. I could not imagine why anyone would have wanted to take them, unless someone other than myself were interested in Dr. Charriere, perhaps with a view to laying claim to the house and property; for these papers were painstaking notes about the longevity of crocodiles and alligators, as well as of related reptiles. It had already begun to be plainly evident to me that the late doctor had been studying reptilian longevity with almost obsessive devotion, and with a view, clearly, to learning how man might lengthen his own life. If the secrets of reptilian longevity had been revealed to Dr. Charriere, there was nothing in his papers thus far to show that it had, though I had come upon two or three disquieting suggestions of 'operations' performed – on whom was not set down – with a view to increasing the life span of the subject.

True, there was one variant vein of notes in what I assumed to be Dr. Charriere's handwriting, treated as a related subject, but, to me, one at variance from the more or less scientific inquiry into the long life of reptiles. This was a sequence of cryptic references to certain mythological creatures, particularly one named 'Cthulhu,' and another named 'Dagon,' who were evidently deities of the sea in some ancient mythology completely unknown to me; and suggestions of long-lived creatures (or people?) who served these ancient Gods, named the 'Deep Ones,' evidently amphibious creatures living in the depths of the seas. Among these notes were photographs of a singularly hideous monolithic statue, of a distinctly saurian cast of feature, labelled 'E. coast Hivaoa Is., Marquesas. Object of worship?' and of a totem pole of the North-west Coast Indians of a disturbingly similar workmanship, also reptilian in aspect, this one being marked, 'Kwakiutl Indian totem. Quatsino Sound. Sim. t. erected by Tlingit Inds.' These curious notes existed as if to show that Dr. Charriere was not averse to examining rites of ancient sorceries and primitive religious beliefs in an effort to bring about some earnestly desired goal.

What that goal might be was soon evident enough. Dr. Charriere had not been interested in the study of longevity for its own sake alone; no, he had also wished to prolong his own life. And there were certain upsetting hints in the writings he had left behind him to suggest that in part, at least, he had succeeded beyond his wildest dreams. This was a disturbing discovery to make because it recalled again the curious history of that first Jean-François Charriere, also a surgeon, about whose later years and death there was fully as much mystery as there was about the birth and early years of the late Dr. Jean-François Charriere, who died in Providence in 1927.

The events of that night, though not frightening me too badly, did result in my purchasing a powerful Luger pistol in a second-hand shop, as well as a new flashlight; the lamp had impeded me in the night, which a flashlight would not do in similar circumstances. If indeed I had a visitor from among the neighbours, I could be sure that the papers he had taken would no more than whet his appetite, and sooner or later he would return. Against that contingency I meant to be fully prepared, and if again I caught a marauder in the study of the house I had leased, I would not hesitate to shoot if my demand to stop where he was were not heeded. I hoped, however, that I would not have occasion to use the weapon in such a manner.

On the next night I resumed my study of Dr. Charriere's books and papers. The books had surely at one time belonged to his forbears, for many of them dated back through the centuries; among them was a book translated into the French from the English of R. Wiseman, testifying to some connection between the Dr. Jean-François Charriere who had studied in Paris under Wiseman, and that other surgeon of similar name who had, until recently, lived in Providence, Rhode Island.

They were *en masse* a singular hodge-podge of books. They seemed to be in every known language, from French to Arabic. Indeed, I could not hope to translate a majority of the titles, though I could read French and had some smattering of other Romance languages. I had at that time no understanding of the meaning of such a title as *Unaussprechlichen Kultein,* by von

Junzt, though I suspected that it was akin to the Comte d'Erlette's *Cules des Goules,* since it stood next to that book on the shelf. But then, books on zoological subjects stood beside weighty tomes about ancient cultures; they bore such titles as *An Inquiry Into the Relationship of the Peoples of Polynesia and the Indian Cultures of the South American Continent with Special Reference to Peru; The Pnakotic Manuscripts, De Furtivis Literarum Notis,* by Giambattista Porta; Thicknesse's *Kryptographik;* the *Daemonolatreia* of Remigius; Banfort's *The Saurian Age;* a file of the Aylesbury, Massachusetts, *Transcript;* another of the Arkham, Massachusetts, *Gazette* – and the like. Some of these books were certainly of immense value, for many of them dated as far back as from 1670 to 1820, and, though all showed much wear from use, all were still in relatively good condition.

These books, however, meant comparatively little to me. In retrospect, I am constrained to believe that, had I examined them more attentively, I might have learned even more than I did; but there is a saying that too much knowledge of matters men are better off without knowing is even more damning than too little. I soon gave over my examination of the books because I discovered, pressed in among them on the shelves, what seemed at first glance to be a diary or journal, but was, on closer examination, manifestly a notebook, for the entries dated too far back to have encompassed Dr. Charriere's life span of years. Yet all were written in a crabbed, tiny script, which was most certainly the late surgeon's, and, despite the age of the first pages, all had been written by the same hand, suggesting that Dr. Charriere had set down these notes in a kind of rough chronology, very probably from some earlier draft. Nor were they jottings alone; some were illustrated with crude drawings which were nevertheless effective, as are on many occasions the primitive paintings of untutored artists.

Thus, upon the very first page of the hand-bound manuscript, I came upon this entry: '1851. Arkham. Aseph Goade, D.O.' and with it a drawing, presumably of the said Aseph Goade, emphasizing certain aspects of his features, which were batrachian in essence, for they were distinguished by an abnormally wide mouth, with peculiar leathery lips, a very low brow, strangely webbed eyes, and a generally squat physiognomy, giving them a distinctly and unmistakably froglike appearance. This drawing took up the majority of the page, and the jotting accompanying it I assumed to be a notation of an encounter – evidently in research, for it could hardly have been in the flesh – with a sub-human type (could the 'D.O.' have been a reference to the 'Deep Ones,' mention of which I had previously encountered?), which, doubtless, Dr. Charriere looked upon as a verification of the trend of his research, a trend to support a belief he probably held that some kinship with batrachia, and hence very probably also saurians, could be traced.

To that end, too, there were other jottings. Most of them were so vague – perhaps purposely so – as to seem to me at that first examination of them virtually meaningless. What was I to make of a page like this, for instance?

'1857. St. Augustine. Henry Bishop. Skin very scaly, but not ichthic. Said to be 107 years old. No deteriorative process. All senses still keen. Ancestry uncertain, but Polynesian trade in background.

'1861. Charleston. Balzac family. Crusted hands. Double jaw construction. Entire family manifesting similar stigmata. Anton 117 years old. Anna 109. Unhappy away from water.

'1863. Innsmouth. Marsh, Waite, Eliot, Gilman families. Captain Obed Marsh a trader in Polynesia, married to a Polynesian woman. All bearing facial characteristics similar to Aseph Goade's. Much secretive living. Women seldom seen in streets, but at night much swimming – entire families, all the rest of the town keeping to their houses, swimming out to Devil Reef. Relationship to D.O. very marked. Considerable traffic between Innsmouth and Ponape. Some dark religious worship.

'1871. Jed Price carnival entertainer. Billed as "Alligator Man." Appears in pool of alligators. Saurian look. Long lantern jaw. Said to have pointed teeth, but whether real or filed unable to determine.'

This was the general tenor of the jottings in the book. Their range was continental – there were notes referring to Canada and Mexico as well as the eastern seaboard of North America. From then, Dr. Jean-François Charriere began to emerge as a man obsessed with a strange compulsion – to establish proof of the longevity of certain human beings seemingly bearing some kinship to saurian or batrachian ancestors.

Admittedly, the weight of the evidence gathered, could one have accepted it all as fact, rather than as wishfully coloured accounts of people with some marked physical defect, seemed to lend to Dr. Charriere and his belief a strange and provocative corroboration. Yet the surgeon had not often gone beyond the realm of pure conjecture. What he sought seemed to be the con-necting link among the various instances which had come to his notice. He had sought this link in three bodies of lore. The most familiar of these was the *vodu* legendry of Negro culture. Next to it, in familiarity, stood the animal worship of ancient Egypt. Finally, and most important, according to the surgeon's notes, was a completely alien culture which was as old as earth, nay, older, involving ancient Elder Gods and their terrible, unceas-ing conflict with equally primeval Old Ones who bore such names as Cthulhu, Hastur, Yog-Sathoth, Shub-Niggurath, and Nyarlathotep, and who were served in turn by such curious beings as the Tcho-Tcho People, the Deep Ones, the Shantaks, the Abominable Snow Men, and others, some of whom ap-peared to have been a sub-order of human being, but others of which were either definite mutations or not human at all. All this fruit of Dr. Charriere's research was fascinating, but in no case had he adduced a definite, provable link. There were certain saurian references in the *Vodu* cult; there were similar connections to the religious culture of ancient Egypt; and there were many obscure and tantalizing suggestions connecting the saurians of the Cthulhu myth-pattern, ranging far deeper into the past than *Crocodylus* and *Gavialis*, embracing *Tyrannosausus* and *Brontosaurus*, *Megalosaurus* and other Mesozoic reptilia.

In addition to these interesting notes, there were diagrams of what seemed to be very odd operations, the nature of which I did not fully comprehend at that time. These were apparently copied out of ancient texts, particularly one given frequently as source entitled, *De Vermis Mysteriis*, by Ludvig Prinn, another of these obscure references completely foreign to me. The operations themselves suggested a *raison d'être* too astounding to accept on face; one of them, for instance, was designed to stretch the skin, consisting of many incisions made to 'permit growth.' Yet another was a simple cross-incision made at the base of the spine for the purpose of 'extension of the tail-bone.' What these fantastic diagrams suggested was too horrible to contemplate, yet it was part and parcel, surely, of the strange research conducted for so many years by Dr. Charriere, whose seclusion was thus readily explicable, since his was a project which could only be conducted in secret lest it bring down upon him the scorn and laughter of his fellow scientists.

Among these papers there were also certain references set down in such a manner that I could not doubt they were the experiences of the narrator. Yet, for all that these antedated 1850, in some cases by decades, they were unmistakably in Dr. Charriere's handwriting, so that – excepting always the possibility that he had transcribed the experiences of someone else – it was evident that he was more than an octogenarian at the time of his death, indeed, far more, so much more that the very anticipation of it made me uneasy, and cast my thoughts back to that other Dr. Charriere who had gone before him.

The sum total of Dr. Charriere's credo amounted to a strongly hypothetical conviction that a human being could, by means of certain operations, together with other unusual practices of a macabre nature, take upon himself something of the longevity that characterized the sauria; that as much as a century and a half, perhaps even two centuries, could be added to a man's life span; and, beyond that, given a period of semi-conscious torpor in some moist place, which would amount to a kind of gestation, the individual could emerge again, somewhat altered in aspect, true, to begin another lengthy span of life, which would, by virtue of the physiological *changes* which had taken place in him, be of necessity somewhat altered from his previous mode of existence. To support this conviction, Dr. Charriere had amassed only a number of legendary tales, certain data of a kindred nature, and highly speculative accounts of curious human mutations known to have existed in the past two hundred and ninety-one years – a figure which later assumed far more meaning, when I realized that this was the exact span of time from the year of the birth of that earlier Dr. Charriere to the date of the later surgeon's death. Nowhere in all this material was there anything resembling a concrete line of scientific research, with adducible proof – only hints, vague intimations, hideous suggestions – sufficient, in truth, to fill a casual reader with horrible doubts and terrible, half-formed convictions, but not nearly enough to warrant the sober interest of any genuine scholar.

How much further I would have gone into Dr. Charriere's research, I do not know.

Had it not been for the occurrence of *that* which sent me screaming in horror from that house on Benefit Street, it was possible that I would have gone much further instead of leaving house and contents to be claimed by a survivor who, I know now, will never come, thus leaving the house to fall to its ultimate destruction by the city.

It was while I was contemplating these 'findings' of Dr. Charriere that I became aware of being under scrutiny, that manifestation people are fond of calling the 'sixth sense.' Unwilling to turn, I did the next best thing; I opened my pocket-watch, set it up before me, and used the inside of the highly polished case as a kind of mirror to reflect the windows behind me. And there I saw, dimly reflected, a horrible travesty of a human face, which so startled me that I turned to view for myself that which I had seen mirrored. But there was nothing at the pane, save the shadow of movement. I rose, put out the light, and hastened to the window. Did I then see a tall, curiously bent figure, crouched and shuffling in an awkward gait into the darkness of the garden? I believed that I did, but I was not given to folly enough to venture out in pursuit. Whoever it was would come again, even as he had come the previous night.

Accordingly, I settled back to watch, a score of possible explanations crowding upon my mind. As the source of my nocturnal visitor, I confess I put at the head of the list the neighbours who had long opposed the continued standing of the house of Dr. Charriere. It was possible that they meant to frighten me away, unaware of the shortness of my lease; it was also possible that there was something in the study they wanted, though this was far-fetched, in view of the time they had had to search the house during its long period of unoccupancy. Certainly the truth of the matter never once occurred to me; I am not by nature any more sceptical than an antiquarian might be expected to be; but the true identity of my visitor did not, I confess, suggest itself to me despite all the curious interlocking circumstances which might have conveyed a greater meaning to a less scientific mind than my own.

As I sat there in the dark, I was more than ever impressed with the aura of the old house. The very darkness seemed alive, but incredibly remote from the life of Providence which swirled all around it. The interior darkness was filled instead with the psychic residue of years – the persistent smell of moisture, accompanied by that musk so commonly associated with reptilian quarters at the zoo; the smell of old wood, old limestone, of which the cellar walls were composed, the odour of decay, for the centuries had begun to deteriorate both wood and stone. And there was something more – the vaporous hint of an animal presence, which seemed indeed to grow stronger with every passing moment.

I sat there well over an hour, before I heard any untoward sound.

Then it was indistinguishable. At first I thought it a bark, akin to that sound made by alligators; but then I thought it rather less a figment of my perfervid imagination than the actual sound of a door closing. Yet it was some time before another sound smote upon my ears – a rustling of papers. Astonishing as it was, an intruder had actually found his way into the study before my very eyes without being seen! I turned on the flashlight, which was directed at the desk I had left.

What I saw was incredible, horrible. It was not a man who stood there, but a travesty of a man. I know that for one cataclysmic moment I thought consciousness would leave me; but a sense of urgency coupled with an awareness of acute danger swept over me, and without a moment's hesitation, I fired four times, at such range that I knew each shot had found harbour in the body of the bestial thing that leaned over Dr. Charriere's desk in that darkened study.

Of what followed I have, mercifully, only the vaguest memory. A wild thrashing about – the escape of the invader – my own uncertain pursuit. I had struck him, certainly, for a trail of blood led from the study to the windows through which he had gone, tearing away glass and frame in one. Outside, the light of my flash gleamed on the drops of blood, so that I had no difficulty following them. Even without this to follow, the strong musk pervading the night air would have enabled me to trace whoever had gone ahead.

I was led – not away from the house – but deeper into the garden, straight to the kerb of the well behind the house. And over the kerb *into the well*, where I saw for the first time in the glow of the flashlight the cunningly fashioned steps which led down into that dark maw. So great was the discharge of blood at the well-kerb, that I was confident I had mortally wounded the intruder. It was that confidence which impelled me to follow, despite the manifest danger.

Would that I had turned at the well-kerb and gone away from that accursed place! For I followed down the rungs of the ladder set into the well-wall – not to the water below, as I had first thought I might be led – but to an aperture opening into a tunnel in the well-wall, leading even deeper into the garden. Compelled now by a burning desire to know the nature of my victim, I pushed into this tunnel, unmindful of the damp earth which stained my clothes, with my light thrust before me, and my weapon in instant readiness. Up ahead I could see a kind of hollowed out cavern – not any larger than enough to permit a man to kneel upright – and in the centre of my flashlight's glow stood a casket, at sight of which I hesitated momentarily, for I recognized the direction of the tunnel away from the well led towards the grave of Dr. Charriere.

But I had come too far to retreat.

The smell in this narrow opening was almost indescribable. Pervading every part of the tunnel was the nauseatingly strong musk of reptiles; indeed, it lay so thickly in the air that I had to force myself to press on towards the casket. I came up to it and saw that it lay uncovered. The trail of blood led to the edge of the casket and into it. Impelled by burning curiosity and a half-formed fear of what I might find, I rose to my knees and forced the light tremblingly into the casket. . . .

It may well be charged that after so many years my memory is no longer to be relied upon. But what I saw there was imprinted indelibly on my memory. For there, in the glow of my light, lay a newly-dead being, the implications of whose existence overwhelmed me with horror. This was the thing I had killed. Half-man, half-saurian, it was a ghastly travesty upon what had once been a human being. Its clothes were split and torn by the horrible mutations of the flesh, but the crusted skin which had burst its bonds, its hands and unshod feet were flat, powerful in appearance, clawlike. I gazed in speechless terror at the shuddersome tail-like appendage which pushed bluntly out from the base of the spine, at the terribly elongated, crocodilian jaw, to which still grew a tuft of hair, like a goat's beard. . . .

All this I saw before a merciful unconsciousness overcame me – *for I had seen enough to recognize what lay in that coffin – him who had laid there in a cataleptic torpor since 1927, waiting his turn to come back in frightfully altered form to live again – Dr. Jean-François Charriere, surgeon, born in Bayonne in 1636, 'died' in Providence in 1927 – and I knew that the survivor of whom he had written in his will was none other than himself, born again, renewed by a hellish knowledge of long-forgotten, eldritch rites more ancient than mankind, as old as that early vernal earth on which great beasts fought and tore!*

Wentworth's Day

North of Dunwich lies an all but abandoned country, one which has returned in large part – after its successive occupation by the old New Englanders, the French-Canadians who moved in after them, the Italians, and the Poles who came last – to a state perilously close to the wild. The first dwellers wrested a living from the stony earth and the forests that once covered all that land, but they were not versed in conservation of either the soil or its natural resources, and successive generations still further depleted that country. Those who came after them soon gave up the struggle and went elsewhere.

It is not an area of Massachusetts in which many people like to live. The houses which once stood proudly there have fallen into such disuse that most of them would not now support comfortable living. There are still farms on the gentler slopes, with gambrel-roofed houses on them, ancient buildings, often brooding in the lee of rocky ledges over the secrets of many New England generations; but the marks of decay are everywhere apparent – in the crumbling chimneys, the bulging side walls, the broken windows of the abandoned barns and houses. Roads criss-cross it, but, once you are off the state highway which traverses the long valley north of Dunwich, you find yourself in byways which are little more than rutted lanes, as little used as most of the houses on the land.

Moreover, there broods eternally about this country an undeniable atmosphere not alone of age and desertion, but also of evil. There are areas of woodland in which no axe has ever fallen, as well as dark, vine-grown glens, where brooks trickle in a darkness unbroken by sunlight even on the brightest day. Over the entire valley there is little sign of life, though there are reclusive dwellers on some of the broken-down farms; even the hawks which soar high overhead never seem to linger long, and the black hordes of crows only cross the valley and never

descend to scavenge or forage. Once, long ago, it had the reputation of being a country in which *Hexerei* – the witch-beliefs
of superstitious people – was practised, and something of this
unenviable reputation lingers about it still.

It is not a country in which to linger overlong, and certainly
not a place in which to be found by night. Yet it was night in
that summer of 1927 when I made my last trip into the valley,
on my way from delivering a stove not far from Dunwich. I
should never have chosen to drive through the region north of
that decayed town, but I had one more delivery to make, and,
rather than follow my impulse to go around the valley and come
in from the far end, I drove into it at late dusk. In the valley
itself the dusk which still prevailed at Dunwich had given way
to a darkness which was soon to be profound, for the sky was
heavily overcast, and the clouds were so low as almost to touch
upon the enclosing hills, so that I rode, as it were, in a kind of
tunnel. The highway was little travelled; there were other roads
to take to reach points on both sides of the valley, and the side-
roads were so overgrown and virtually abandoned in this place
that few drivers wanted to take the risk of having to use them.

All would have been well, for my course led straight through
the valley to the farther end, and there was no need for me to
leave the state highway, had it not been for two unforeseen fac-
tors. Rain began to fall soon after I left Dunwich; it had been
hanging heavy over the earth throughout the afternoon, and
now at last the heavens opened and the torrent came down. The
highway was soon agleam in the glow of my headlamps. And
that glow, too, soon shone upon something other. I had gone
perhaps fifteen miles into the valley when I was brought up
short by a barrier on the highway, and a well-marked directive
to detour. Beyond the barrier I could see that the highway had
been torn up to such an extent that it was truly impassable.

I turned off the highway with misgivings. If I had only followed my impulse to return to Dunwich and take another road,
I might be free of the accursed nightmares which have troubled
my sleep since that night of horror! But I did not. Having
gone so far, I had no wish to waste the time it would take to

return to Dunwich. The rain was still coming down as a wall of water, and driving was extremely difficult. So I turned off the highway and immediately found myself on a road which was only partially surfaced with gravel. The highway crew had been along this way, and had widened the detour a little by cutting away overhanging limbs which had all but shut off the road before, but they had done little for the road itself, and I had not gone very far before I realized that I was in trouble.

The road on which I travelled was rapidly worsening because of the rain; my car, though one of the sturdiest of Fords, with relatively high, narrow wheels, cut deep ruts where it passed along, and from time to time, splashed into rapidly deepening puddles of water, which caused my motor to sputter and cough. I knew that it was only a question of time before the downpour would seep through the hood of the car and stop my engine altogether, and I began to look around for any sign of habitation, or, at least, some cover which would afford shelter for the car and myself. Indeed, knowing the loneliness of this isolated valley, I would have preferred an abandoned barn, but, in truth, it was impossible to make out any structure without some guidance, and thus I came at last to a pale window square of light shining not far off the road, and by a lucky chance found the driveway in the fading glow of my headlamps.

I turned in, passing a mailbox on which the owner's name had been crudely painted; it stood out, fading now: *Amos Stark*. The headlamp's glow swept the face of the dwelling there, and I saw that it was ancient, indeed, one of those houses which are all of a piece – house, ell, summer kitchen, barn, all in one long structure, under roofs of various heights. Fortunately, the barn stood wide open to the weather and, seeing no other shelter, I drove my car under that cover, expecting to see cattle and horses. But the barn wore an air of long-time desertion, for there were neither cattle nor horses, and the hay which filled it with its aroma of past summers must have been several years old.

I did not linger in the barn, but made my way to the house through the driving rain. From the outside, the house, as much as I could see of it, had the same appearance of desolation as the barn. It was of but one storey, with a low verandah out in front, and the floor of that verandah was, as I discovered just in time, broken here and there, with dark gaps to show where there had once been boards.

I found the door and pounded on it.

For a long time there was no sound but the voice of the rain falling upon the roof of the porch and into the water gathered in the yard just beyond. I knocked again and raised my voice to shout, 'Is anybody home?'

Then a quavering voice rose from inside. 'Who be ye?'

I explained that I was a salesman seeking shelter.

The light began to move inside, as a lamp was picked up from where it stood. The window grew dim, and from under the door a line of yellow grew stronger. There was the sound of bolts and chains being withdrawn, and then the door was opened, and my host stood there, holding a lamp high; he was a wizened old man with a scraggly beard half covering his scrawny neck. He wore spectacles, but peered out at me over them. His hair was white, and his eyes black; seeing me, his lips drew back in a kind of feral grin, exposing the stumps of teeth.

'Mr. Stark?' I asked.

'Storm ketched ye, eh?' he greeted me. 'Come right in the haouse an' dry off. Don't reckon the rain'll last long naow.'

I followed him into the inner room from which he had started away, though not before he had carefully bolted and locked the door behind us, a procedure which touched me with a faint unease. He must have seen my look of inquiry, for, once he had set the lamp down on a thick book which lay on a round table in the centre of the room to which he led me, he turned and said with a dry chuckle,

'This be Wentworth's day. I thought yew might be Nahum.'

His chuckle deepened into the ghost of a laugh.

'No, sir. My name is Fred Hadley. I'm from Boston.'

'Ain't never been ta Boston,' said Stark. 'Never been as fur as Arkham, even. Got my farm work ta keep me ta home.'

'I hope you don't mind. I took the liberty of driving my car into your barn.'

'The caows won't mind.' He cackled with laughter at his little joke, for he knew full well that no cow was in the barn. 'Wouldn't drive one a them new-fangled contraptions myself, but yew taown people are all alike. Got ta hev yer automobiles.'

'I didn't imagine I looked like a city slicker,' I said, in an attempt to meet his mood.

'I kin tell a taown man right off – onct in a while we get one movin' inta the deestrick but they move out suddent; guess they daon't like it here. Ain't never been ta no big taown; ain't sure I want ta go.'

He rambled on in this fashion for such an interminable time that I was able to look around me and make a kind of inventory of the room. In those years the time I did not spend on the road I put in at the warehouse in Boston, and there were few of us who could be counted better at inventory than myself; so it took me no time at all to see that Amos Stark's living room was filled with all kinds of things that the antique collectors would pay well to get their hands on. There were pieces of furniture that went back close to two hundred years, if I were any judge, and fine bric-à-brac, whatnots, and some wonderful blown glass and Haviland china on the shelves and on the whatnots. And there were many of the old handiwork pieces of the New England farm of decades before – candle-snuffers, wooden-pegged cork inkwells, candle-moulds, a book rest, a turkey-call of leather, pitchpine and tree gum calabashes, samplers – so that it was plain to see that the house had stood there for many years.

'Do you live alone, Mr. Stark?' I asked, when I could get a word in.

'Naow I do, yes. Onct thar was Molly an' Dewey. Abel went off when he war a boy, an' Ella died with lung fever. I bin alone naow for nigh on ta seven years.'

Even as he spoke, I observed about him a waiting, watchful air. He seemed constantly to be listening for some sound above the drumming of the rain. But there was none, save one small crepitant sound, where a mouse gnawed away somewhere in the old house – none but this and the ceaseless rune of the rain. Still he listened, his head cocked a little, his eyes narrowed as if against the glow of the lamp, and his head agleam at the bald crown which was ringed round by a thin, straggly tonsure of white hair. He might have been eighty years old, he might have been only sixty with his narrow, reclusive way of life having prematurely aged him.

'Ye war alaone on the road?' he asked suddenly.

'Never met a soul this side of Dunwich. Seventeen miles, I figure.'

'Give or take a half,' he agreed. Then he began to cackle and chuckle, as with an outburst of mirth that could no longer be held within. 'This be Wentworth's day, Nahum Wentworth.' His eyes narrowed again for a moment. 'Yew been a salesman in these parts long naow? Yew must a knowed Nahum Wentworth?'

'No, sir. I never knew him. I sell mostly in the towns. Just once in a while in the country.'

'Might' near everybody knowed Nahum,' he went on. 'But thar weren't none knowed him as well as I did. See that thar book?' He pointed to a well thumbed paper-covered book I could just make out in the ill-lit room. 'That thar's the *Seventh Book of Moses* – it's got a sight more larnin' in it than any other book I ever seen. That thar was Nahum's book.'

He chuckled at some memory. 'Oh, that Nahum was a queer one, all right. But mean – an' stingy, too. Don't see as haow ye could miss knowin' him.'

I assured him I had never heard of Nahum Wentworth before, though I admitted privately to some curiosity about the object of my host's preoccupation, in so far as he had been given to reading the *Seventh Book of Moses*, which was a kind of Bible for the supposed hexes, since it purported to offer all manner of spells, incantations, and charms to those readers who were gullible enough to believe in them. I saw, too, within the circle of lamplight, certain other books I recognized – a Bible, worn as much as the textbook of magic, a compendious edition of Cotton Mather's works, and a bound volume of the *Arkham*

Advertiser. Perhaps these, too, had once belonged to Nahum Wentworth.

'I see ye lookin' at his books,' said my host, as if he had indeed divined my thoughts. 'He said as haow I could have 'em; so I took 'em. Good books, too. Only that I need glasses, I'd a read 'em. Yew're welcome ta look at 'em, though.'

I thanked him gravely and reminded him that he had been talking of Nahum Wentworth.

'Oh, that Nahum!' he replied at once, renewing his chuckle. 'I don't reckon he'd a lent me all that money if he a knowed what was ta happen ta him. No, sir, I don't reckon he would. An' never ta take a note fer it, neither. Five thousand it was. An' him tellin' me he didn't have no need fer a note or any kind a paper, so thar warn't no proof I ever had the money off'n him, not a-tall, jest the two of us knowin' it, and he settin' a day five years after fer him ta come fer his money an' his due. Five years, an' this is the day, this is Wentworth's day.'

He paused and favoured me with a sly glance out of eyes that were at one and the same time dancing with suppressed mirth and dark with withheld fear. 'Only he can't come, because it warn't no less'n two months after that day that he got shot out huntin'. Shotgun in the back o' the head. Pure accident. O' course, thar was them that said as haow I done it a-purpose, but I showed 'em haow ta shet up, 'cause I druv in ta Dunwich an' went straight ta the bank an' I made out my will so's his daughter – that's Miss Genie – was ta git all I die ownin'. Didn't make no secret of it, either. Let 'em all know, so's they could talk their fool heads off.'

'And the loan?' I could not forbear asking.

'The time ain't up till midnight tonight.' He chuckled and cackled with laughter. 'And it don't seem like Nahum can keep his 'pointment, naow, does it? I figure, if he don't come, it's mine. An' he can't come. An' a good thing he can't, 'cause I ain't got it.'

I did not ask about Wentworth's daughter, and how she fared. To tell the truth, I was beginning to feel the strain of the day and the evening's drive through the downpour. And this must have been evident to my host, for he ceased talking and sat watching me, speaking again only after what seemed a long time.

'Yew're peaked lookin'. Yew tired?'

'I guess I am. But I'll be going as soon as the storm abates a little.'

'Tell yew what. That's no need a yew a-settin' here listenin' ta me jaw yew. I'll git ye another lamp, an' yew kin lie down on the couch inside the next room. If it stops rainin', I'll call ye.'

'I'm not taking your bed, Mr. Stark?'

'I set up late nights,' he said.

But any protest I might have made would have been futile. He was already up and about, lighting another kerosene lamp, and in a few moments he was conducting me into the adjoining room and showing me the couch. On the way in, I picked up the *Seventh Book of Moses*, impelled by curiosity inspired by decades of hearing talk of the potent wonders between its covers; though he eyed me strangely, my host made no objection, and returned to his wicker rocking chair in the next room again, leaving me to my own devices.

Outside, the rain still came down in torrential gusts. I made myself comfortable on the couch, which was an old-fashioned leather-covered affair, with a high head-rest, moved the lamp over close – for its light was very feeble – and commenced to read in the *Seventh Book of Moses*, which, I soon found, was a curious rigmarole of chants and incantations to such 'princes' of the nether world as Aziel, Mephistopheles, Marbuel, Barbuel, Aniquel, and others. The incantations were of many kinds; some were designed to cure illness, others to grant wishes; some were meant for success in undertakings, others for vengeance upon one's enemies. The reader was repeatedly warned in the text of how terrible some of the words were, so much so that perhaps because of these adjurations, I was compelled to copy the worst of the incanations which caught my eye – *Aila himel adonaij amara Zebaoth cadas yeseraije haralius* – which was nothing less than an incantation for the assemblage of devils or spirits, or the raising of the dead.

And, having copied it, I was not loath to say it aloud several times, not for a moment expecting anything untoward to take place. Nor did it. So I put the book aside and looked at my watch. Eleven o'clock. It seemed to me that the force of the rain had begun to diminish; it was no longer such a downpour; that lessening which always foretells the end of a rain storm within a reasonably short time had begun. Marking the appointments of the room well, so that I would not stumble over any object of furniture on my way back to the room where my host waited, I put out the light to rest a little while before taking to the road once more.

But, tired as I was, I found it hard to compose myself.

It was not alone that the couch on which I lay was hard and cold, but that the very atmosphere of the house seemed oppressive. Like its owner, it had about it a kind of resignation, an air of waiting for the inevitable, as if it, too, knew that sooner rather than later its weather-beaten siding would buckle outwards and its roof fall inwards to bring an end to its increasingly precarious existence. But there was something more than this atmosphere of so many old houses which it possessed; it was a resignation tinged with apprehension – that same apprehension which had caused old Amos Stark to hesitate about answering my knock; and soon I caught myself listening, too, as Stark did, for more than the patter of the rain, steadily diminishing now, and the incessant gnawing of mice.

My host did not sit still. Every little while he rose, and I could hear him shuffle from place to place; now it was the window, now the door; he went to try them, to make sure they were locked; then he came back and sat down again. Sometimes he muttered to himself; perhaps he had lived too long alone and had fallen into that common habit of isolated, reclusive people, of talking to himself. For the most part what he said was indistinguishable, almost inaudible, but on occasion some words came through, and it occurred to me that one of the things which occupied his thoughts was the amount of interest that would be due on the money he owed Nahum Wentworth, were it now collectable. 'A hundred an' fifty dollars a year,' he kept saying. 'Comes ta seven-fifty' – said with something akin to awe. There was more of this, and there was something more which troubled me more than I cared to admit.

Something the old man said was upsetting when pieced together; but he said none of it consecutively. 'I fell,' he muttered, and there followed a sentence or two of inanities. 'All they was to it.' And again many indistinguishable words. 'Went off – quick-like.' Once more a round of meaningless or inaudible words. 'Didn't know 'twas aimed at Nahum.' Followed once again by indistinct mutterings. Perhaps the old man's conscience troubled him. Certainly the brooding resignation of the house was enough to stir him to his darkest thoughts. Why had he not followed the other inhabitants of the stony valley to one of the settlements. What was there to prevent his going?

He had said he was alone, and presumably he was alone in the world as well as in the house, for had he not willed his earthly possessions to Nahum Wentworth's daughter?

His slippers whispered along the floor, his fingers rustled papers.

Outside the whippoorwills began to call, which was a sign that in some quarters the sky was beginning to clear; and soon there was a chorus of them fit to deafen a man. 'Heer them whipperwills,' I heard my host mutter. 'Callin' fer a soul. Clem Whateley's dyin'.' As the voice of the rain fell slowly away, the voices of the whippoorwills rose in volume, and soon I grew drowsy and dozed off.

I come now to that part of my story which makes me doubt the evidence of my own senses, which, when I look back upon it now, seems impossible of occurrence. Indeed, many times now, with added years, I wonder whether I did not dream it all – yet I know it was not a dream, and I still have certain corroborating newspaper clippings to adduce in proof that mine was not a dream – clippings about Amos Stark, about his bequest to Genie Wentworth – and, strangest of all – about a hellish molestation of a grave half forgotten on a hillside in that accursed valley.

I had not been dozing long when I awoke. The rain had ceased, but the voices of the whippoorwills had moved closer to the house and were now in thunderous chorus. Some of the birds sat immediately under the window of the room in which I lay, and the roof of the shaky verandah must have been covered with the nocturnal creatures. I have no doubt that it was their clamour which had brought me out of the light sleep into which I had fallen. I lay for a few moments to collect myself, and then moved to rise, for, the rain having now come to an end, driving would be less hazardous, and my motor was in far less danger of going out on me.

But just as I swung my feet to the floor, a knock fell upon the outer door.

I sat motionless making no sound – and no sound came from the adjoining room.

The knock came again, more peremptorily this time.

'Who be ye?' Stark called out.

There was no reply.

I saw the light move, and I heard Stark's exclamation of triumph. 'Past midnight!' He had looked at his clock, and at the same time I looked at my watch. His clock was ten minutes fast.

He went to answer the door.

I could tell that he set down the lamp in order to unlock the door. Whether he meant to take it up again, as he had done to peer at me, I could not say. I heard the door open – whether by his hand or by another's.

And then a terrible cry rang out, a cry of mingled rage and terror in Amos Stark's voice. 'No! No! Go back. I ain't got it – ain't got it, I tell yew. Go back!' He stumbled back and fell, and almost immediately after there came a horrible, choking cry, a sound of laboured breathing, a gurgling gasp . . .

I came to my feet and lurched through the doorway into that room – and then for one cataclysmic moment I was rooted to that spot, unable to move, to cry out, at the hideousness of what

I saw. Amos Stark was spread on the floor on his back, and sitting astride him, was a mouldering skeleton, its bony arms bowed above his throat, its fingers at his neck. And in the back of the skull, the shattered bones where a charge of shot had once gone through. This I saw in that one terrible moment — then, mercifully, I fainted.

When I came to a few moments later, all was quiet in the room. The house was filled with the fresh musk of the rain, which came in through the open dront door; outside, the whip-poorwills still cried, and a wan moonlight lay on the ground like pale white wine. The lamp still burned in the hall, but my host was not in his chair.

He lay where I last had seen him, spread on the floor. My whole impulse was to escape that horrible scene as quickly as possible, but decency impelled me to pause at Amos Stark's side, to make sure that he was beyond my help. It was that fateful pause which brought the crowning horror of all, that horror which sent me shrieking into the night to escape that hellish place as were all the demons of the nether regions at my heels. For, as I bent above Amos Stark, ascertaining that he was indeed dead, I saw sticking into the discoloured flesh of his neck the whitened finger bones of a human skeleton, and, *even as I looked upon them, the individual bones detached themselves, and went bounding away from the corpse, down the hall, and out into the night to rejoin that ghastly visitor who had come from the grave to keep his appointment with Amos Stark!*

I

I never knew my great-grandfather Asaph Peabody though I was five years old when he died on his great old estate northeast of the town of Wilbraham, Massachusetts. There is a childhood memory of once visiting there, at a time when the old man was lying ill; my father and mother mounted to his bedroom, but I remained below with my nurse, and never saw him. He was reputed to be wealthy, but time whittles away at wealth as at all things, for even stone is mortal, and surely mere money could not be expected to withstand the ravages of the ever-increasing taxation, dwindling a little with each death. And there were many deaths in our family, following my great-grandfather's in 1907. Two of my uncles died after – one was killed on the Western front, and another went down on the *Lusitania*. Since a third uncle had died before them, and none of them had ever married, the estate fell to my father on my grandfather's death in 1919.

My father was not a provincial, though most of his forbears had been. He was little inclined to life in the country, and made no effort to take an interest in the estate he had inherited, beyond spending my great-grandfather's money on various investments in Boston and New York. Nor did my mother share any of my own interest in rural Massachusetts. Yet neither of them would consent to sell it, though on one occasion, when I was home from college, my mother did propose that the property be sold, and my father coldly dismissed the subject; I remember his sudden freezing – there is no more fitting word to describe his reaction – and his curious reference to 'the Peabody heritage,' as well as his carefully phrased words: 'Grandfather predicted that one of his blood would recover the heritage.' My mother had asked scornfully: 'What heritage? Didn't your father just about spend it all?' to which my father made no reply, resting his case in his icy inference that there were certain good reasons why the property could not be sold, as if it were entailed beyond any process of law. Yet he never went near the property; the taxes were paid regularly by one Ahab Hopkins, a lawyer in Wilbraham, who made reports on the property to my parents, though they always ignored them, dismissing any suggestion of 'keeping up' the property by saying it would be like 'Throwing good money after bad.'

The property was abandoned, to all intents and purposes; and abandoned it remained. The lawyer had once or twice made a half-hearted attempt to rent it, but even a brief boom in Wilbraham had not brought more than transient renters to the old homestead, and the Peabody place yielded inexorably to time and the weather. It was thus in a sad state of disrepair when I came into the property on the sudden death by automobile accident of both my parents in the autumn of 1929. Nevertheless, what with the decline in property values which took place subsequent to the inauguration of the depression that year, I determined to sell my Boston property and refurbish the house outside of Wilbraham for my own use. I had enough of a competence on my parents' death so that I could afford to retire from the practice of law, which had always demanded of me greater preciseness and attention than I wished to give to it.

Such a plan, however, could not be implemented until at least part of the old house had been got ready for occupation once more. The dwelling itself was the product of many generations. It had been built originally in 1787, at first as a simple colonial house, with severe lines, an unfinished second storey, and four impressive pillars at the front. But, in time, this had become the basic part of the house, the heart, as it were. Subsequent generations had altered and added to it – at first by the addition of a floating stairway and a second storey; then by various ells and wings, so that at the time I was preparing to make it my residence, it was a large rambling structure, which occupied over an acre of land, adding to the house itself the lawn and gardens, which were in as great a state of disuse as the house.

The severe colonial lines had been softened by age and less regardful builders, and the architecture was no longer pure, for gambrel roof vied with mansard roof, small-paned windows with large, figured and elaborately sculptured cornices with plain, dormers with unbroken roof. Altogether the impression the old house conveyed was not displeasing, but to anyone of architectural sensibilities, it must have appeared a woeful and unhappy conglomeration of architectural styles and kinds of ornament. Any such impression, however, must surely have been softened by the tremendously spreading ancient elms and oaks which crowded upon the house from all sides save the garden, which had been taken over among the roses, so long grown untended, by young poplar and birch trees. The whole effect of the house, therefore, despite the accretions of time and differing tastes, was of faded magnificence, and even its unpainted walls were in harmony with the great-girthed trees all around.

The house had no less than twenty-seven rooms. Of these, I selected a trio in the south-east corner to be rehabilitated, and all that autumn and early winter, I drove up from Boston to keep an eye on the progress of the venture. Cleaning and waxing the old wood brought out its beautiful colour, installing electricity removed the dark gloom of the rooms, and only the waterworks delayed me until late winter; but by February twenty-fourth, I was able to take up my residence in the ancestral Peabody home. Then for a month I was occupied with plans for the rest of the house, and, though I had initially thought of having some of the additions torn down and the oldest parts of the structure retained, I soon abandoned this project in favour of the decision to keep the house as it was, for it had a pervasive charm born, no doubt, of the many generations which had lived there, as well as of the essence of the events which had taken place within its walls.

Within that month, I was quite taken with the place, and what had been primarily a temporary move was gladly embraced as a lifelong ideal. But alas, this ideal grew to such proportions that it soon brought about a grandiose departure which

subtly altered my direction and threw me off the track on a
course I had never wished to take. This scheme was the determination to move to the family vault, which had been cut into
a hillside within sight of the house, though away a little from
the highway which passed in front of the estate, the remains
of my parents, who had been decently interred in a Boston plot.
This was in addition to my resolve to make an attempt also to
bring back to the United States the bones of my dead uncle,
which reposed somewhere in France, and thus re-unite the family, as far as possible, on the ancestral acres near Wilbraham. It
was just such a plan as might occur to a bachelor who was also
a reclusive solitary, which I had become in the short space of
that month, surrounded by the architect's drawings and the lore
of the old house which was about to begin a new lease of life in
a new era, far removed from that of its simple beginnings.

It was in pursuit of this plan that I made my way one day
in March to the family vault, with the keys the lawyer for the
estate had delivered into my hands. The vault was not obtrusive; indeed, no part of it was ordinarily visible except the massive door, for it had been built into a natural slope, and was
almost concealed by the trees which had grown without pruning
for decades. The door and the vault, as well, had been built to
last for centuries; it dated back almost as far as the house, and
for many generations every member of the Peabody family
from old Jedediah, the first to occupy the house, onward, had
been interred here. The door offered me some resistance, since
it had not been opened for years, but at length it yielded to my
efforts and the vault lay open to me.

The Peabody dead lay in their coffins – thirty-seven of them,
some in cubicles where the earliest Peabodys had lain held only
the remains of coffins, while that reserved for Jedediah was
completely empty, with not even the dust to show that coffin
and body had once reposed in that place. They were in order,
however, save for the casket which bore the body of my great-
grandfather Asaph Peabody; this seemed curiously disturbed,
standing out of line with the others, among those more recent
ones – my grandfather's and my one uncle's – which had no

cubicles of their own but were simply on a ledge extended outward from the cubicled wall. Moreover, it seemed as if someone had lifted or attempted to lift the cover, for one of the hinges was broken, and the other loosened.

My attempt to straighten my great-grandfather's coffin was instinctive, but in so doing, the cover was still further jostled and slipped partially off, revealing to my startled gaze all that remained of Asaph Peabody. I saw that through some hideous error, he had been buried face downward – I did not want to think, even at so long a time after his death, that the old man might have been buried in cataleptic state and so suffered a painful death in that cramped, airless space. Nothing but bones survived, bones and portions of his garments. Nevertheless, I was constrained to alter mistake or accident, whichever it might be; so I removed the cover of the coffin, and reverently turned skull and bones over so that the skeleton of my great-grandfather lay in its rightful position. This act, which might have seemed grisly in other circumstances, seemed only wholly natural, for the vault was aglow with the sunlight and shadows that speckled the floor through the open door, and it was not at that hour a cheerless place. But I had come, after all, to ascertain how much room remained in the vault, and I was gratified to note that there was ample room for both my parents, my uncle – if his remains could be found and brought thither from France – and, finally, myself.

I prepared, therefore, to carry on with my plans, left the vault well locked behind me, and returned to the house pondering ways and means of bringing my uncle's remains back to the country of his birth. Without delay, I wrote to the authorities in Boston on behalf of the disinterment of my parents, and to those of the county in which I now resided for permission to re-inter my parents in the family vault.

II

The singular chain of events which seemed to centre about the old Peabody homestead began, as nearly as I can recall, on that very night. True, I had had an oblique kind of warning that something might be amiss with the old house, for old Hopkins, on surrendering his keys, had asked me insistently when I came to take possession whether I was sure I wanted to take this step, and had seemed equally intent upon pointing out that the house was 'a lonely sort of place,' that the farming neighbours 'never looked kindly on the Peabodys,' and that there had always been a 'kind of difficulty keeping renters there.' It was one of those places, he said, almost with relish at making a distinct point, 'to which nobody ever goes for a picnic. You'll never find paper plates or napkins *there*!' – a plethora of ambiguities which nothing could persuade the old man to reduce to facts, since, evidently, there were no facts, but that the neighbours frowned upon an estate of such magnitude in the midst of what was otherwise good farming land. This, in truth, stretched out on all sides of my property of but forty acres, most of it woods – a land of neat fields, stone walls, rail fences, along which trees grew and shrubbery made adequate cover for birds. An old man's talk, I thought it, given rise to by his kinship with the farmers who surrounded me: solid, sturdy Yankee stock, no whit different from the Peabodys, save that they toiled harder and perhaps longer.

But on that night, one on which the winds of March howled and sang among the trees about the house, I became obsessed with the idea that I was not alone in the house. There was a sound not so much of footsteps as of *movement* from somewhere upstairs, one that defies description, save that it was of someone moving about in a narrow space, forward and back, forward and back. I remember that I went out in the great dark space into which the floating stairway descended, and listened to the darkness above; for the sound seemed to drift down the stairs, sometimes unmistakable, sometimes a mere

whisper; and I stood there listening, listening, listening, trying
to identify its source, trying to conjure up from my rationalization some explanation for it, since I had not heard it before, and
concluded at last that in some fashion a limb of a tree must be
driven by the wind to brush against the house, forward and
back. Settled on this, I returned to my quarters, and was no
more disturbed by it – not that it ceased, for it did not, but
that I had given it a rational excuse for existence.

I was less able to rationalize my dreams that night. Though
ordinarily not at all given to dreams, I was literally beset by
the most grotesque phantasms of sleep, in which I played a
passive role and was subjected to all manner of distortions of
time and space, sensory illusions, and several frightening glimpses of a shadowy figure in a conical black hat with an equally
shadowy creature at his side. These I saw as through a glass,
darkly, and the twilight landscape as through a prism. Indeed,
I suffered not so much dreams as fragments of dreams, none of
them having either beginning or ending, but inviting me into
an utterly bizarre and alien world, as through another dimension of which I was not aware in the mundane world beyond
sleep. But I survived that restless night, if somewhat haggardly.

On the very next day I learned a most interesting fact from
the architect who came out to discuss my plans for further
renovation, a young man not given to the quaint beliefs about
old houses common to isolated, rural areas. 'One who came
to look at the house would never think,' he said, 'that it had a
secret room – well, hidden – would you?' he said, spreading his
drawings before me.

'And has it,' I asked.

'Perhaps a "priest's hole",' he guessed. 'For runaway slaves.'

'I've never seen it.'

'Nor I. But look here . . .' And he showed me on the plans
he had reconstructed from the foundations and the rooms as
we knew them, that there was a space unaccounted for along
the north wall upstairs, in the oldest part of the house. No
priest's hole, certainly: there were no Papists among the Pea-

bodys. But runaway slaves – perhaps. If so, however, how came it there so early, before there were enough slaves to make the run for Canada to justify the room's coming into being? No, not that, either.

'Can you find it, do you think?' I asked.

'It has to be there.'

And so indeed it was. Cleverly concealed, though the absence of a window in the north wall of the bedroom ought to have warranted an earlier examination. The door to it was hidden in the finely-wrought carvings which decorated that entire wall, which was of red cedar; had one not known the room must have been there, one would hardly have seen the door which had no knob and worked only by pressure upon one of the carvings, which the architect found, not I, for I have never had an adeptness at things of that kind. However it lay rather within the province of an architect than my own and I paused only long enough to study the rusty mechanism of the door before stepping into the room.

It was a small confining space. Yet it was not as small as a priest's hole; a man could walk upright in it for a distance of ten feet or so, though the slant of the roof would cut off any walking in the direction opposed to it. The long way, yes; across to the wall, no. What was more, the room bore every sign of having been occupied in past time, for it was left undisturbed, there were still books and papers about, as well as chairs which had been used at a small desk against one wall.

The room presented the most singular appearance. Though it was small, its angles seemed to be awry, as if the builder were subtly determined to confound its owner. Moreover, there were curious designs drawn upon the floor, some of them actually cut into the planking in a crudely barbarous fashion, roughly circular in plan, with all manner of oddly repellent drawings around the outer and inner edges. There was a similar repulsiveness about the desk, for it was black, rather than brown, and it had the surprising appearance of having been burned; it looked, indeed, as if it served in more than the capacity of a desk. On it, moreover, was a stack of what looked at first glance to be very ancient books, bound in some sort of leather, as well as a manuscript of some kind, likewise bound.

There was little time for any examination, however, for the architect was with me and, having seen all he wished, which was just sufficient to verify his suspicion of the room's existence, he was eager to be off.

'Shall we plan to eliminate it, cut in a window,' he asked, and added, 'Of course, you won't want to keep it.'

'I don't know,' I answered. 'I'm not sure. It depends on how old it is.'

If the room were as ancient as I thought it to be, then I would be quite naturally hesitant to destroy it. I wanted a chance to poke around it a little, to examine the old books. Besides, there was no haste; this decision did not need to be made at once; there were other things the architect could do before either of us need think about the hidden room upstairs. It was there that the matter rested.

I had fully intended to return to the room next day, but certain events intervened. In the first place, I spent another very troubled night, the victim of recurrent dreams of a most disturbing nature, for which I could not account, since I had never been given to dreams except as a concomitant of illness. These dreams were, perhaps not unnaturally, of my ancestors, particularly of one long-bearded old fellow, wearing a conical black hat of strange design, whose face, unfamiliar to me in dream, was in actuality that of my great-grandfather Asaph, as a row of family portraits in the lower hall verified next morning. This ancestor seemed to be involved in an extraordinary progression through the air, quite as if he were flying. I saw him walking through walls, walking on the air, silhouetted among treetops. And wherever he went, he was accompanied by a large black cat which had the same ability to transcend the laws of time and space. Nor did my dreams have any progression or even, each within itself, any unity; they were a mixed-up sequence of scenes in which my great-grandfather, his cat, his house, and his property took part as in unrelated tableaux. They were distinctly related to my dreams of the previous night, and accompanied again by all the extra-dimensional trappings of those first nocturnal experiences, differing only in that they possessed greater clarity. These dreams insistently disturbed me throughout the night.

I was thus in no mood to learn from the architect that there would be some further delay in the resumption of work at the Peabody place. He seemed reticent or reluctant to explain, but I pressed him to do so, until at last he admitted that the workmen he had hired had all notified him early this morning that none of them wished to work on this 'job.' Nevertheless, he assured me, he would have no difficulty hiring some inexpensive Polish or Italian labourers from Boston, if I would be a little patient with him. I had no alternative, but, in fact, I was not as much annoyed as I pretended to be, for I began to have certain doubts about the wisdom of making all the alterations I had intended. After all, a part of the old house must necessarily stand with no more than re-enforcement, for much of the charm of the old place lay in its age; I adjured him, therefore, to take his time, and went out to make such purchases as I had intended to make when I came into Wilbraham.

I had hardly begun to do so before I was aware of a most sullen attitude on the part of the natives. Whereas, heretofore, they had either paid me no attention at all, since many of them did not know me, or they had greeted me perfunctorily, if they had made my acquaintance, I found them on that morning of one mind – no one wished to speak to me or to be seen speaking to me. Even the storekeepers were unnecessarily short, if not downright unpleasant, their manner suggesting plainly that they would appreciate my taking my trade elsewhere. It was possible, I reflected, that they had learned of my plans to renovate the old Peabody house, and might be opposed to it on twin grounds – either that renovation would contribute to the destruction of its charm, or that it would on the other hand, give another and longer lease of life to a piece of property that surrounding farmers would much have preferred to cultivate, once the house and the woods were gone.

My first thoughts, however, soon gave way to indignation.

I was not a pariah, and I did not deserve to be shunned like one, and when finally, I stopped in at the office of Ahab Hopkins, I unburdened myself to him rather more volubly than was my custom, even though, as I could see, I made him uneasy.

'Ah, well, Mr. Peabody,' he said, seeking to soothe my ruffled composure, 'I would not take that too seriously. After all, these people have had a grievous shock, and they are in an ugly, suspicious mood. Besides, they are basically a superstitious lot. I am an old man, and I have never known them to be otherwise.'

Hopkins' gravity gave me pause. 'A shock, you say. You must forgive me – I've heard nothing.'

He favoured me with a most curious look, at which I was quite taken aback. 'Mr. Peabody, two miles up the road from your place lives a family by the name of Taylor. I know George well. They have ten children. Or perhaps I had better say "had". Last night, their second youngest, a child of slightly over two years of age, was taken from his bed and carried off without a trace.'

'I am sorry to hear it. But what has that got to do with me?'

'Nothing, I'm sure, Mr. Peabody. But you're a comparative stranger here, and well – you must know it sooner or later –the name of Peabody is not looked on with pleasure – in fact, I may say it is hated – by many people of the community.'

I was astounded and did not attempt to hide it. 'But why?'

'Because there are many people who believe every kind of gossip and muttered talk, no matter how ridiculous it is,' Hopkins answered. 'You are an old enough man to realize that it is so, even if you're unfamiliar with our rural countryside, Mr. Peabody. There were all manner of stories common about your great-grandfather, when I was a child, and, since during the years of his incumbency of the homestead, there were certain ugly disappearances of little children, of whom no trace was ever found, there is possibly a natural inclination to connect these two events – a new Peabody on the homestead, and a recurrence of a kind of event associated with another Peabody's residence there.'

'Monstrous!' I cried.

'Undoubtedly,' Hopkins agreed with an almost perverse ami-
ability, 'but so it is. Besides, it is now April. Walpurgis Night is
scarce a month away.'

I fear my face must have been so blank as to disconcert him.

'Oh, come, Mr. Peabody,' said Hopkins with false joviality,
'you are surely aware that your great-grandfather was considered to be a warlock!'

I took my leave of him, gravely disturbed. Despite my shock
and outrage, despite my indignation at the manner in which
the natives showed their scorn and – yes, fear – of me, I was
even more upset by the nagging suspicion that there was a disquieting logic to the events of the previous night and this day.
I had dreamed of my great-grandfather in strange terms indeed,
and now I heard him spoken of in far more significant terms.
I knew only enough to know that the natives had looked upon
my great-grandfather superstitiously as the male counterpart of
a witch – a warlock or wizard; by whatever name they called
him, so they had seen him. I made no further attempt to be even
decently courteous to the natives who turned their heads when
I came walking towards them, but got into my car and drove
out to the homestead. There my patience was still further
tried, for I found nailed to my front door a crude warning –
a sheet of tablet paper upon which some illiterate, ill-inten-
tioned neighbour had scrawled in pencil: *'Git out – or els.'*

III

Possibly because of these distressing events, my sleep that night
was far more troubled by dreams than it had been on previous
nights. Save for one major difference – there was more continu-
ity in the scenes I saw while I tossed in restless slumber. Again
it was my great-grandfather, Asaph Peabody, who occupied
them, but he seemed now to have grown so sinister in appearance as to be threatening, and his cat moved with him with the
hair of its neck ruffled, its pointed ears forward, and tail erect –

a monstrous creature, which glided or floated along beside or behind him. He carried something – something white, or flesh-coloured, but the murkiness of my dream would not permit me to recognize it. He went through woods, over countryside, among trees; he travelled in narrow passageways, and once, I was certain, he was in a tomb or vault. I recognized, too, certain parts of the house. But he was not alone in his dreams – lingering always in the background was a shadowy, but monstrous Black Man – not a Negro, but man of such vivid black-ness as to be literally darker than night, but with flaming eyes which seemed to be of living fire. There were all manner of lesser creatures about the old man – bats, rats, hideous little beings which were half human, half rat. Moreover, I was given to auditory hallucinations simultaneously, for from time to time, I seemed to hear muffled crying, as if a child were in pain, and, at the same time, a hideous, cackling laughter, and a chanting voice saying: 'Asaph will *be* again. Asaph will *grow* again.'

Indeed, when at last I awoke from this continuing nightmare, just as the dawn light was making itself manifest in the room, I could have sworn that the crying of a child still sounded in my ears, as if it came from within the very walls itself. I did not sleep again, but lay wide-eyed, wondering what the coming night would bring, and the next, and the next after that.

The coming of the Polish workmen from Boston put my dreams temporarily from my mind. They were a stolid, quiet lot. Their foreman, a thick-set man named Jon Cieciorka, was matter-of-fact and dictatorial with the men under him; he was a well-muscled fellow of fifty or thereabouts, and the three men whom he directed moved in haste at his command, as if they feared his wrath. They had told the architect that they could not come for a week, the foreman explained, but another job had been postponed, and here they were; they had driven up from Boston after sending the architect a telegram. But they had his plans, and they knew what must be done.

Their very first act was to remove the plaster from the north wall of the room immediately beneath the hidden room. They had to work carefully, for the studding which supported the second storey could not be disturbed, nor need it be. Plaster and lathing, which, I saw as they began, was of that old-fashioned kind made by hand, had to be taken off and replaced; the plaster had begun to discolour and to break loose years before, so that the room was scarcely habitable. It had been so, too, with that corner of the house which I now occupied, but, since I had made greater changes there, the alterations had taken longer.

I watched the men work for a while, and had just become accustomed to the sounds of their pounding, when suddenly, they ceased. I waited a moment, and then started up and went out into the hall. I was just in time to see all four of them, clustered near the wall, cross themselves superstitiously, back away a little, and then break and run from the house. Passing me, Cieciorka flung an epithet at me in horror and anger. Then they were out of the house, and while I stood as if rooted to the spot, I heard their car start and leap away from my property.

Utterly bewildered, I turned towards where they had been working. They had removed a considerable section of the plaster and lathing; indeed, several of their tools were still scattered about. In their work, they had exposed that section of the wall which lay behind the baseboard, and all the accumulated detritus of the years which had come to rest in that place. It was not until I drew close to the wall that I saw what they must have seen and understood what had sent these superstitious louts running in fear and loathing from the house.

For at the base of the wall, behind the baseboard, there lay, among long yellowed papers half gnawed away by mice, yet still bearing on their surfaces the unmistakably cabalistic designs of some bygone day, among wicked implements of death and destruction – short, dagger-like knives rusted by what must surely have been blood – *the small skulls and bones of at least three children!*

I stared unbelievingly, for the superstitious nonsense I had heard only a day before from Ahab Hopkins now took on a more sinister cast. So much I realized on the instant. Children had disappeared during my great-grandfather's aegis; he had been suspected of wizardry, of witchcraft, of playing roles in which the sacrifice of little children was an integral part; now here, within the walls of his house, were such remains as lent weight to the native suspicions of his nefarious activities!

Once my initial shock had passed, I knew I must act with dispatch. If this discovery were made known, then indeed my tenure here would be bitterly unhappy, made so by the God-fearing natives of the neighbourhood. Without hesitating further, I ran for a cardboard box and, returning to the wall with it, gathered up every vestige of bone I could find, and carried this gruesome burden to the family vault, where I emptied the bones into the cubicle which had once held the remains of Jedediah Peabody, now long since gone to dust. Fortunately, the small skulls disintegrated, so that anyone searching there would find only the remains of someone long dead, and only an expert would have been able to determine the origin of the bones which remained sufficiently unimpaired to offer any key. By the time any report from the Polish workingmen came back to the architect, I would be able to deny the truth of them, though for this report I was destined to wait in vain, for the fear-ridden Poles never revealed to the architect a word of their real reason for deserting their job.

I did not wait to learn this from the architect, who was bound eventually to find someone who would undertake such alterations as I wished made, but, guided by an instinct I did not know I possessed, I made my way to the hidden room, carrying a powerful flashlight, determined to subject it to the most painstaking examination. Almost at once upon entering it, however, I made a spine-chilling discovery; though the marks the architect and I had made in our brief foray into the room were still identifiably evident, there were other, more recent marks which suggested that someone – or something – had been in this room since I had last entered it. The marks were plain to be seen – of a man, bare of foot, and, equally unmistakably, the prints of a cat. But these were not the most terrifying evidences of some sinister occupation – they began out of the northeast corner of the curiously-angled room, at a point where it was impossible for a man to stand, and scarcely high enough for a cat; yet it was here that they materialized in the room, and from this point that they came forward, proceeding in the direction of the black desk – where there was something far worse, though I did not notice it until I was almost upon the desk in following the footsteps.

The desk had been freshly stained. A small pool of some viscous fluid lay there, as if it had boiled up out of the wood – scarcely more than three inches in diameter, next to a mark in the dust as if the cat or a doll or a bundle of some kind had lain there. I stared at it, trying to determine what it might be in the glow of my flashlight, sending my light ceilingward to detect, if possible, any opening through which rain might have come, until I remembered that there had been no rainfall since my first and only visit to this strange secret room. Then I touched my index finger to the pool and held it in the light. The colour was red – the colour of blood – and simultaneously I knew without being told that this was what it was. Of how it came there I dared not think.

By this time the most terrifying conclusions were crowding to mind, but without any logic. I backed away from the desk, pausing only long enough to snatch up some of the leather-bound books, and the manuscript which reposed there; and with these in my possession, I retreated from the room into the more prosaic surroundings outside – where the rooms were not constructed of seemingly impossible angles, suggesting dimensions beyond the knowledge of mankind. I hastened almost guiltily to my quarters below, hugging the books carefully to my bosom.

Curiously, as soon as I opened the books, I had an uncanny conviction that I knew their contents. Yet I had never seen them before, nor, to the best of my knowledge, had I ever encountered such titles as *Malleus Maleficarum* and the *Daemonialitas* of Sinistrari. They dealt with witch-lore and wizardry, with all manner of spells and legends, with the destruction of witches and warlocks by fire, with their methods of travel –

'Among their chief operations are being bodily transported from place to place . . . seduced by the illusions and phantasms of devils, do actually, as they believe and profess, ride in the night-time on certain beasts . . . or simply walk upon the air out of the openings built for them and for none other. Satan himself deludes in dreams the mind which he holds captive, leading it through devious ways . . . They take the unguent, which they made at the devil's instruction from the limbs of children, particularly of those whom they have killed, and anoint with it a chair or a broomstick; whereupon they are immediately carried up into the air, either by day or by night, and either visibly or, if they wish, invisibly . . .' But I read no more of this, and turned to Sinistrari.

Almost at once my eye fell upon this disturbing passage – '*Promittunt Diabolo statis temporibus sacrificia, et oblationes; singulis quindecim diebus, vel singulo mense saltem, necem alicujus infantis, aut mortale veneficium, et singulis hebdomadis alia mala in damnum humani generis, ut grandines, tempestates, incendia, mortem animalium . . .*' setting forth how warlocks and witches must bring about, at stated intervals, the murder of a child, or some other homicidal act of sorcery, the mere reading of which filled me with an indescribable sense of alarm, as a result of which I did no more than glance at the other books I had brought down, the *Vitae sophistrarum* of Eunapius, Anania's *De Natura Daemonum*, Stampa's *Fuga Satanae*, Bouget's *Discours des Sorciers*, and that untitled work by Olaus Magnus, bound in a smooth black leather, which only later I realized was human skin.

The mere possession of these books betokened a more than ordinary interest in the lore of witchcraft and wizardry; indeed, it was such manifest explanation for the superstitious beliefs about my great-grandfather which abounded in and about Wilbraham, that I understood at once why they should have persisted for so long. Yet there must have been something more, for few people could have known about these books. What more? The bones in the wall beneath the hidden chamber spoke damningly for some hideous connection between the Peabody house and the unsolved crimes of other years. Even so, this was surely not a public one. There must have been some overt feature of my great-grandfather's life which established the connection in their minds, other than his reclusiveness and his reputation for parsimony, of which I knew. There was not likely to be any key to the riddle among these things from the hidden room, but there might well be some clue in the files of the Wilbraham *Gazette,* which were available in the public library.

Accordingly, half an hour later found me in the stacks of that institution, searching through the back issues of the *Gazette.* This was a time-consuming effort, since it involved a blind search of issue after issue during the later years of my great-grandfather's life, and not at all certain to be rewarding, though the newspapers of his day were less hampered and bound by legal restrictions than those of my own time. I searched for over an hour without coming upon a single reference to Asaph Peabody, though I did pause to read accounts of the 'outrages' perpetrated upon people – primarily children – of the countryside in the vicinity of the Peabody place, invariably accompanied by editorial queries about the 'animal' which was 'said to be a large black creature of some kind, and it has been reported to be of different sizes – sometimes as large as a cat, and sometimes as big as a lion' – which was a circumstance no doubt due solely to the imagination of the reporting witnesses, who were principally children under ten, victims of mauling or biting, from which they had made their escape, happily more fortunate in this than younger children who had vanished without trace at intervals during the year in which I read: 1905. But throughout all this, there was no mention of my great-grandfather; and, indeed, there was nothing until the year of his death.

Then, and only then, did the editor of the *Gazette* put into print what must have represented the current belief about Asaph Peabody. 'Asaph Peabody is gone. He will be long remembered. There are those among us who have attributed to him powers which belonged rather more to an era in the past than to our own time. There was a Peabody among those charged at Salem; indeed, it was from Salem that Jedediah Peabody removed when he came to build his home near Wilbraham. The pattern of superstition knows no reason. It is perhaps mere coincidence that Asaph Peabody's old black cat has not been seen since his death, and it is undoubtedly mere ugly rumour that the Peabody coffin was not opened before interment because there was some alteration in the body tissues or in the conventions of burial to make such opening unwise. This is again lending credence to old wives' tales – that a warlock must be buried face downward and never thereafter disturbed, save by fire. . . .'

This was a strange, oblique method of writing. Yet it told me much, perhaps uncomfortably more than I had anticipated. My great-grandfather's cat had been looked upon as his familiar – for every witch or warlock has his personal devil in any shape it might care to assume. What more natural than that my great-grandfather's cat should be mistaken for his familiar, for it had evidently in life been as constant a companion to him as it was in my dreams of the old man? The one disturbing note struck by the editorial comment lay in the reference to his interment, for I knew what the editor could not have known – that Asaph Peabody had indeed been buried face downward. I knew more – that he had been disturbed, and should not have been. And I suspected yet more – that something other than myself walked at the old Peabody homestead, walking in my dreams and over the countryside and in the air!

IV

That night, once more, the dreams came, accompanied by that same exaggerated sense of hearing, which made it seem as if I were attuned to cacophonous sound from other dimensions. Once again my great-grandfather went about his hideous business, but this time it seemed that his familiar, the cat, stopped several times and turned to face squarely at me, with a wickedly triumphant grin on its evil face. I saw the old man in a conical black hat and a long black robe walking from woodland seem-

ingly through the wall of a house, coming forth into a darkened
room, spare of furnishings, appearing then before a black altar,
where the Black Man stood waiting for the sacrifice which was
too horrible to watch, yet I had no alternative, for the power of
my dreams was such that I must look upon this hellish deed.
And I saw him and his cat and the Black Man again, this time
in the midst of a deep forest, far from Wilbraham, together
with many others, before a large outdoors altar, to celebrate the
Black Mass and the orgies that followed upon it. But they were
not always so clear; sometimes the dreams were only arrow-
swift descents through unlimited chasms of strangely coloured
twilight and bafflingly cacophonous sound, where gravity had
no meaning, chasms utterly alien to nature, but in which I was
always singularly perceptive on an extrasensory plane, able to
hear and see things I would never have been aware of while
waking. Thus I heard the eldritch chants of the Black Mass, the
screams of a dying child, the discordant music of pipes, the
inverted prayers of homage, the orgiastic cries of celebrants,
though I could not always see them. And on occasion, too, my
dreams conveyed portions of conversations, snatches of words,
meaningless of themselves, but capable of dark and disquieting
explication.

'Shall he be chosen?'

'By Belial, by Beelzebub, by Sathanus . . .'

'Of the blood of Jedediah, of the blood of Asaph, compan-
ioned by Balor.'

'Bring him to the Book!'

Then there were those curious figments of dreams in which
I myself appeared to be taking part, particularly one in which
I was being led, alternately by my great-grandfather and by
the cat, to a great black-bound book in which were written
names in glowing fire, countersigned in blood, and which I was
instructed to sign, my great-grandfather guiding my hand,
while the cat, whom I heard Asaph Peabody call Balor, having
clawed at my wrist to produce blood into which to dip the pen,
capered and danced about. There was about this dream one
aspect which had a more disturbing bond to reality. In the

course of the way through the woods to the meeting place of the coven, the path led beside a marsh where we walked in the black mud of the sedge, near to foetid sloughs in a place where there was a charnel odour of decay; I sank into the mud repeatedly in that place, though neither the cat nor great-grandfather seemed to more than float upon its surface.

And in the morning, when at last I awoke after sleeping over long, I found upon my shoes, which had been clean when I went to bed, a drying black mud which was the substance of my dream! I started from bed at sight of them, and followed the tracks they had made easily enough, tracing them backwards, out of the room, up the stairs, into the hidden room on the second storey – and, once there, back, inexorably, to that same bewitched corner of peculiar angle from which the footprints in the dust had led into the room! I stared in disbelief, yet my eyes did not deceive me. This was madness, but it could not be denied. Nor could the scratch on my wrist be wished out of existence.

I literally reeled from the hidden room, beginning at last vaguely to understand why my parents had been loath to sell the Peabody homestead; something had come down to them of its lore from my grandfather, for it must have been he who had had great-grandfather buried with his face downward in the family crypt. And, however much they may have scorned the superstitious lore they had inherited, they were unwilling to chance its defiance. I understood, too, why periods of rental had failed, for the house itself was a sort of focal point for forces beyond the comprehension or control of any one person, if indeed any human being; and I knew that I was already infected with the aura of the habitation, that, indeed, in a sense I was a prisoner of the house and its evil history.

I now sought the only avenue of further information open to me. The manuscript of the journal kept by my great-grandfather. I hastened to it directly, without pausing for breakfast, and found it to be a sequence of notes, set down in his flowing script, together with clippings from letters, newspapers, magazines, and even books, which had seemed to him pertinent, though these were peculiarly unconnected, yet all dealing with inexplicable events – doubtless, in great-grandfather's eyes, sharing a common origin in witchcraft. His own notes were spare, yet revealing.

'Did what had to be done today. J. taking on flesh, incredibly. But this is part of the lore. Once turned over, all begins again. The familiar returns, and the clay takes shape again a little more with each sacrifice. To turn him back would be futile now. There is only the fire.'

And again:

'Something in the house. A cat? I see him, but cannot catch him.'

'Definitely a black cat. Where he came from, I do not know. Disturbing dreams. Twice at a Black Mass.'

'In dream the cat, led me to the Black Book. Signed.'

'In dream an imp called Balor. A handsome fellow. Explained the bondage.'

And, soon after:

'Balor came to me today. I would not have guessed him the same. He is as handsome a cat as he was a young imp. I asked him whether this was the same form in which he had served J. He indicated that it was. Led the way to the corner with a strange and extra-dimensional angle which is the door to outside. J. had so constructed it. Showed me how to walk through it . . .'

I could bear to read no further. Already I had read far too much.

I knew now what had happened to the remains of Jedediah Peabody. And I knew what I must do. However fearful I was of what I must find, I went without delay to the Peabody crypt, entered it, and forced myself to go to the coffin of my great-grandfather. There, for the first time, I noticed the bronze plate attached beneath the name of Asaph Peabody, and the engraving upon it: 'Woe betide him who disturbs his rest!'

Then I raised the lid.

Though I had every reason to expect what I saw, I was horrified no less. For the bones I had last seen were terribly altered. What had been but bone and fragments, dust and tatters of clothing, had begun a shocking alteration. Flesh was beginning to grow once again on the remains of my great-grandfather, Asaph Peabody – flesh that took its origin from the evil upon which he had begun to live anew when I had so witlessly turned over his mortal remains – and from that other thing within his coffin – the poor, shrivelling body of that child which, though it had vanished from the home of George Taylor less than ten days ago, already had a leathern, parchment appearance, as were it drained of all substance, and partially mummified!

I fled the vault, numb with horror, but only to build the pyre I knew I must gather together. I worked feverishly, in haste lest someone surprise me at my labours, though I knew that people had shunned the Peabody homestead for decades. And then, this done, I laboured alone to drag Asaph Peabody's coffin and its hellish contents to the pyre, just as, decades before, Asaph himself had done to Jedediah's coffin and what it had contained! Then I stood by while the holocaust consumed coffin and contents, so that I alone heard the high shrill wail of rage which rose from the flames like the ghost of a scream.

All that night the diminishing ashes of that pyre still glowed. I saw it from the windows of the house.

And inside, I saw something else.

A black cat which came to the door of my quarters and leered wickedly in at me.

And I remembered the path through the marsh I had taken, the muddied footprints, the mud on my shoes. I remembered the scratch on my wrist, and the Black Book I had signed. Even as Asaph Peabody had signed it.

I turned to where the cat lurked in the shadows and called it gently. 'Balor!'

It came and sat on its haunches just inside the door.

I took my revolver from the drawer of my desk and deliberately shot it.

It kept right on regarding me. Not so much as a whisker twitched.

Balor. One of the lesser devils.

This, then, was the Peabody heritage. The house, the grounds, the woods – these were only the superficial material aspects of the extra-dimensional angles in the hidden room, the path through the marsh to the coven, the signatures in the Black Book . . .

Who, I wonder, after I am dead, if I am buried as the others were, will turn me over?

The Gable Window

I

I moved into my cousin Wilbur's home less than a month after his untimely death, not without misgivings, for its isolation in a pocket of the hills off the Aylesbury Pike was not to my liking. Yet I moved with a sense of fitness that this haven of my favourite cousin should have descended to me. As the old Wharton place, the house had been untenanted for many years. It had fallen into disuse after the grandson of the farmer who had built it had left the soil for the seaside city of Kingston, and my cousin had bought it from the estate of that heir disgruntled with the meagre living to be made on that sadly depleted land. It was not a calculated move, for the Akeleys did nothing but by sudden impulse.

Wilbur had been for many years a student of archaeology and anthropology. He had been graduated from Miskatonic University in Arkham, and immediately following his graduation, had spent three years in Mongolia, Tibet, and Sinkiang Province, followed by an equal number of years divided among South and Central America, and the south-western part of the United States. He had come home to reply in person to an offer to join the staff of Miskatonic University, but instead, he had bought the old Wharton farm, and set about to remodel it, tearing down all but one of the outbuildings, and imposing upon the central structure an even more curious shape than it had gathered to itself in the course of the twenty decades it had been standing. Indeed, the extent of these alterations was not fully apparent to me until I myself took possession of the house.

It was then that I learned that Wilbur had retained unaltered only one face of the old house, that he had completely rebuilt the front and one side, and had erected a gable room over the south wing of the ground floor. The house had originally been a low building, of but one storey, with a large attic, which had in its time been hung with all the impedimenta of the rural life

of New England. In part, it had been constructed of logs; and
some of this construction had been carefully retained by Wilbur,
which was testimony to my cousin's respect for the handiwork
of our forbears in this country, for the Akeley family had been
in America fully two hundred years when Wilbur had decided
to forswear his wanderings and settle in his native milieu. The
year, as I recall it, was 1921; he had lived but three years thereafter, so that it was 1924 – on April 16 – that I took possession
of the house in accordance with the terms of his will.

The house was still very much as he left it, an anomaly in the
New England landscape, for, though it still bore the marks of
its ancestry in its stone foundations and the logs of its sub-
structure, as well as in the square stone chimney which rose
from its fireplaces, it had been so much altered as to seem a
product of several generations. Though the majority of these
alterations had apparently been made to contribute to Wilbur's
comfort, there was one change which had baffled me at the time
that Wilbur had made it, and for which he never offered any
explanation; this was the installation in the south wall of his
gable room of a great round window of a most curious clouded
glass, of which he said only that it was a work of great antiquity,
which he had discovered and acquired in the course of his travels in Asia. He referred to it at one time as 'the glass from Leng'
and at another as 'possibly Hyadean in origin,' neither of which
enlightened me in the slightest, though, to tell the truth, I was
not sufficiently interested in my cousin's vagaries to press inquiries.

I soon wished, however, that I had done so, for I discovered
rapidly, once I had taken up my existence in the building, that
my cousin's entire living seemed to revolve not about the central rooms of the house on the ground floor, which one might
have expected, since these were appointed for maximum effect
and comfort, but about the south gable room, for it was here
that he kept his rack of pipes, his favourite books, records, and
most comfortable pieces of furniture, and it was here that he
worked on such manuscripts pertinent to his studies as he had

in progress at the time that he was struck down with a coronary ailment while he was at work in the stacks of Miskatonic University Library.

That some adjustment between what had been his regimen and what was mine would have to be made, I knew; and it must be made in my favour. It seemed therefore, that the first order of business was a restoration of the rightful way of existence in the house, a resumption of life on the ground floor, for, to tell the truth, I found myself from the beginning curiously repelled by the gable room, in part certainly because it reminded me so strongly of the living presence of my dead cousin who could never again occupy his favourite corner of the house, in part also because the room was to me unnaturally alien and seemed cold, holding me off as by some physical force I could not understand, though this was surely consistent with my attitude about the room, for I could understand it no more than I ever really understood my cousin Wilbur.

The alteration I wished to bring about, however, was not as easily accomplished as I had hoped it might be, for I was soon aware that my cousin's old 'den' cast an aura over the entire house. There are those who hold that houses inevitably assume something of the character of their owners; if the old house had worn any of the characteristics of the Whartons, who had lived in it for so long, it was certain that my cousin had effectively obliterated them when he remodelled the house, for now it seemed often literally to speak of Wilbur Akeley's presence. It was not often an obtrusive feeling – only rather an uneasy conviction I experienced of being no longer alone, or of being watched, under some scrutiny, the source of which was not known to me.

Perhaps it was the very isolation of the house which was responsible for this fancy, but it came to seem to me that my cousin's favourite room was like something alive, waiting on his return, like an animal unaware that death had intervened and the master for whom it waited would not again come back. Perhaps because of this obsession, I gave the room more attention than in fact it deserved. I had removed from it certain articles, such as a very comfortable lounging chair; but I was curiously impelled to bring them back, out of compulsions which arose from different and often conflicting convictions – the fancy that this chair, for instance, which at first proved to be so comfortable, was made for someone of a different shape from my own, and thus was uncomfortable to my person, or the belief that the light was not as good downstairs as above, which was responsible for my returning to the gable room the books I had removed from it.

The fact was, undeniably, that the character of the gable room was subtly at variance with that of the remainder of the house. My cousin's home was in every way prosaic enough, except for that one room in the south gable. The ground floor of the house was filled with creature comforts, but gave little evidence of having been extensively used, save for that room given over to the preparation of food. In contrast, the gable room, while also comfortable, was comfortable in a different way, difficult to explicate; it was as if the room, manifestly a 'den' built by one man for his use, had been used by many different kinds of people, each of whom left something of himself within these walls, without, however, any identifying mark. Yet I knew that my cousin had lived the life of a recluse, save for his journeys to the Miskatonic at Arkham and the Widener Library in Boston. He had gone nowhere else, he had received no callers, and even, on the rare occasions when I stopped at his home – as an accountant I did sometimes find myself in his vicinity – he seemed always willing that I be gone, though he was unfailingly courteous, and though I never remained longer than fifteen minutes at most.

Truth to tell, the aura of the gable room diminished my resolve. The lower floor was ample for my purposes; it afforded me a commodious home, and it was easy to put the gable room and the alterations I hoped to make in it out of my mind, to defer and postpone it until it came to seem too minor a matter to trouble about. Moreover, I was still frequently away for days and nights at a time, and there was nothing pressing I needed to do about the house. My cousin's will had been probated, the estate had been settled, and no one challenged my possession.

All might have been well, for, with my resolve put by, I was much less aware of my unfinished plans for the gable room, had it not been for the succession of little incidents which occurred to disturb me. These were of no consequence at first; they began as tiny, almost unnoticed things. I believe that the first of them took place when I had been in possession scarcely a month, and it was such an infinitesimal thing that it did not occur to me to connect it to the later events I experienced until many weeks had gone by. It happened one night when I sat reading before my fireplace in the ground-floor living-room, and it was surely nothing more, I was certain, than a cat or some similar animal scratching at the door to be let in. Yet it was so distinct that I got up and made the rounds, from the front door to the back, and even to a little side door which was a relic of the oldest part of the house, but I could find neither cat nor trace of one. The animal had vanished into the darkness. I called to it several times, but it neither replied nor made any other sound. Yet I had no sooner seated myself again before the scratching began anew. No matter how I tried, I failed utterly to catch any sight of the cat, though I was disturbed in this fashion fully half a dozen times, until I was so upset that, had I caught sight of the cat, I would probably have shot it.

Of itself, this was an incident so trivial that no one would think twice about it. Could it not have been a cat familiar with my late cousin, and unfamiliar enough with me to be frightened away by my appearance? Indeed, it could. I thought no more of it. However, in less than a week, a similar incident took place, differing in one marked exception to the first. This time, instead of there being the clawing or scratching of a cat, there was a slithering, groping sound that sent a chill of apprehension through me, just as if a giant snake or an elephant's trunk were moving along the glass of the windows and doors. The pattern of its sounding and my reactions were exactly similar. I heard, but saw nothing; I listened, but could find nothing – only the intangible sounds. A cat, a snake? What more?

But there was yet more, quite apart from the occasions on which the cat or the snake seemed to have returned for another try. There was the time when I heard what sounded like hoof beats, or the tramping of some gigantic animal, or the twittering of birds pecking at the windows, or the slithering of some vast body, or the sucking sounds of lips or suckers. What was I to make of all this? I considered hallucination, and dismissed it as an explanation, for the sounds occurred in all kinds of weather and at all hours of the night and day, so that, had there actually been an animal of any size at door or window, I should certainly have caught sight of it before it vanished into the wooded hills which rose on all sides of the house, for the fields had long since been reclaimed by new growths of poplar, birch, and ash trees.

This mysterious cycle might never have been interrupted if I had not chanced one evening to open the stair door leading up to the gable room, on account of the heat of the ground floor; for it was then, when the clawing of a cat came once more, that I realized the sound came not from one of the doors, but from the window in the gable room. I bounded up the stairs in unthinking haste, never stopping to realize that it would have been a remarkable cat indeed which could or would climb to the second floor of the house and demand entrance through the round window, which was the only opening into the room from outside. And, since the window did not open, either in whole or in part, and, since it was clouded glass, I saw nothing, even though I stood there and continued to hear, just as close by as the other side of the glass, the sounds made by the cat clawing the glass.

I raced downstairs, snatched up a powerful flashlight, and went out into the hot summer night to throw a beam of light to the side wall in which the window stood. But now all sound had ceased, and now there was nothing whatsoever to be seen but the bland house wall and the equally bland window, which looked as black from the outside as it looked like clouded white from within. I might have remained for ever baffled – and often I think it would surely have been for the best had it been so – but it was not meant to be.

It was at about this time that I received from an elderly aunt a prize cat named Little Sam, which had been a pet of mine as a kitten two years before. My aunt had fretted about my insistence on living alone, and had finally sent along one of her cats to keep me company. Little Sam now belied his name; he ought to have been called 'Big Sam,' for he had added pounds since I last saw him, and he was in every way a fierce, tawny feline, a credit to his species. But, while Little Sam rubbed me with affection, he was of two minds about the house. There were times when he slept in comfort and ease on the hearth; there were others when he was like a cat possessed, demanding to be out. And, at such times as the curious sounds as of some other animal seeking entry were to be heard, Little Sam was virtually mad with fear and fury, and I had to let him out of the house at once, whereat he would streak to the one outbuilding left after my cousin's remodelling was done and there he would spend the night – there or in the woods, and not come out again until dawn, when hunger drove him back to the house. And into the gable room he absolutely refused to set foot!

II

It was the cat, in fact, which was responsible for my decision to probe a little deeper into my cousin's work, since Little Sam's antics were so manifestly genuine that I had no recourse but to seek, among the scattered papers my cousin had left, some explanation for the phenomena so common to the house. Almost at once I came upon an unfinished letter in the drawer of a desk in one of the downstairs rooms; it was addressed to me, and it was apparent that Wilbur must have been aware of his coronary condition, for I saw at a glance that the letter was meant to be one of those instructions in case of death, though Wilbur was clearly not cognizant of how short his time was to be, for the letter had been begun only about a month before his death, and, once pushed into the drawer, had not been taken up again, though ample time had been afforded him in which to finish it.

'Dear Fred,' he wrote, 'The best medical authorities tell me I have not long to live, and, since I have already set down in my will that you are to be my heir, I want to supplement that document now with a few final instructions, which I adjure you not to dismiss and want you to carry out faithfully. There are specifically three things you must do without fail, as follows:

'1. All my papers in Drawers A, B and C of my filing cabinet are to be destroyed.

'2. All books on shelves H, I, J, and K are to be turned over to the library of Miskatonic University at Arkham.

'3. The round glass window in the gable room upstairs is to be broken. It is not to be simply removed and disposed of elsewhere, but it must be shattered.

'You must accept my decision that these things must be done, or you may ultimately be responsible for loosing a terrible scourge upon the world. I shall say no more of this, for there are other matters of which I wish to write here while I am still able to do so. One of these is the question . . .'

But here my cousin had been interrupted and left his letter.

What was I to make of these strange instructions? I could understand that his books ought to go to the Miskatonic Library, since I had no especial interest in them. But why destroy his papers? Should they not also go there? And as for the glass – its destruction was surely a piece of wanton folly, since it would entail a new window and thus additional expense. This fragment of a letter had the unfortunate effect of whetting my curiosity even further, and I determined to look into his things with more attention.

That very evening I began with the books on the designated shelves, which were all in the south gable room upstairs. My cousin's interest in archaeological and anthropological subjects was clearly reflected in his choice of books, for he possessed many texts related to the civilizations of the Polynesians, the Easter Islanders, the Mongolians, and various primitive peoples, as well as books about the migrations of peoples and the cult – and myth-patterns of primitive religions. These, however, were but a prelude to his shelves of books designated for disposal to the university library, for some of these appeared to be fabulously old, so old, in fact, that they bore no dates, and must have descended, to judge from their appearance and their written characters, from medieval times. The more recent ones among them – and none of these dated beyond 1850 – had been assembled from various places; some had belonged to our fathers' cousin, Henry Akeley, of Vermont, who had sent them down to Wilbur; some bore the ownership stamps of the Bibliotheque Nationale of Paris, suggesting that Wilbur had not been above abstracting them from the shelves.

These books were in various languages; they bore titles such as *Pnakotic Manuscripts*, the *R'lyeh Text*, the *Unaussprechlichen Kulten* of von Junzt, the *Book of Eibon*, the *Dhol Chants*, the *Seven Cryptical Books of Hsan*, Ludvig Prinn's *De Vermis Mysteriis*, the *Celaeno Fragments*, the *Cultes des Goules* of the Comte d'Erlette, the *Book of Dzyan*, a photostat copy of the *Necronomicon*, by an Arabian, Abdul Alhazred, and many others, some of them apparently in manuscript form. I confess that these books baffled me, for they were filled – such of them as I could read – with an incredible lore of myths and legends, related beyond question to the ancient, primitive religious beliefs of the race – and, if I could read it correctly, of other and alien races as well. Of course, I could not hope to do justice to the Latin, French, and German texts; it was difficult enough to read the old English of some of the manuscripts and books. In any case, I soon lost patience with this task, for the books postulated a belief so bizarre that only an anthropologist would be likely to give enough credence to it to amass so much literature on the subject.

Yet it was not uninteresting, though it represented a familiar pattern. It was the old credo of the force of light against the force of darkness, or at least, so I took it to be. Did it matter

whether you called it God and the Devil, or the Elder Gods and
the Ancient Ones, Good and Evil or such names as the Nodens,
Lord of the Great Abyss, the only named Elder God, or these
of the Great Old Ones – the idiot god, Azathoth, that amorphous blight of nethermost confusion which blasphemes and
bubbles at the centre of all infinity; Yog-Sothoth, the all-in-
one and one-in-all, subject to neither the laws of time nor of
space, co-existent with all time and co-terminous with space;
Nyarlathotep, the messenger of the Ancient Ones; Great Cthulhu, waiting to rise again from hidden R'lyeh in the depths of the
sea; the unspeakable Hastur, Lord of the Interstellar Spaces;
Shub-Niggurath, the black goat of the woods with a thousand
young. And, just as the races of men who worshipped various
known gods bore sectarian names, so did the followers of the
Ancient Ones, and they included the Abominable Snow Men
of the Himalayas and other Asian mountain regions; the Deep
Ones, who lurked in the ocean depths to serve Great Cthulhu,
though ruled by Dagon; the Shantaks; the Tcho-Tcho people;
and many others, some of whom were said to stem from the
places to which the Ancient Ones had been banished – as was
Lucifer from Eden – when once they revolted against the Elder
Gods – such places as the distant stars of the Hyades, Unknown
Kadath, the Plateau of Leng, the sunken city of R'lyeh.

    Throughout all this, there were two disturbing notes which
suggested that my cousin took this myth-pattern more seriously
than I had thought. The repeated references to the Hyades,
for instance, reminded me that Wilbur had spoken of the glass
in the gable window as 'possibly Hyadean in origin.' Even more
specifically, he had referred to it as 'the glass from Leng.' It is
true that these references might have been coincidental, and for
a while I took comfort in telling myself that 'Leng' might well
be some Chinese dealer in antinques, and the word 'Hyadean'
might readily have been misunderstood. Yet this was a mere
pretence on my part, for there was indeed everything to show
that Wilbur had had more than a passing interest in this utterly
alien mythos. If his possession of the books and manuscripts
were not enough, his notes left me in no doubt whatsoever.

For there were in his notes far more than strange references, which I found oddly disturbing; there were crude, yet effective drawings of shockingly outré settings and alien creatures, such beings as I could never, in my wildest dreams, have conceived. Indeed, for the most part, the creatures beggared description; they were winged, bat-like beings of the size of a man; they were vast, amorphous bodies, hung with tentacles, looking at first glance octopoid, but very definitely far more intelligent than an octopus; they were clawed half-man, half-bird creatures; they were horrible, batrachian-faced things walking erect, with scaled arms and a hue of pale green, like sea-water. There were also more recognizable human beings, however distorted – stunted and dwarfed Orientals living in a cold place, to judge by their attire, and a race born of miscegenation, with certain characteristics of the batrachian beings, yet unmistakably human. I had never dreamed that my cousin was possessed of such imagination; I had long known that Uncle Henry was convinced of the most patently imagined delusions, but no taint had ever shown in Wilbur, to my knowledge; I saw now, however, that he had skilfully concealed from all of us the essentials of his true nature, and I was more than a little astonished at this revelation.

For certainly no living creatures could ever have served as models for his drawings, and there were no such illustrations in the manuscripts and books which he had left behind. Moved by my curiosity, I delved deeper and deeper into his notes, and finally put aside certain cryptic references which seemed, however remotely, to bear upon my immediate quest, arranging them into a sequence, which was easy, for all were dated.

'Oct. 15, '21. Landscape coming clearer. Leng? Suggestive of south-western America. Caves filled with hordes of bats which begin to come out – like a dense cloud – just before sundown, blot out the sun. Low shrub growth, twisted trees. A place of much wind. Snow-capped mountains in distance, right, along the rim of the desert region.

'Oct. 21, '21. Four Shantaks mid-scene. Average height exceeding that of a man. Furred, bat-like bodies, bat wings, extending three feet above head. Face beaked, vulture-like, but otherwise resembling bat. Crossed landscape in flight, pausing to rest on crag in middle distance. Not *aware*. Did one have a rider? Cannot be sure.

'Nov. 7, '21. Night. Ocean. A reef-like island in the foreground. Deep Ones together with humans of partly similar origin: hybrid white. Deep Ones scaled, walk with frog-like gait, a cross between a hop and a step, somewhat hunched, too, as most batrachia. Others seem to have swum to reef. Possibly Innsmouth? No coast line evident, no town lights. Also no ship. Rise from below, beside reef. *Devil Reef?* Even hybrids ought not to be able to swim too far without some resting-place. Possibly coast foreground, out of sight.

'Nov. 17, '21. Utterly alien landscape. Not of earth so far as I know. Black heavens, some stars. Crags of porphyry or some similar substance. Foreground a deep lake. Hali? In five minutes the water began to ripple where something rose. Facing inward. A titanic aquatic being, tentacled. Octopoid, but far, far larger – ten – twenty times larger than the giant *Octopus apollyon* of the west coast. What was its neck was alone easily fifteen rods in diameter. Could not risk chance of seeing its face and destroyed the star.

'Jan. 4, '22. An interval of nothingness. *Outer space?* Planetary approach, as were I seeing through the eyes of some being coming in to an object in space. Sky dark, few stars, but the surface of the planet soon looming close. Coming closer, saw barren landscape. No vegetation, as on the dark star. A circle of worshippers facing a stone tower. Their cries: *Iä! Shub-Niggurath!*

'Jan. 16, '22. Undersea region. *Atlantis?* Doubtful. A vast, cavernous temple-like structure, broken by depth-charges. Massive stones, similar to pyramid stones. Steps leading down to black maw below. Deep Ones in background. Movement in darkness of stair-well. A huge tentacle moving up. Far back two liquid eyes, many rods apart. *R'lyeh?* Fearful at approach of thing from below, and destroyed star.

'Feb. 24 '22. Familiar landscape. *Wilbraham country?* Run-down farm houses, ingrown family. Foreground, old man listening. Time: evening. Whippoorwills calling in great volume. Woman approaches holding stone replica of star in hand. Old man flees. Curious. Must look up.

'Mar. 21, ' 22. Unnerving experience today. Must be more careful. Constructed star and spoke the words: *Ph'nglui mglw'nafh Cthulhu R'lyeh wgah'nagl fhtagn.* Opened immediately on hugh shantak in foreground. Shantak *aware,* and at once moved forward. I could actually hear its claws. Managed to break the star in time.

'Apr. 7, ' 22. I know now they will actually come through if I am not careful. Today the Tibetan landscape, and the Abominable Snowmen. Another attempt made. But what of their masters? If the servants make the attempt to transcend time and space, what of Great Cthulhu – Hastur – Shub-Niggurath? I intend to abstain for a while. Shock profound.'

Nor did he again turn to whatever had been his odd pursuit until early the next year. Or, at least, so his notes indicate. An abstention from his obsessive preoccupation, followed once more with a period of brief indulgence. His first entry was just short of a year later.

'Feb. 7, '23. There seems now no doubt but that there is a general awareness of the door. Very risky to look in at all. Safe only when landscape is clear. And, since one never knows upon what scene the eye will turn, the risk is all the more grave. Yet I hesitate to seal the opening. I constructed the star, as usual, spoke the words, and waited. For a while I saw only the familiar south-western American landscape, at the hour of evening – bats, owls, night-prowling kangaroo rats and wild · south-western American landscape, at the hour of evening – cats. Then out of one of the caves, came a Sand-Dweller – rough-skinned, large-eyed, large-eared, with a horrible, distorted resemblance to the koala bear facially, though his body had an appearance of emaciation. He shambled towards the foreground, manifestly eager. Is it possible that the door makes this side as visible to them as they are to me? When I saw that he was heading straight for me, I destroyed the star. All vanished, as usual. But later – the house *filled with bats*! Twenty-seven of them! I am no believer in mere coincidence!'

There occurred now another hiatus, during which my cousin wrote cryptic notes without reference to his visions or to the mysterious 'star' of which he had written so often. I could not doubt that he was the victim of hallucinations inspired, no doubt, by his intensive study of the material in the books he had assembled from all corners of the world. These paragraphs were in the nature of substantiation, though they were in essence an attempt to rationalize what he had 'seen.'

They were interspersed with newspaper clippings, which my cousin obviously sought to relate to the myth-pattern to which he was so devoted – accounts of strange happenings, unknown objects in the heavens, mysterious disappearances into space, curious revelations regarding hidden cults, and the like. It was painfully patent that Wilbur had come to believe intensely in certain facets of the ancient primitive credos, particularly that there were contemporary survivals of the hellish Ancient Ones and their worshippers and followers; and it was this, more than anything else, that he was trying to prove. It was as if he had taken the writings, printed or written in the old books he possessed and, accepting them for literal truth, were trying to adduce the weight of evidence from his own time to add to that from the past. It was true, there was a disturbing element of similarity between the ancient accounts and many of those my cousin had managed to find, but these were doubtless capable of being explained as coincidence. Cogent as they were, I reproduced none of them before sending them to Miskatonic Library for the Akeley Collection, but I remember them vividly – and all the more so in the light of that unforgettable climax to my somewhat aimless inquiry into my cousin Wilbur's preoccupation.

III

I would never have known about the 'star' if it had not been accidentally brought to my attention. My cousin had written repeatedly about 'making,' 'breaking,' 'constructing' and 'destroying' the star as a necessary adjunct to his illusions, but this reference was utterly meaningless to me and would perhaps have remained so had I not chanced to see in the slanting light across the floor of the gable room the faint marks which seemed to outline a five-pointed star. This had been invisible before, because it had been covered by a large rug; but the rug had got moved in the course of my packing the books and papers to be taken to Miskatonic University Library, and thus my sight of the markings was an accident.

Even then it did not dawn upon me that these markings represented a star. Not until I finished my work with the books and papers and could push back the rug from the entire centre of the floor did the whole design present itself. I saw then that it was a star of five points, decorated with various ornamental designs, the whole of sufficient size to permit its being drawn from within it. This then, I knew at once, was the explanation for a box of chalk for which I had previously found no reason for being in my cousin's favourite room. Pushing books, papers, and all else out of the way, I went for the chalk, and set about faithfully copying the star design and all the decorations within the star. It was clearly meant for some kind of cabalistic drawing, and it was equally evident that the performer was required to sit within its outlines.

So, having completed the drawing in accordance with the impress left by frequent reconstructions, I sat within the design. Quite possibly I expected something to happen, though I was still puzzled by my cousin's references in his notes as to the breaking of the design each time he thought himself menaced, for, as I recalled cabalistic rituals, it was the breaking of such designs which brought about the danger of psychic invasion. However, nothing whatsoever took place, and it was not until several minutes had passed that I remembered 'the words.' I had copied them, and now I rose to find my copy, and, finding it, returned with it to the star and gravely spoke the words —

'*Ph'nglui mglw'nafh Cthulhu R'lyeh wgah'nagl fhtagn.*' . . .

Instantly a most extraordinary phenomenon took place. I was seated, facing the round window of clouded glass in the south wall, so that I saw everything that happened. The cloudiness vanished from the glass, and I found myself, to my astonishment, looking upon a sunbaked landscape — though the hour was night, a few minutes past nine o'clock of a late summer evening in the state of Massachusetts. Yet the landscape which appeared through the glass was one which could not have been found anywhere in New England — an arid country, a land of sandy rocks, of desert vegetation — which was spare — of caverns, and, in the background, of snowcapped mountains — just such a landscape as had been described more than once in my cousin's cryptic notes.

Upon this landscape I gazed in the utmost fascination, my mind in turmoil. Life seemed to be going on in the landscape to which I looked, and I picked out one aspect after another — the rattlesnake crawling sinuously along, the sharp-eyed hawk soaring overhead — which enabled me to see that the hour was not long before sundown, for the reflection of the sunlight on the hawk's breast was indicative — the Gila monster, the road-runner — all those prosaic aspects of the American south-west I saw. Where was the scene, then? Arizona? New Mexico?

But the events of that alien landscape kept on without reference to me. The snake and Gila monster crawled away, the hawk plummeted downward and came up with a snake in his talons, the roadrunner was joined by another. And the sunlight drew away, making of that land a face of great beauty. Then, from the mouth of one of the largest caverns came the bats. They came flowing from that black maw by the thousands in an endless stream, and it seemed to me that I could hear their chittering. How long it took for them to fly out into the gathering twilight, I do not know. They had hardly gone before something more made its appearance — a kind of human being, rough of skin, as if the desert's sand had been encrusted upon the surface of his body, with abnormally large eyes and ears. He seemed to be emaciated, with ribs showing through his skin, but what was particularly repellent was the look of his face – for he resembled an Australian toy bear called the koala. And at this, I remembered what my cousin had called these people – for there were others following that first, some of them female. Sand-Dwellers!

They came from the cavern, blinking their great eyes, but soon they came in greater haste, and scattered to both sides, crouching behind the bushes – then, little by little, an incredible monster made its appearance – at first a probable tentacle, then another, and presently half a dozen cautiously exploring the cave's mouth. And then, from out of the darkness of the cavern's well, an eldritch head showed dimly. Then as it thrust forth, I almost screamed aloud in horror – for the face was a ghastly travesty on everything civilized; it rose from a neckless body which was a mass of jelly-like flesh, rubbery to the eye, and the tentacles which adorned it took rise from that area of the creature's body which was either its lower jaw or what passed for a neck.

Moreover, the thing had intelligent perception, for from the first it seemed to be aware of me. It came sprawling out of the cavern, its eyes fixed upon me, and then began to move with unbelievable rapidity towards the window over that rapidly darkening landscape. I suppose I had no real concept of the danger in which I sat, for I watched with rapt attention, and only when the thing was blotting out all the landscape, when its tentacles were reaching towards the gable window – and through it! – that I recognized the paralysis of fright.

Through it! Was this, then, the ultimate illusion?

I remember breaking through the icy fear which held me long enough to pull off a shoe and hurl it with all my might at the glass; and at the same time, recalled my cousin's frequent references to breaking the star; so I slouched forward and wiped part of the design into oblivion. Even as I heard the sound of shattering glass, I slipped into merciful darkness.

I know now what my cousin knew.

If only I had not waited quite so long, I might have been spared that knowledge, I might have continued able to believe in illusion, in hallucination. But I know that the clouded glass in the gable window was a potent door into other dimensions – to alien space and time, an opening to landscapes Wilbur Akeley sought at will, a key to those hidden places of the earth and the star spaces where the followers of the Ancient Ones – and the Old Ones themselves! – lurk for ever, awaiting their time to rise again. The glass from Leng – which might have come out of the Hyades, for I never learned where my cousin had got it – was capable of being rotated within its frame, it was not subject to mundane laws save only that its direction was altered by the earth's movement on its axis. And if I had not shattered it, I would have loosed upon the earth indeed a scourge from other dimensions, unwittingly called forth by my ignorance and curiosity.

For I know now that the models from which my cousin drew the illustrations, however crude, among his notes, were *alive*, and not the product of his imagination. The final, crowning proof is indisputable. The bats I found in the house when I regained consciousness might have come in through the broken window. That the clouded glass had cleared might have been an optical illusion – if it were not that I know better. For I know beyond doubt that what I saw was not the product of my feverish fancy, because nothing could demolish that final damning proof which I found near the shattered glass on the floor of the gable room – *the cut tentacle, ten feet in length, which had been caught between dimensions when the door had been shut against that monstrous body to which it belonged, the tentacle no living savant could identify as belonging to any known creature, living or dead, on the face or in the subterrene depths of the earth!*

The Ancestor

I

When my cousin, Ambrose Perry, retired from the active practice of medicine, he was still a comparatively young man, ruddy
and vigorous and in his fifties. He had had a very lucrative
practice in Boston, and, though he was fond of his work, he was
somewhat more given to the development of certain of his theories, which – and he was an individualist in this – he did not
inflict upon his colleagues, whom, truth to tell, he was inclined
to look down upon as too bound by the most orthodox methods,
and too timid to venture forth upon experiments of their own
without the sanction of the American Medical Association. He
was a cosmopolitan in every sense of the word, for he had studied extensively in Europe – in Vienna, at the Sorbonne, at
Heidelberg - and he had travelled widely, but for all that he
was content to lose himself in wild country in Vermont, when
at last he chose retirement to climax his brilliant career.

He went into virtual seclusion at his home, which he had
built into the middle of a dense wood, and outfitted with as
complete a laboratory as money could buy. No one heard from
him, and for three years not a word of his activities reached the
public prints or the private correspondence of his relatives and
friends. It was thus with considerable surprise that I received
a letter from him – I found it waiting on my return from a
sojourn in Europe – asking me to come and spend some time
with him, if possible. I replied regretfully that I had now to
set about finding a position for myself, and expressed my pleasure at hearing from him and the hope that some day I might be
able to avail myself of his invitation, which was as kind as it
was unexpected. His answer came by return mail, offering me
a handsome emolument if I would accept the position of secretary – by which, I was certain, he meant me to do everything
about the house as well as take notes.

Perhaps my motivation was as much curiosity as the attractiveness of the remuneration, which was generous; I accepted as quickly, almost fearful lest he withdraw his offer, and within a week I presented myself at my cousin's rambling house, built in the Pennsylvania Dutch farm manner, though of but one storey with sharply pointed gables and deeply pitched roofs. I had had some difficulty finding it, even after receiving my cousin's explicit instructions, for he was at least ten miles from the nearest village, which was a hamlet called Tyburn, and his house was set so far back from the little-travelled road, and had so slight a lane leading up to it, that I was constrained to believe for some time that I had travelled past it in my eagerness to arrive at the hour I had promised.

An alert German shepherd dog guarded the premises, but, though he was chained, he was not at all vicious, for apart from watching me intently, he neither growled nor made any move in my direction when I went up to the door and rang the bell. My cousin's appearance, however, shocked me, for he was thin and gaunt; the hale, ruddy man I had last seen almost four years ago had vanished, and in his place stood a mere travesty of his former self. His hearty vigour, too, seemed sadly diminished, though his handshake was firm and strong, and his eyes no less keen.

'Welcome, Henry,' he cried at sight of me. 'Even Ginger seems to have accepted you without so much as a bark.'

At the mention of his name, the dog came bounding forward as far as his long chain would reach, tail wagging.

'But come in. You can always put your car up later on.'

I did as I was bidden and found the interior of his house very masculine, almost severe in its appointments. A meal was on the table, and I learned that, far from expecting me to do other than serve as his 'secretary,' my cousin had a cook and a handyman, who lived above his garage, and had no intention whatsoever that I should do more than take down such notes as he intended to give me, and to file the results of his experiments. For he was experimenting; he made so much clear at once, though he said nothing of the nature of his experiments, and all during our meal, in the course of which I met both

Edward and Meta Reed, the couple who took care of the house and grounds, he asked only about myself, what I had been doing, what I hoped to do – at thirty, he reminded me, there was considerably less time to dawdle about deciding on one's future – and occasionally, though only as my own answers to his questions brought up their names, about other members of the family, who were, as always, widely scattered. Yet I felt that he asked about me only to satisfy the amenities of the situation, and without any real interest, though he did once hint that if only I could turn to medicine for a career, he might be persuaded to see me through college in pursuit of my degree. But all this, I felt sure, was only the superficiality, the politeness of the moment, representing those aspects of our first meeting in some years which were to be got over with at the earliest opportunity; there was, moreover, that in his manner which suggested a suppressed impatience at this subject he himself had initiated, an impatience with me for my preoccupation with his questions, and at himself for having so far yielded to the conventionalities of the situation as to have asked questions about matters in which he was plainly not interested at all.

The Reeds, man and wife, who were both in their sixties, were subdued. They made little conversation, not only because Mrs. Reed both cooked and served her dinner, but because they were plainly accustomed to carrying on an existence apart from their employer's, for all that they ate at his table. They were both greying, yet they managed to look far more youthful than Ambrose, and they showed none of the signs of the physical deterioration which had come upon my cousin. The meal went on with only the dialogue between Ambrose and myself to break the silence; the Reeds partook of the meal not in subservience, but with a mask of indifference, though I did notice, two or three times, that quick, sharp glances passed from one to the other of them at something my cousin said, but that was all.

It was not until we had retired to Ambrose's study that he touched upon that subject closest to his thoughts. My cousin's study adjoined his laboratory, which was at the rear of the house; the kitchen and large dining and living room combination came next, and the bedrooms, curiously, were at the front of the house; once in the cosy study, Ambrose relaxed, his voice filled with the tremor of excitement.

'You will never guess the direction my experiments have taken since I left practice, Henry,' he began, 'and I dare to wonder at my temerity in telling you. Were it not, indeed, that I need someone to set down these amazing facts, I would not do so. But now that I am on the road to success, I must think of posterity. I have, in short, made successful efforts to recapture all my past, down to the most minute nooks and crannies of human memory, and I am now further convinced that, by the same methods, I can extend this perceptive process to *hereditary* memory and re-create the events of man's heredity. I see your expression – you doubt me.'

'On the contrary, I am astounded at the possibilities in it,' I answered, quite truthfully – though I failed to admit that a sharp stab of alarm possessed me simultaneously.

'Ah, good, good! I sometimes think that, because of the means I must use to induce the state of mind necessary to this ceaseless probing of past time, I have gravely disappointed the Reeds, for they look upon all experimentation on human beings as fundamentally un-Christian and treading upon forbidden ground.'

I wanted to ask what means he had reference to, but I knew that in good time he would tell me if he had a mind to; if he had not, no question of mine would bring the answer. And presently he came to it.

'I have found that a combination of drugs and music, taken at a time when the body is half-starved, induces the mood and makes it possible to cast back in time and sharpen all the faculties to such a degree that memory is regained. I can tell you, Henry, I have achieved the most singular and remarkable results; I have actually gone back to memory of the womb, incredible as it may seem.'

He spoke with great intensity; his eyes shone, his voice trembled. Plainly, he was exhilarated beyond ordinary stimulation by his dreams of success. This had been one of his goals when he was still in practice; now he had used his considerable means to further his ambition to achieve success in this, and he seemed to have accomplished something. So much I was ready to admit, however cautiously, for his experiments explained his appearance – drugs and starvation could easily account for his gauntness, which was in fact a kind of emaciation – he had starved himself so frequently and so steadily that he had not only lost his excess weight but had reduced beyond the point of wisdom and health. Furthermore, as I sat listening to him, I could not help observing that he had all the aspects of fanaticism, and I knew that no demurrer I could offer would affect him in the slightest or bring about any deviation whatsoever in his direction. He had his eyes fixed on this strange goal, and he would permit nothing and no one to deflect him from it.

'But you will have the task of transcribing my shorthand notes, Henry,' he went on, less intensely. 'For, of course, I have kept them – some of them written in a trance-like state, quite as if I were possessed by some spirit guide, which is an absurdity, naturally. They range backward in time to just before my birth, and I am now engaged in probing ancestral memory. You shall see how far I have got when you have had time to examine and transcribe such data as I have set down.'

With that, my cousin turned to other matters, and soon excused himself, vanishing into his laboratory.

II

It took me fully a fortnight to assimilate and copy Ambrose's notes, which were more extensive than he had led me to believe, and also disturbingly revelatory. I had already come to look upon Ambrose as extremely quixotic, but now I was convinced that a strong vein of aberration was manifest in his make-up as well, for the relentless driving of himself to achieve an end which was incapable of proof, for the most part, and promised no boon to mankind even if his goal were reached, seemed to me to border on irrational fanaticism. He was not interested so much for the information he might obtain in this incessant probing of memory as he was in the experiment for its sake alone, and what was most disturbing about it was the patent evidence that his experiment, which might at first have had only the proportions of a hobby, was becoming obsessive, to such an extent that all other matters were relegated to second place – not excluding his health.

At the same time, I was forced to admit that the material the notes contained was often deeply surprising. There was no question but that my cousin had found some way to tap the stream of memory; he had established beyond doubt that everything that happened to a human being was registered in some compartment of the brain, and that it needed but the proper bridge to its place of storage in memory to bring it to consciousness once more. By recourse to drugs and music, he had gone back into the past to such a degree that his notes, as finally put together, constituted an exact biography which was in no way complicated by the glossing over of wish-fulfilment dreams, the enchantment of distance, or the ego-gratifications which always play a part in adjustment of the individual personality to life's disappointments which have dealt blows to the ego.

My cousin's course so far was undeniably fascinating. For the immediate past years, his notes mentioned many people we knew in common; but soon the two decades between us began to become obvious and his memory concerned strangers to me and events in which I had no part, even indirectly. The notes were especially revealing in what they conveyed of my cousin's dominant thoughts during his youth and early manhood – in their cryptic references to the themes which were constantly uppermost in his thoughts.

'Argued vehemently with de Lesseps about the primal source. The chimpanzee linkage too recent. Primal fish?' So he wrote of his days at the Sorbonne. And, at Vienna – ' "Man did not always live in trees" – so says Von Wiedersen. Agreed. Presumably he swam. What role, if any, did man's ancestors have in the age of the brontosaur?' Such notes as these, including many far more detailed, were interspersed with the daily record of his years, mingling with accounts of parties, romances, an adolescent duel, differences with his parents, and the like – all the assorted trivia of one man's life. This subject appeared to hold my cousin's interest with an astonishing consistency; his more recent years, of course, were filled with it, but it recurred all the way through his life from the age of nine onwards, when on one occasion he had asked our grandfather to explain the family tree and demanded to know what was beyond the registered beginnings of the line.

There was, too, in these notes, certain evidence of how much he was taxing himself in this obsessive experiment, for his handwriting had undergone a marked decrease in legibility from the time he had first begun to chronicle his memories to the present; that is, as he went backwards through time to his earliest years – and indeed, into the place of darkness which was the womb, for he had accomplished this return, if his notes were not a skilful fabrication – his script grew steadily more illegible, quite as if there were a change in degrees with the change in the age of his memories which was as fantastic a concept as, I felt then, my cousin's belief that he could reach back into ancestral and hereditary memory, both involving the memory of his forbears for many generations, and presumably transmitted in the genes and chromosomes from which he had sprung.

To a very large extent, however, I suspended judgment while I was putting his notes in order, and there was no mention of the notes, except for the help I asked once or twice when I could not decipher a word in Ambrose's script. Read over, when at last it was completed, the transcript was impressive and cogent, and I handed it to my cousin at last with mixed feelings and not without some suspension of belief.

'Are you convinced?' he asked me.

'As far as you've gone, yes,' I admitted.

'You shall see,' he replied imperturbably.

I undertook to remonstrate with him about the diligence with which he pursued this dream of his. In the two weeks it had taken me to assimilate and copy his notes, he had plainly driven himself beyond the bounds of reason. He had taken so little food and had slept so little that he had grown noticeably thinner and more haggard than he had been on the day of my arrival. He had been secluded in his laboratory day and night, for long hours at a time; indeed, on many occasions in that fortnight there were but three of us at the table for meals – Ambrose had not come out of the laboratory. His hands had a tendency to tremble, and there was a hint of palsy too about his mouth, while his eyes burned with the fire of the fanatic, to whom all else but the goal of his fanaticism had ceased to exist.

The laboratory was out of bounds for me. Though my cousin had no objection to showing me about the extensive laboratory, he required the utmost solitude when he was conducting his experiments. Nor had he any intention of setting down exactly what drugs he had recourse to – though I had reason to believe that *Cannabis indica*, or Indian hemp, commonly known as hashish, was one of them – in the punishment he inflicted on his body in pursuit of his wild dream to recapture his ancestral and hereditary memory, a goal he sought daily and often nightly, as well, without surcease, so much so that I saw him with increasing rarity, though he sat for a long time with me on the night I finally gave him the transcript of his notes tracing the course of his life through his recaptured memory, going over each page with me, making certain small corrections and additions, striking out a few passages here and there, and, in general, improving the narrative as I had transcribed it. A retyping was obviously necessary, but what then, if I were not to attend him in the actual course of his experiments?

But my cousin had yet another sheaf of notes ready for me when the retyping was finished. And this time the notes were not of his own memories, but ranged back through time; they were the memories of his parents, his grandparents, of his forbears even before them – not specific, as were his own, but only general, yet enough to convey an amazing picture of the family before his own generation. They were memories of great cataclysms, of major events of history, of the earth in its youth;

they were such re-creations of time past as I would have thought impossible for one man to set down. Yet here they were, undeniably, impressive and unforgettable: an accomplishment by any standard. I was convinced that they were a skilful fabrication, yet I dared not pass judgment on Ambrose, whose fanatical belief brooked no doubt. I copied them as carefully as I had copied his earlier notes, and in but a few days I finished and handed the new transcript to him.

'You need not doubt me, Henry,' he said, smiling grimly. 'I see it in your eyes. What would I have to gain by making a false record? I am not prone to self-deception.'

'I am not qualified to judge, Ambrose. Perhaps not even to believe or disbelieve.'

'That is well enough put,' agreed my cousin.

I pressed him to tell me what I must do next, but he suggested that I wait on his pleasure. I might take the time to explore the woods or roam the fields on the far side of the road, until he had more work ready for me. I planned to take his suggestion and explore the adjoining woods, but this was never to be done, for other events intervened. That very night I was set in a different direction, providing a decided change from the routine of my cousin's increasingly difficult notes, for in the middle of the night Reed came to awaken me and tell me that Ambrose wanted me in his laboratory.

I dressed and went down at once.

I found Ambrose stretched out on an operating table, clad in the worn mouse-coloured dressing-gown he usually wore. He was in semi-stuporous state, yet not so far gone that he failed to recognize me.

'Something's happened to my hands,' he said with effort. 'I'm going under. Will you take down anything I may say?'

'What is it?' I asked.

'A temporary nerve block, perhaps. A muscular cramp. I don't know. They'll be all right tomorrow.'

'All right,' I said. 'I'll take down anything you may say.'

I took his pad and pencil and sat waiting.

The atmosphere of the laboratory, ill-lit with but one low

red light near to the operating table, was eerie. My cousin looked far more like a corpse than a man under the influence of drugs. Moreover, there was playing in one corner an electric phonograph, so that the low, discordant strains of Stravinsky's *Le Sacre du Printemps* flowed through the room and took possession of it. My cousin lay perfectly still, and for a long time not a sound escaped him; he had sunk into the deep drugged sleep in which he carried on his experiment, and I could not have awakened him had I tried.

Perhaps an hour elapsed before he began to speak, and then he spoke so disjointedly that I was hard put to it to catch his words.

'Forest sunk into earth,' he said. 'Great ones fighting, tearing. Run, run. . . .' And again, 'New trees for old. Footprint ten feet across. We live in cave, cold, damp, fire. . . .'

I put down everything he said in so far as I could catch his muttered words. Incredibly, he seemed to be dreaming of the saurian age, for his hints were of great beasts that roamed the face of his land and fought and tore, walking through forests as though they were of grass, seeking out and devouring mankind, the dwellers in caves and holes under the surface of the earth.

But the effort of driving himself back so far into the past was a singular strain on my cousin Ambrose, and, when at last he came back to consciousness that night, he shuddered, directing me to turn off the phonograph, and muttered something about 'degenerative tissues' curiously allied to 'my dreams – my memories,' and announced that we would all rest for a while before he resumed his experiments.

III

It is possible that if my cousin could have been persuaded to rest his experiment on the admitted probability of ultimate success, and taken care of himself, he might have avoided the consequences of pushing himself beyond the boundaries of mortal man was meant to go. But he did not do so; indeed, he scorned my every suggestion, and reminded me that he was the doctor, not I. My retort that like all doctors he was more careless of himself as patient than he would have been of anyone else fell on deaf ears. Yet even I could not have foreseen what was to take place, though Ambrose's vague hint about 'degenerative tissues' ought to have lent direction to my contemplation of the harm he was doing to himself by the addiction to drugs which had made him their victim.

For a week he rested.

Then he resumed his experiments, and soon I was once more putting his notes into typescript. But this time his notes were increasingly difficult to decipher; his script was indeed deteriorating, even as he had hinted, and, moreover, their subject was often very difficult to follow, though it was evident that Ambrose had gone far back in time. The possibility remained, of course, and was strong, that my cousin had fallen victim to a kind of self-hypnosis, and that, far from experiencing any such memory as he chronicled, he was reproducing from the memory of books he had read the salient aspects of the lives of ancient cave- and tree-dwellers; yet there were disturbingly clear indications from time to time that the observations he made were not made from any printed text or the memory of such a text, though I had no way of seeking out such possible sources for my cousin's bizarre chroniclings.

I saw Ambrose increasingly seldom, but on the rare occasions when I did see him, I could not avoid noticing the alarming degree to which he had yielded to drugs and starvation; his emaciation was complicated by certain repellent signs of degeneration. He tended to slaver at his food and his eating habits became so deplorable that Mrs. Reed was pointedly absent from the table at more than one occasion; though, because of Ambrose's growing dislike of leaving his laboratory, we were not often more than three at table.

I do not remember just when the drastic alteration in Ambrose's habits came about, but I believe I had been at the house just over two months. Now that I think back to it, it seems to me that events were signalled by Ginger, my cousin's dog, which began to act up most restlessly. Whereas hitherto he had been a singularly well-behaved dog, now he began to bark often at night, and by day he whined and moved about house and yard with an air of alarm. Mrs. Reed said of him. 'That dog smells or hears something he don't like.' Perhaps she spoke truly, for all that I paid little attention.

It was about this time that my cousin elected to remain in his laboratory altogether, instructing me to leave his food on a tray outside the laboratory door. I took issue with him, but he would neither open the door nor come out, and very often he let his food stand for some time before he took it in, so that Mrs. Reed made ever less attempts to serve him hot food, for most of the time it had grown cold by the time he took it in. Curiously, none of us ever saw Ambrose take his food; the tray might stand there for an hour, two hours, even three – then suddenly it would be gone, only to be replaced later by an empty tray.

His eating habits also underwent a change; though he had formerly been a heavy coffee drinker, he now spurned it, re-turning his cup untouched so many times that Mrs. Reed no longer troubled to serve it. He seemed to grow ever more partial to simpler foods – meat, potatoes, lettuce, bread – and was not attracted to salads or most casserole dishes. Sometimes his empty tray contained notes, but these were growing fewer and further between, and such as there were I found almost im-possible to transcribe, for in his handwriting now, as well as in the content of his notes, there was the same distressing deterio-ration. He seemed to have difficulty properly holding a pencil, and his lines were scrawled in large letters over all the sheets of paper without any sense of order, though this was not en-tirely unexpected in one heavily dosed with drugs.

The music which welled forth from the laboratory was even more primitive. Ambrose had obtained certain records of ethnic music – Polynesian, ancient Indian, and the like – and it was these he now played to the exclusion of all else. These were weird sounds, indeed, and peculiarly trying in endless repeti-tion, however interesting they were at first hearing, and they prevailed with monotonous insistence, night and day for over a week, when one night the phonograph began to manifest every indication of having run down or worn out, and then abruptly stopped; it was not thereafter heard again.

It was at about this time that the notes ceased to appear, and, concomitant with this development, there were two others. The dog, Ginger, erupted into frantic barking during the night, at fairly regular intervals, as if someone were invading the property; I got up once or twice, and once I did think I saw some unpleasantly large animal scuttling into the woods, but nothing came of this; it was gone by the time I had got outside, and, however wild this portion of Vermont was, it was not bear country, nor, for that matter, was there any likelihood of encountering in the woods anything larger or more dangerous than a deer. The other development was more disturbing: Mrs. Reed noticed it first, and called my attention to it – a pervasive and highly repellent musk, clearly an animal odour, which seemed to emanate from the laboratory.

Could my cousin somehow have brought an animal in from the woods through the back door of the laboratory, which opened out upon the woods? This was always a possibility, but in truth, I knew of no animal which might give out so powerful a musk. Efforts to question Ambrose from this side of the door were of no avail; he resolutely refused to make any answer, and even the threat of the Reeds that they would leave, unable any longer to work in such a stench, did not move him. After three days of it, the Reeds departed with their belongings, and I was left alone to take care of Ambrose and his dog.

In the shock of discovery, the exact sequence of events thereafter is no longer very clear. I know that I determined to reach my cousin by one way or other, though all my pleadings remained unanswered. I lightened my burdens as much as possible by unchaining the dog that morning, and letting him roam. I made no attempt to undertake the various tasks Reed had performed, but spent my time going to and from the laboratory door. I had long ago given up trying to look into the laboratory from the outside, for its windows were high rectangles parallel to the roof, and, like the single window in the door, they were covered over so as to make it impossible to look in upon any experiment under way inside.

Though my cajolery and pleadings had no effect on Ambrose, I knew that ultimately he must eat, and that, if I withheld food from him, he would finally be forced to come out of the laboratory. So for all of one day I set no food before his door; I sat grimly watching for him to appear, despite the almost nauseating animal musk which invaded the house from behind the laboratory door. But he did not appear. Determinedly, I continued to keep my vigil at the door, fighting sleep, which was not difficult, for in the quiet of the night I was aware of peculiarly disturbing movements within the laboratory – awkward, shuffling sounds, as if some large creature were crawling about – combined with a guttural mewing sound, as if some mute animal were trying to speak. Several times I called out, and as often I tried the laboratory door anew, but it still resisted my efforts, being not only locked, but also barred by some heavy object.

I decided that, if this refusal to serve my cousin the food to which he had become accustomed did not bring him out, I would tackle the outer door of the laboratory in the morning, and force it by whatever means I could devise. I was now in a state of high alarm, since Ambrose's persistent silence seemed wholly unlike him.

But this decision had hardly been made, when I was aware of the frantic excitement of the dog. This time, unhampered by the chain which had hitherto bound him, he streaked along one side of the house and made for the woods, and in a moment I heard the furious snarling and growling which always accompanied an attack.

Momentarily forgetting my cousin, I made for the nearest door, snatching up my flashlight as I ran, and, running outside, I was on my way to the woods when I stopped short. I had come around the corner of the house, in view of the back of the laboratory – and I saw that the door to the laboratory stood open.

Instantly I turned and ran into the laboratory.

All was dark inside. I called my cousin's name. There was no response. With the flashlight I found the switch and turned up the light.

The sight that met my eyes startled me profoundly. When last I had been in the laboratory, it had been a conspicuously neat and trim room – yet now it was in a shocking state. Not only were the impedimenta of my cousin's experiments tipped over and broken, but there were scattered over instruments and floor fragments of partly decayed food – some that was clearly recognizable as having come prepared, but also a disturbing amount of wild food – remains of partially-consumed rabbits, squirrels, skunks, wood-chucks, and birds. Above all the laboratory bore the nauseatingly repellent odour of a primal animal's abode – the scattered instruments bespoke civilization, but the smell and sight of the place were of sub-human life.

Of my cousin Ambrose there was no sign.

I recalled the large animal I had seen faintly in the woods, and the first thought that came to mind was that somehow the creature had broken into the laboratory and made off with Ambrose, the dog in pursuit. I acted on the thought, and ran from the laboratory to the place in the woods from which still came the throaty, animal sounds of a lethal battle which ended only as I came running up. Ginger stepped back, panting, and my light fell upon the kill.

I do not know how I managed to return to the house, to call the authorities, even to think coherently for five minutes at a time, so great was the shock of discovery. For in that one cataclysmic moment, I understood everything that had taken place – I knew why the dog had barked so frantically in the night when the 'thing' had gone to feed, I understood the source of that horrible animal musk. I realized that what had happened to my cousin was inevitable.

For the thing that lay below Ginger's bloody jaws was a sub-human caricature of a man, a hellish parody of primal growth, with horrible malformations of face and body, giving off an all-pervasive and wholly charnel musk – but it was clad in the rags of my cousin's mouse-coloured dressing-gown, and it wore on its wrist my cousin's watch.

By some unknown primal law of nature, in sending his memory back to that prehuman era, into man's hereditary past, Ambrose had been trapped in that period of evolution, and his body had retrograded to the level of man's prehuman existence on the earth. He had gone nightly to forage for food in the woods, maddening the already alarmed dog; and it was by my hand that he had come to this horrible end – for I had unchained Ginger and made it possible for Ambrose to come to his death at the jaws of his own dog!

The Shadow out of Space

*'The most merciful thing in the world ... is the inability of
the human mind to correlate all its contents. We live on an
island of ignorance in the midst of black seas of infinity,
and it was not meant that we should voyage far ...'*

I

If it is true that man lives for ever on the edge of an abyss, then
certainly most men must experience moments of awareness –
of a kind of precognition, as it were – when the vast, unplumbed
depths which exist for ever on the rim of man's little world
become for one cataclysmic moment tangible, when the terrible,
boundless well of knowledge of which even the most brilliant
man has only tasted, assumes a shadowy being capable of striking the most primal terror into even the stoutest heart. Does
any living man know the true beginnings of mankind? Or man's
place in the cosmos? Or whether man is doomed to the worm's
ignominious end?

There are terrors that walk the corridors of sleep each night,
that haunt the world of dreams, terrors which may indeed be
tenuously bound to the more mundane aspects of daily life.
Increasingly, I have known such an awareness of a world outside this world – coterminous, perhaps, yet not impossibly completely hallucinatory. Yet it was not always so. It was not so
until I met Amos Piper.

My name is Nathaniel Corey. I have been in the practice of
psychoanalysis for more than fifty years. I am the author of one
textbook and uncounted monographs published in the journals
devoted to such learned papers. I practised for many years in
Boston, after studying in Vienna, and only within the last
decade, in semi-retirement, removed to the university town of
Arkham, in the same state. I have a hard-earned reputation for
integrity, which I fear this paper may seem to challenge. I
pray that it may do more than that.

It is a steadily disturbing sense of premonition that drives me at last to setting down some record of what is perhaps the most interesting and provocative problem I have faced in all my years of practice. I am not in the habit of making public statements regarding my patients, but I am forced by the peculiar circumstances attending the case of Amos Piper to set forth certain facts, which, in the light of other, seemingly unrelated data, may quite possibly assume a greater importance than they appeared to have when first I made their acquaintance. There are powers of the mind which are shrouded in darkness, and perhaps also there are powers in darkness beyond the mind – not witches and warlocks, not ghosts and goblins, or any such desiderata of primitive civilizations, but powers infinitely more vast and terrible, beyond the concept of most men.

The name of Amos Piper will not be unfamiliar to many people, particularly to those who recall the publication of anthropological papers, bearing his byline a decade or more ago. I met him for the first time when his sister, Abigail, brought him to my office one day in 1933. He was a tall man who had the look of once having been fleshy, but upon whose large-boned frame the clothes now hung as if he had lost much weight in a comparatively short time. Indeed, this proved to be the case, for, while Piper seemed to need medical attention far more than the services of a psychoanalyst, his sister explained that he had sought out the best medical care, and one and all the doctors he had seen had concluded that his trouble was primarily mental and beyond their curative powers. Several of my colleagues had recommended me to Miss Piper, and at the same time some of Piper's fellow savants on the faculty of Miskatonic University had added their commendations to those of the medical counsel Piper had sought out, hence the coming of the Pipers to fulfil an appointment.

Miss Piper prepared me a little with her statement of her brother's problem, while he was composing himself in my consultation room. She set forth the background with admirable succinctness. Piper appeared to be the victim of certain terrifying hallucinations, which took the shape of visions whenever he closed his eyes or lowered his eyelids while in a waking state, and of dreams when he slept. He had not slept, however, for three weeks, during which time he had lost so much weight that both of them had become profoundly alarmed at his condition. As a prelude, Miss Piper recalled to my mind that her brother had suffered a nervous collapse while at the theatre three years before; this collapse had been of such duration that it was actually only for the past month that Piper had seemed once more to have become his normal self. His new obsession – if such it was – had begun scarcely a week after his return to normal; it seemed to Miss Piper that there might be some logical connection between his former state and this occurrence following a brief normalcy. Drugs had proved successful in inducing sleep, but even they had not eliminated the dreams, which seemed to Dr. Piper to be of a peculiarly horrible nature, so much so that he hesitated to speak of them.

Miss Piper answered frankly such questions as I asked her, but betrayed the lack of any real knowledge of her brother's condition. She assured me that he had never been violent at any time, but he was frequently distrait and apparently separated from the world in which he lived, with a manifest line of demarcation, as if he existed in a shell enclosing him from the world.

After Miss Piper took her leave, I looked in on my patient. I found him sitting wide-eyed beside my desk. His eyes had an hypnotic quality, and appeared to be held open by force of will, for the eyeballs were extremely bloodshot, and the irises seemed to be clouded. He was in an agitated condition, and began at once to apologize for being there, explaining that his sister's determined insistence had left him no recourse but to yield to her. He was all the more unwilling to heed her demands because he knew that nothing could be done for him.

I told him that Miss Abigail had briefly outlined his trouble, and sought to calm his fears. I spoke soothingly in generalized terms. Piper listened with patient respect, apparently yielding to the casual yet reassuring manner with which I have always sought to inspire confidence, and when at last I asked why he could not close his eyes, he answered without hesitation, and quite simply, that he was afraid to do so.

'Why?' I wanted to know. 'Can you say – if you will?'

I remember his reply. 'The moment I close my eyes, there appear on the retina strange geometrical figures and designs, together with vague lights and even more sinister shapes beyond, as of great creatures past the conception of mankind – and the most frightening thing about them is that they are creatures of intelligence – immeasurably alien.'

I urged him then to make an attempt to describe these beings. He found it difficult to do so. His descriptions were vague, but startling in what they suggested. None of his beings seemed clearly formed, except for certain rugose cones which might as readily have been vegetable in origin as animal. Yet he spoke with such conviction, striving to limn for me the astonishing creatures of which he dreamed so insistently, that I was struck by the vividness of Piper's imagination. Perhaps there was a connection between these visions and the long illness which had beset him? Of this he was reluctant to speak, but after a while he began to go back to it, somewhat uncertainly, speaking of it disconnectedly, so that it was left for me to piece together the sequence of events.

His story began properly in his forty-ninth year. This was when his illness came upon him. He had been attending a performance of Maugham's *The Letter* when, in the middle of the second act, he had fainted. He had been carried to the manager's office, and efforts were there made to revive him. These were futile, and finally he was removed to his home by police ambulance; there medical men spent some further hours in an attempt to bring him to. As a result of their failure, Piper was hospitalized. He lay in a comatose state for three days, at the end of which he returned to consciousness.

It was immediately observed, however, that he was 'not himself.' His personality seemed to have suffered a profound disorientation. It was at first believed by his medical attendants that he had been the victim of a stroke of some kind, but this theory was reluctantly abandoned for lack of corroborative symptoms. So profound was his ailment that some of the most ordinary acts of man were performed by him with the utmost difficulty. For instance, it was noticed at once that he seemed to have difficulty grasping objects; yet nothing seemed wrong with his physical structure and his articulation appeared to be normal. His approach in grasping things was not that of a creature with fingers, but a motion of opening fingers and thumb as if to pick up and handle objects without finger mobility, in a motion that was claw-like rather than manual. Nor was this the only aspect of his disturbing 'recovery.' He had to learn to walk all over again, for he seemed to attempt to inch along as if he had no locomotive power. He had, too, a most extraordinary difficulty in learning to speak; his first attempts to do so were made with his hands, in the same claw-like motion with which he sought to grasp objects; at the same time, he made curious whistling sounds, the meaninglessness of which visibly troubled him. Yet it was perceived that his intelligence did not appear to have suffered any impairment, for he learned rapidly, and in a week's time he had mastered all those prosaic acts which are part of any man's daily life.

But, if his intelligence had not been impaired, his memory for the events of his life had been all but wiped out. He had not recognized his sister, nor had he known any of his fellow faculty members on the staff at Miskatonic University. He professed to know nothing of Arkham, of Massachusetts, and but little of the United States. It was necessary to make all this knowledge available to him anew, though it was only a short time – less than a month – before he had assimilated all that had been put before him, rediscovering human knowledge in an amazingly brief time, and manifesting a phenomenally accurate memory of everything he had been told and read. Indeed, if anything, his memory during his illness – once indoctrination had been completed – was infinitely superior to the functioning of that part of his mind before.

It was only after Piper had made these necessary adjustments to his situation that he began to follow what he himself described as 'an inexplicable' course of action. He was on indefi-

nite leave from Miskatonic University, and he began to travel
extensively. Yet he had no direct and personal knowledge of
these travels at the time of his visit to my office, or at any time
since his 'recovery' from the illness which had afflicted him for
three years. There was nothing remotely resembling memory
in his account of these travels, and what he did on these journeys he did not know; this was extraordinary, in view of the
astounding memory he had displayed during that illness. He
had been told since his 'recovery' that he had gone to strange,
out-of-the-way places on the globe – the Arabian desert, the
fastnesses of Inner Mongolia, the Arctic Circle, the Polynesian
Islands, the Marquesas, the ancient Inca country of Peru, and
the like. Of what he did there he had no recollection whatever,
nor was there anything in his luggage to show, save for one or
two curious scraps of what might have been antique hiero-
glyphic writings, most of them on stone, such as any tourist
might be interested in adding to a small collection.

When not engaged on these mysterious journeys, he had spent
his time reading very widely, and with almost inconceivable
rapidity at the great libraries of the world. Beginning with that
of Miskatonic University in Arkham – one well known for
certain forbidden manuscripts and books gradually accumulated over a period of centuries begun in colonial times – he
had ranged as far as Cairo, Egypt, in such studies, though he
had spent most of his time at the British Museum in London
and the Bibliotheque Nationale in Paris. He had consulted in-
numerable private libraries, wherever he could gain admittance.

In every case, the records which he had subsequently troubled
to check in that single brief week of his 'normalcy' – using
every available means: cablegram, wireless, radio, in the sense
of urgency which, he said, impelled him – showed that he had
read avidly of certain very old books, of but a few of which he
had had only the remotest knowledge prior to the onset of his
illness. They were such books related to ancient lore as the
Pnakotic Manuscripts, the *Necronomicon* of the mad Arab
Adul Alhazred, the *Unaussprechlichen Kulten of* von Junzt,
the Comte d'Erlette's *Cultes des Goules,* Ludvig Prinn's *De*

Vermis Mysteriis, the *R'lyeh Text,* the *Seven Cryptical Books of Hsan,* the *Dhol Chants,* the *Liber Ivoris,* the *Celaeno Fragments,* and many others, similar texts, some of which existed only in fragmentary form, all of which were scattered over the globe. Of course, there was also a leavening of history, but it was to be noted, according to the records of withdrawals in such libraries as Piper had been able to check, that reading in any given library had always begun with books accounted to be of legendry and of supernatural lore, and from them progressed into studies of history and anthropology, in a direct progression, as if Piper assumed that the history of mankind began not with ancient times but with the incredibly old world which existed before man's measured time as known to historians, and which was written about in certain dreaded and terrible lore to be found only in eldritch books held of an occult nature.

He was also known to have made contacts with other persons with whom he had had no prior acquaintance, but whom he now met as by prearrangement at various places, persons of similar pursuits, also engaged in somewhat macabre research, or affiliated with the faculty of some college or university. Yet there had been always one affinity among them, as Piper had learned by dint of telephoning across oceans and continents to people whose communications he found among his papers when he had returned to 'normalcy' – each of them had suffered a seizure either identical with or very similar in nature to that which had come upon Piper at the theatre.

Though this course of action was not related to Piper's way of life before the illness came upon him, it remained fairly consistent for the duration of that illness, once it had been set. The strange and unaccountable trips he had undertaken soon after he had once again accustomed himself to living among his fellow men after his initial 'recovery' had continued throughout the three years he had been 'not himself.' Two months at Ponape, a month at Angkor-Vat, three months in Antarctica, a conference with a fellow-savant in Paris, and only brief periods in Arkham between journeys; such was the pattern of his life, this was the way in which he had spent the three years prior to full and complete recovery, which in turn had been followed by another period of profound displacement, which permitted Amos Piper no memory of what he had done during those three years, and subjected him to a dread of closing his eyes lest he see that which suggested to his subconscious mind something awe-inspiring and terrible, coupled with his dreams.

II

It was only after three visits that I managed to persuade Amos Piper to set down for me a sequence of his strangely vivid dreams, those nocturnal adventures of his subconscious mind which troubled him and disturbed him so deeply. They were very similar to one another in nature, and each of them was unconnected and fragmentary, since none had any transitional phase from waking to dream. Yet, in the light of Piper's illness, they were challengingly significant. The most common of them was a repetitive dream of place; this, in one variation or an other, occurred repeatedly in the sequence which Piper set down. I reproduce here his own account of the repetitive dream.

'I was a scholar at work in a library in a colossal building. The room in which I sat transcribing something in a book in a language which was not English was so large that the tables in it were as high as an ordinary room. The walls were not of wood, but of basalt, though the shelves which lined the walls were of a kind of dark wood I did not know. The books were not printed, but entirely in holograph, many of them written in the same strange language which I wrote. But there were some which were in recognizable languages – this recognition, however, seemed to spring from an ancestral memory – in Sanscrit, Greek, Latin, French – even English, but English of much variation, from the time of Piers Plowman to our own time. The tables were lit with large globes of luminous crystal together with strange machines made of vitreous tubes and metal rods, without connecting wires of any kind.

'Apart from the books on the shelves, there was an austere

barrenness about the place. The exposed stonework showed some odd carvings, invariably in curvilinear mathematical designs, together with inscriptions in the same hieroglyphs which were written in the books. The masonry was megalithic; convex-topped blocks fitted the concave-bottomed courses which rested upon them; and all rose from a floor composed of great octagonal flagstones of a similar basalt. Nothing was hung upon the walls, and nothing decorated the floors. The shelves rose from floor to ceiling, and between the walls were only the tables at which we worked at a standing position, since nothing resembling chairs was in evidence, nor was the inclination to sit down felt.

'By day I could see outside a vast forest of fernlike trees. By night I could look upon the stars, but none was recognizable; no single constellation of those skies even remotely resembled the familiar stars which were the nocturnal companions of Earth. This filled me with terror, for I knew that I was in an utterly alien place, far removed from the terrestrial surroundings I had once known, and which now seemed a memory of an incredibly far existence. Yet I knew that I was an integral part of all this, and at one and the same time wholly distinct from it; or, as if part of me belonged to this milieu, and part did not. I was very much confused, and all the more so to recognize that the material I was writing was nothing more or less than a history of Earth of a time I believed was one I had lived – that is, the twentieth century; I was setting this down in the minutest detail, as if for study, but I knew not for what purpose, save to add to the tremendous accumulation of knowledge already in those countless books in the room in which I sat as well as in adjoining rooms, for the entire building of which this room was but one was a vast storehouse of knowledge. Nor was it the only one, for I knew from such conversation as went on around me that there were others far removed, and that in them all there were other writers such as ourselves, similarly engaged, and that the work we were doing was vital to the return of the Great Race – which was the race to which we belonged – to the places in the universes which had once, aeons gone by, served us as home until the war with the Ancient Ones had forced us into flight.

'I worked always under great fear and an inspired terror. I was afraid to look at myself. There was omnipresent a lurking fear that some hideous discovery was implicit in even the most fleeting glance at my body, which sprang from the conviction that I had stolen such a glance at some past time and had been profoundly frightened at sight of myself. Perhaps I feared that I was like the others, for my fellow-workers were all around me, and all were alike. They were great rugose cones, resembling a vegetable in structure, more than ten feet in height, with heads and claw-like hands attached to thick limbs which were ringed around the apex of their bodies. They walked by expanding and contracting the viscous layer attached to their bases, and, though they did not speak a language I recognized, yet I was able to understand the sounds they made because, as I knew in my dream, I had been instructed in that language from the moment of my arrival at that place. They did not speak with anything that resembled a human voice at all, nor did I, rather by a combination of strange whistlings and the clicking or scraping of huge claws attached to the end of their four limbs, which radiated from what supposedly would have been their necks, save that no such part of their bodies was visible.

'Part of my fear arose from the dim understanding that I was a prisoner within a prisoner, that even as I was imprisoned within a body similar to those around me, so this body was imprisoned within the great library. I sought in vain for any familiar thing. Nothing was there to suggest the Earth I had known since childhood, and everything hinted at a point as far out in space as that which we now occupied. I understood that all my fellow-workers were captives of some kind, too, though there were occasional appearances by warders who, though they were similar in form to the others, nevertheless wore an air of authority, and came walking among us, often to assist us. These warders were not menacing, but courteous, if firm.

'Though our warders were not supposed to engage us in conversation, there was one among them who was under no restrictions. He was evidently an instructor, and moved among us with more importance than the others, and I noticed that even the other warders deferred to him. This was not alone because he was an instructor, but also because he was held to be doomed for the Great Race was not yet ready to move, and the body he inhabited was destined to die before the migration would take place. He had known other men, and he was in the habit of stopping at my table – at first with only a few words of encouragement, but finally to talk for longer periods of time.

'From him I learned that the Great Race had existed on Earth and on other planets of our own universe as well as those of others, billions of years before recorded history. The rugose cones which made their present form had been occupied for only a few centuries, and were far from their true form, which was more kin to a shaft of light, for they were a race of free minds, capable of invading any body and displacing the mind which inhabited it. They had occupied Earth until they had become involved in the titanic struggle between the Elder Gods and the Ancient Ones for the domination of the cosmos, a struggle which, he told me, accounted for the Christian Mythos among mankind, for the simple minds of early men had conceived of their ancestral memories of this struggle as one between elemental Good and elemental Evil. From Earth, the Great Race had fled outward into space, at first to the planet Jupiter, and then farther, to that star on which they now were, a dark star in Taurus, where they remained ever watchful for invasion from the region of the Lake of Hali, which was the place of banishment for Hastur of the Ancient Ones, after the defeat of the Ancient Ones by the Elder Gods. But now their star was dying, and they were preparing for a mass migration to another star, either backward or forward in time, and for the occupation of the bodies of creatures more long-lived than the rugose cones which now afforded them housing.

'Their preparation consisted of the displacing of minds of creatures who existed at various times and in many places among the universes. There were among my companions, he asserted, not only tree-men from Venus, but also members of the half-vegetable race of paleogean Antarctica; not only representatives of the great Inca civilization of Peru, but also members of the race of men who were to live on post-atomic earth, horribly altered by mutations caused by the fall-out of radio-active materials from the hydrogen and cobalt bombs of the atomic wars; not only ant-like beings from Mars, but also men from ancient Rome and men from a world fifty thousand years in the future. There were countless others from all races, from all walks of life, from worlds I knew and from worlds separated from my time by thousands upon thousands of years. For the Great Race could travel at will in time or space, and the rugose cones which now constituted their bodies were but a temporary dwelling, briefer than most, and the place where they now carried on their vast researches, filling their archives with the history of life in all time and all places, was for them but a short residence before they went on to a newer and continuing existence elsewhere, in some other form, on some other world.

'All of us who worked in the great library were assisting in the gathering of the archives, for each of us wrote the history of his own time. By sending their members forth into the void, the Great Race could both see for itself what life was like in other times and places, and achieve an account of it in terms of the beings who lived then and there, for these were the minds which had been sent back to take the place of the missing members of the Great Race until such time as they were ready to return. The Great Race had built a machine which aided them in their flight through time and space, but it was not such a machine as had been crudely imagined by mankind, but rather one that operated on the body to separate and project the mind; and whenever a journey forward or backward in time was contemplated, the voyager submitted to the machine and the project was accomplished. Then, wherever they went in mass migration, they went unfettered; all the appurtenances, the artifacts, the inventions, even the great library would be left behind; the Great Race would begin to build its civilization, always hoping to escape the holocaust which would come about when the Ancient Ones – great Hastur, the Unspeakable; and Cthulhu, who lies in the watery depths; and Nyarlathotep, the Messenger; and Azathoth and Yog-Sothoth and all their terrible progeny – escaped their bondage and joined again in titanic battle with the Elder Gods in their remote fastnesses among distant stars.'

This was Piper's most recurrent dream. Actually, it was very probably not a continuing dream in the sense that it took place at one time, but rather one which was repeated, adding details, until the final version which he had set down seemed to him one repetitive dream, when in truth it had been cumulative, adding details with each recurrence. The pattern of his actions on his brief period of 'normalcy' in relation to the dream was significant, for it represented a signal reversal of the proper order – in life he imitated the actions of what he later described as rugose cones inhabiting dreams which came subsequently into peripheral existence. The order should have been, normally, reversed to this; had his actions – his attempts to grasp objects as with claws, and to speak with his hands, and so on – taken place after the occurrence of these vivid dreams, the normal progression would have been observed. It was significant that it did not happen in this manner.

A second recurring dream appeared to be merely an appendage to his first. Once more Piper was at work at the high table in the great library, unable to sit because there were no chairs and because the rugose cone was not meant to sit. Once again the doomed instructor had stopped to talk with him, and Piper had questioned him about the life of the Great Race.

'I asked him how the Great Race could hope to keep secret its plans, if it replaced the displaced minds. He said this would be done in two ways. First, all trace of memory of this place would be carefully expunged before any displaced mind was returned, whether it were sent back or forward in time and space. Second, if traces remained, they were likely to be so diffuse and unconnected as to be meaningless, and, if something could be pieced together from them, it would be so incredible to others as to be considered the workings of an overwrought imagination, if not, indeed, illness.

'He went on to tell me that the minds of the Great Race were permitted to select their habitats. They were not sent forth haphazardly to occupy the first "dwellings" to which they came, but had the power of choosing among the creatures they saw which they would occupy. The mind so displaced would be sent back to the present home of the Great Race, while the member of that race who had gone forth would adjust himself to the life of the civilization to which he had gone until he had sought out the traces of the aeon-old culture which had culminated in the great upheaval between the Elder Gods and the Ancient Ones. Even after the return had been effected, and the Great Race had learned all it wished to learn of the ways of life and the points of contact with the Ancient Ones, particularly of their minions who might oppose the Great Race, whose members had always striven for solitude and peace, but who were more closely akin to the Elder Gods than to the Ancient Ones, there were times when minds were sent out to make sure that the displaced minds had been washed clear of memory, and to reclaim them by affecting another displacement if they had not.

'He took me into the subterranean rooms of the great library. There were books everywhere, all in holograph. Cases of them were stored in tiers of rectangular vaults wrought of some unknown lustrous metal. The archives were arranged in the order of life forms, and I took note of the fact that the rugose creatures of the dark star were held to be of a higher order than man, for the race of man was not very far from the reptilian orders which immediately preceded it on Earth. When asked about this, the instructor confirmed that it was so. He explained that contact with Earth was maintained only because it had once been the centre of the great battleground between the Elder Gods and the Ancient Ones, and the minions of the latter existed there unknown to most men – the Deep Ones in the ocean depths, the batrachian people of Polynesia and the Innsmouth country of Massachusetts, the dreaded Tcho-Tacho people of Tibet, the shantaks of Kadath in the Cold Waste, and many others, and because it might now be necessary for the Great Race to retreat once more to that green planet which had first been their home. Only yesterday, he said – a time which seemed infinitely long ago, for the length of the days and nights was equivalent to a week on Earth – one of the minds had returned from Mars and reported that that planet was farther along the way towards death even than their own star, and thus one more prospective haven had been lost.

'From these subterranean reaches, he took me to the top of the building. This was a great tower domed in a substance like glass, from which I could look out over the landscape below. I saw then that the forest of fernlike trees which I had seen was of dried green leaves, not fresh, and that, far from the edge of the forest stretched an interminable desert which descended into a dark gulf, which, my guide explained, was the dried bed of a great ocean. The dark star had come within the outermost orbit of a nova and was now slowly and surely dying. How strange indeed that landscape looked! The trees were stunted, in comparison to the great buildings of megalithic stone out of which we peered; no bird flew across that grey heaven; no cloud was there; no mist hung above the abyss; and the light of the distant sun which illuminated the dark star came indirectly out of space, so that the landscape was bathed for ever in a grey unreality.

'I shuddered to look upon it.'

Pipers' dreams grew steadily more fraught with fright. This fear seemed to exist on two planes – one which bound him to Earth, another which bound him to the dark star. There was seldom much variation. A secondary theme which occurred two or three times in his dream sequence was that of being permitted to accompany the instructor-warder to a curious circular room which must have been at the very bottom of the colossal tower. In each such case one of their number was stretched out upon a table between glittering domes of a machine which shone a blinking and wavering light as if it were of some kind of electricity, though, as with the lamps on the working table, there were no wires leading to or from it.

As the light pulsations increased and brightened, the rugose cone on the table became comatose and remained so for some time, until the light wavered and the hum of the machine failed. Then the cone came to life once more, and immediately began an excited jabbering of whistling and clicking sounds. This scene was invariable. Piper understood what was being said, and he believed that what he had witnessed in each case was the return of a mind belonging to the Great Race, and the sending back of the displaced mind which had occupied the rugose cone in its absence. The substance of the rapid talk of the revived cone was always quite similar; it amounted to a report in summary of the great mind's sojourn away from the dark star. In one instance the great mind had just come back from Earth after five years as a British anthropologist, and he pretended to have himself seen the places where the minions of the Ancient Ones lay in wait. Some had been partially destroyed – as, for instance, were a certain island not far from Ponape, in the Pacific, and Devil Reef off Innsmouth, and a mountain cavern and pool near Machu Pichu – but other minions were widespread, with no organization, and the Ancient Ones who remained on Earth were imprisoned under the five-pointed star which was the seal of the Elder Gods. Of the places which were reported potentially future homes for the Great Race, Earth was always a leading contender, despite the danger of atomic war.

It was clear, in the progression of Piper's dreams, despite their confusion, that the Great Race contemplated flight to some planet or star far distant from the dying star which they occupied, and that vast regions of the green planet where few men lived – places covered with ice, great sandy regions in the hot countries – offered a haven to the Great Race. Basically, Piper's dreams were all very similar. Always there was the vast structure of megalithic basalt blocks, always the interminable working by those peculiar beings who had no need of sleep, invariably the feeling of imprisonment, and, in real life concomitantly, the omnipresent fear of which Piper could not shake himself free.

I concluded that Piper was the victim of a very deep confusion, unable to relate dream to reality, one of those unhappy men who could no longer know which was the real world – that of his dreams or that in which he walked and talked by day. But even in this conclusion I was not wholly satisfied, and how right I was to question my judgment I was soon to learn.

III

Amos Piper was my patient for a period just short of three weeks. I observed in him throughout that time, however much to my dismay and to the discredit of such treatment as I attempted, a steady deterioration in his condition. Hallucinatory data – or what I took to be such – began to make their appearance, particularly in the development of the typical paranoid delusions of being followed and watched. This development reached its climax in a letter Piper wrote to me and sent by the hand of a messenger. It was a letter obviously written in great haste . . .

'Dear Dr. Corey, Because I may not see you again, I want to tell you that I am no longer in any doubt about my position. I am satisfied that I have been under observation for some time – not by any terrestrial being, but by one of the minds of the Great Race – for I am now convinced that all my visions and all my dreams derive from that three-year period when I was displaced – or "not myself," as my sister would put it. The Great Race exists apart from my dreams. It has existed for longer than mankind's measure of time. I do not know where they are – whether in the dark star in Taurus or farther away. But they are preparing to move again, and one of them is nearby.

'I have not been idle between visits to your office. I have had time to make some further private enquiries of my own. Many connecting links to my dreams have alarmed and baffled me.

What, for instance, actually happened at Innsmouth in 1928 that caused the federal government to drop depth charges off Devil Reef in the Atlantic coast just out of that city? What was it in that sea-coast town that brought about the arrest and subsequent banishing of half the citizenry? And what was the connecting link between the Polynesians and the people of Innsmouth? Too, what was it that the Miskatonic Antarctic Expedition of 1930-31 discovered at the Mountains of Madness, of such a nature that it had to be kept quiet and secret from all the world except the savants at the university? What other explanation is there for the Johannsen narrative but a corroborative account of the legendry of the Great Race? And does this not also exist in the ancient lore of the Inca and Aztec nations?

'I could go on for many pages, but there is no time. I discovered scores of such subtly disturbing related incidents, most of them hushed up, kept secret, suppressed, lest they disturb an already sorely troubled world. Man, after all, is only a brief manifestation on the face of but a single planet in only one of the vast universes which fill all space. Only the Great Race knows the secret of eternal life, moving through space and time, occupying one habitation after another, becoming animal or vegetable or insect, as the circumstances demand.

'I must hurry – I have so little time. Believe me, my dear doctor, I know whereof I write . . .'

I was not, in view of this letter, particularly surprised to learn from Miss Abigail Piper that her brother had suffered a 'relapse' within a few hours, apparently, of the writing of this letter. I hastened to the Piper home only to be met at the door by my one-time patient. But he was now completely changed.

He presented to me a self-assurance he had not shown in my consultation room or at any time since first I had met him. He assured me that he had won control of himself at last, that the visions to which he had been subjected had vanished, and that he could now sleep free of the disturbing dreams which had so troubled him. Indeed, I could not doubt that he had made a recovery, and I was at a loss to understand why Miss Piper should have written me that frantic note, unless she had become so accustomed to her brother in his disoriented state that she had mistaken his improvement for a 'relapse.' This recovery was all the more remarkable since every evidence – his increasing fears, his hallucinations, his mounting nervousness, and, finally, his hasty letter – combined to indicate, as surely as any physical symptom ever did a disease, a collapse of what remained of his sanity.

I was pleased with his recovery, and congratulated him. He accepted my congratulations with a faint smile, and then excused himself, saying there was much for him to do. I promised to call once again in a week or so, to watch against any return of the earlier symptoms of his distressed state.

Ten days later I called on him for the last time. I found him affable and courteous. Miss Abigail Piper was present, somewhat distraught, but uncomplaining. Piper had had no further dreams or visions, and was able to talk quite frankly of his 'illness,' deprecating any mention of 'disorientation' or 'displacement' with an insistence that I could interpret only as great anxiety that I should not retain such impressions. I spent a very pleasant hour with him; but I could not escape the conviction that whereas the troubled man I had known in my office was a man of matching intelligence, the 'recovered' Amos Piper was a man of far vaster intelligence than my own.

At the time of my visit, he impressed me with the fact that he was making ready to join an expedition to the Arabian desert country. I did not then think of relating his plans to the curious journeys he had made during the three years of his illness. But subsequent happenings brought this forcibly to mind.

Two nights later, my office was entered and rifled. All the original documents pertaining to the problem of Amos Piper were removed from my files. Fortunately, impelled by an intuition for which I could not account, I had presence of mind enough to make copies of the most important of his dream accounts, as well as of the letter he had written to me at the end, for this, too, was removed. Since these documents could have had no meaning or value to anyone but Amos Piper and since Piper was now presumably cured of his obsession, the only conclusion that presented itself in explanation of this strange robbery was in itself so bizarre that I was reluctant to entertain it. Moreover, I ascertained that Piper departed on his journey on the following day, establishing the possibility in addition to the probability of his having been the instrument – I write 'instrument' advisedly – of the theft.

But a recovered Piper would have no valid desire for the return of the data. On the other hand, a 'relapsed' Piper would have every reason to want these papers destroyed. Had Piper, then, suffered a second disorientation, one which was this time not obvious, since the mind displacing his would have no need to accustom itself again to the habits and thought-patterns of man?

However incredible this hypothesis, I acted on it by initiating some inquiries of my own. I intended originally to spend a week – possibly a fortnight – in pursuit of the answers to some of the questions Amos Piper had put to me in his last letter. But weeks were not enough; the time stretched into months, and by the end of a year, I was more perplexed than ever. More, I trembled on the edge of that same abyss which had haunted Piper.

For something had indeed taken place at Innsmouth in 1928, something which had involved the federal government at least, and about which nothing but the most vaguely terrifying hints of a connection to certain batrachian people of Ponape – none of this official – ever seeped out. And there were oddly disquieting discoveries made at some of the ancient temples at Angkor-Vat, discoveries which were linked to the culture of the Polynesians as well as to that of certain Indian tribes of North-western America, and to certain other discoveries made at the Mountains of Madness by an expedition from Miskatonic University.

There were scores of similar related incidents, all shrouded in mystery and silence. And the books – the forbidden books Amos Piper had consulted – these were at the library of Miskatonic University, and what was in such pages as I read was hideously suggestive in the light of all Amos Piper had said, and all I had subsequently confirmed. What was there set forth, however indirectly, was that somewhere there did exist a race of infinitely superior beings – call them gods or the Great Race or any other name – who could indeed send their free minds across time and space. And if this were accepted as a premise, then it could also be true that Amos Piper's mind had once again been displaced by that mind of the Great Race sent to find out whether all memory of his stay among the Great Race had been expunged.

But perhaps the most damningly disturbing facts of all have only gradually come to light. I took the trouble to look up everything I could discover about the members of the expedition to the Arabian desert which Amos Piper had joined. They came from all corners of the earth, and were all men who might be expected to show an interest in an expedition of that nature – a British anthropologist, a French paleontologist, a Chinese scholar, an Egyptologist – there were many more. And I learned that each of them, like Amos Piper, had some time within the past decade suffered some kind of seizure, variously described, but which was undeniably a personality displacement precisely the same as Piper's.

Somewhere in the remote wastes of the Arabian desert, the entire expedition vanished from the face of the earth!

Perhaps it was inevitable that my persistent inquiries should stir interest in quarters beyond my reach. Yesterday, a patient came to my office. There was that in his eyes which made me think of Amos Piper, when I last saw him – a patronizing, aloof superiority, which made me cringe mentally, together with a certain awkwardness of the hands. And last night I saw him again, passing under the streetlight across from the house. Once more this morning, like a man studying another's every habit for some reason too devious for his intended victim to know . . .

And now, coming across the street . . .

The scattered pages of the above manuscript were found on

the floor of Dr. Nathaniel Corey's office, when his resident
nurse summoned police as a result of an alarming disturbance
behind the locked door of the office. When the police broke in,
Dr. Corey and an unidentified patient were found on their
knees on the floor, both trying vainly to push the sheets of
paper towards the flames of the fireplace in the north wall of
the room.

The two men seemed unable to grasp the pages, but were
nudging them forward with strange, crablike motions. They
were oblivious of the police, and were bent only on the destruction of the manuscript, continuing their unnatural efforts towards that end with a frenzied haste. Neither man was able to
give an intelligible account of himself to the police or to medical
attendants, nor was either even coherent in what he did say.

Since, after competent examination, both appeared to have
suffered a profound personality displacement, they have been
removed for indefinite confinement in the Larkin Institute, the
well-known private asylum for the insane . . .

The Lamp of Alhazred

It was seven years after his Grandfather Whipple's disappearance that Ward Phillips received the lamp. This, like the house on Angell Street where Phillips lived, had belonged to his grandfather. Phillips had had the living of the house ever since his grandfather's disappearance, but the lamp had been in the keeping of the old man's lawyer until the elapsing of the required seven years for the presumption of death. It had been his grandfather's wish that the lamp be safely kept by the lawyer in the event of any untoward circumstance, whether death or any other, so that Phillips should have sufficient time to browse as he pleased in the sizeable Whipple library, in which a great store of learning waited for Phillips' attention. Once he had read through the many volumes on the shelves, Phillips would be mature enough to inherit his grandfather's 'most priceless treasure' – as old Whipple himself had put it.

Phillips was then thirty, and in indifferent health, though this was but a continuation of the sickliness which had so often made his childhood miserable. He had been born into a moderately wealthy family, but the savings which had once been his grandfather's had been lost through injudicious investments, and all that remained to Phillips was the house on Angell Street and its contents. Phillips had become a writer for the pulp magazines, and had eked out a spare living by undertaking in addition the revision of countless almost hopeless manuscripts of prose and verse by writers far more amateur than he, who sent them to him, hopeful that through the miracle of his pen they in turn might see their work in print. His sedentary life had weakened his resistance to disease; he was tall, thin, wore glasses and was prey to colds and once, much to his embarrassment, he came down with the measles.

He was much given on warm days to wandering out into the country where he had played as a child, taking his work outdoors, where often he sat on the same lovely wooded riverbank which had been his favourite haunt since infancy. This Seekonk River shore had changed not at all in the years since then, and Phillips, who lived much in the past, believed that the way to defeat the sense of time was to cling close to unaltered early haunts. He explained his way of life to a correspondent by writing, 'Amongst those forest paths I know so well, the gap between the present and the days of 1899 or 1900 vanishes utterly – so that sometimes I almost tend to be astonished upon emergence to find the city grown out of its *fin de siècle* semblance!' And, in addition to the Seekonk's banks, he went often to a hill, Nentaconhaunt, from the slope of which he could look down upon his native city and wait there for the sunset and the enchanting panoramas of the city springing to its life by night, with the steeples and gambrel roofs darkening upon the orange and crimson, or mother-of-pearl and emerald afterglow, and the lights winking on, one by one, making of the vast, sprawling city a magical land to which, more than to the city by day, Phillips fancied himself bound.

As a result of these diurnal excursions, Phillips worked far into the night, and the lamp, because he had long ago given up the use of electricity to conserve his meagre income, would be of use to him, for all that it was of an odd shape and manifestly very old. The letter which came with this final gift from the old man, whose attachment to his grandson had been unbounded and was cemented by the early death of the boy's parents, explained that the lamp came from a tomb in Arabia of the dawn of history. It had once been the property of a certain half-mad Arab, known as Abdul Alhazred, and was a product of the fabulous tribe of Ad – one of the four mysterious, little-known tribes of Arabia, which were Ad – of the south, Thamood – of the north, Tasm and Jadis – of the centre of the peninsula. It had been found long ago in the hidden city called Irem, the City of Pillars, which had been erected by Shedad, last of the despots of Ad, and was known by some as the Nameless City, and said to be in the area of Hadramant, and, by others, to be buried under the ageless, ever-shifting sands of the Arabian deserts, invisible to the ordinary eye but sometimes encountered by chance by the favourites of the Prophet. In concluding his long letter, old Whipple had written: 'It may bring pleasure equally by being lit or by being left dark. It may bring pain on the same terms. It is the source of ecstasy or terror.'

The lamp of Alhazred was unusual in its appearance. It was meant for burning oil, and seemed to be of gold. It had the shape of a small oblong pot, with a handle curved up from one side, and a spout for wick and flame on the other. Many curious drawings decorated it, together with letters and pictures arranged into words in a language unfamiliar to Phillips, who could draw upon his knowledge for more than one Arabian dialect, and yet knew not the language of the inscription on the lamp. Nor was it Sanscrit which was inscribed upon the metal, but a language older than that – one of letters and hieroglyphs, some of which were pictographs. Phillips worked all one afternoon to polish it, inside and out, after which he filled it with oil.

That night, putting aside the candles and the kerosene lamp by the light of which he had worked for many years, he lit the lamp of Alhazred. He was mildly astonished at the warmth of its glow, the steadiness of its flame, and the quality of its light, but, since he was behind in his work, he did not stop to ponder these things, but bent at once to the task in hand, which was the revision of a lengthy creation in verse, which began in this manner:

> Oh, 'twas on a bright and early morn
> Of a year long 'fore I was born,
> While earth was yet being torn,
> Long before by strife 'twas worn . . .

and went on even more archaically in a style long ago out of fashion. Ordinarily, however, the archaic appealed to Phillips. He lived so definitely in the past that he had pronounced views, and a philosophy all his own about the influence of the past. He had an idea of impersonal pageantry and time-and-space-defying fantasy which had always from his earliest consciousness been so inextricably bound up with his inmost thoughts and feeling, that any searching transcript of his moods would sound highly artificial, exotic, and flavoured with conventional images, no matter how utterly faithful it might be to truth. What had haunted Phillips' dreams for decades was a strange sense of adventurous expectancy connected with landscapes and architecture and sky-effects. Always in his mind was a picture of himself at three, looking across and downward from a railway bridge at the densest part of the city, feeling the imminence of some wonder which he could neither describe nor fully conceive – a sense of marvel and liberation hidden in obscure dimensions and problematically reachable at rare instances still through vistas of ancient streets across leagues of hill country, or up endless flights of marble steps culminating in tiers of balustraded terraces. But, however much Phillips was inclined to retreat to a time when the world was younger and less hurried, to the eighteenth century or even further back, when there was still time for the art of conversation, and when a man might dress with a certain elegance and not be looked at askance by his neighbours, the lack of invention in the lines over which he struggled, and the paucity of ideas, together with his own weariness, soon combined to tire him to such an extent that he found it impossible to continue, and recognizing that he could not do justice to these uninspired lines, he pushed away at last and leaned back to rest.

Then it was that he saw that a subtle change had come upon his surroundings.

The familiar walls of books, broken here and there by windows, over which Phillips was in the habit of drawing the curtains tight so that no light from outside – or sun or moon or even the stars – invaded his sanctuary, were strangely overlaid not only with the light of the lamp from Arabia, but also by certain objects and vistas in that light. Wherever the light fell, there, superimposed upon the books on their serried shelves, were such scenes as Phillips could not have conjured up in the wildest recesses of his imagination. But where there were shadows – as, for instance, where the shadow of the back of a chair was thrown by the light upon the shelves — there was nothing but the darkness of the shadow and the dimness of the books on the shelves in that darkness.

Phillips sat in wonder and looked at the scenes unfolded before him. He thought fleetingly that he was the victim of a curious optical illusion, but he did not long entertain this explanation of what he saw. Nor, curiously, was he in want of an explanation; he felt no need of it. A marvel had come to pass, and he looked upon it with but a passing question, only the wonder at what he saw. For the world upon which he looked in the light of the lamp was one of great and surpassing strangeness. It was like nothing he had ever seen before, nor like anything he had read or dreamed about.

It seemed to be a scene of the earth when young, one in which the land was still in the process of being formed, a land where great gouts of steam came from fissures and rocks, and the trails of serpentine animals showed plainly in the mud. High overhead flew great beasts that fought and tore, and from an opening in a rock on the edge of a sea, a tremendous animal appendage, resembling a tentacle, uncoiled sinuously and menacingly into the red, wan sunlight of that day, like a creature from some fantastic fiction.

Then, slowly, the scene changed. The rocks gave way to wind-swept desert, and, like a mirage, rose the deserted and hidden city, the lost City of the Pillars, fabled Irem, and Phillips knew that, while no human foot any longer walked the streets of that city, certain terrible beings still lurked among the ancient stone piles of the dwellings, which stood not in ruins, but as they had been built, before the people of that ancient city had been destroyed or driven forth by the things which came out of the heavens to lay siege to and possess Irem. Yet nothing was to be seen of them; there was only the lurking fear of a movement, like a shadow out of time. And far beyond the city and the desert rose the snowcapped mountains; even as he looked upon them, names for them sprang into his thoughts. The city on the desert was the Nameless City and the snow peaks were the Mountains of Madness or perhaps Kadath in the Cold Waste. And he enjoyed keenly bestowing names upon these landscapes, for they came to him with ease, they sprang to his mind as if they had always been lingering on the perimeter of his thoughts, waiting for this moment to come to being.

He sat for a long time, his fascination unbounded, but presently a vague feeling of alarm began to stir in him. The landscapes passing before his eyes were no less of the quality of dreams, but there was a disquieting persistence of the malign, together with unmistakable hints of horrible entities which inhabited those landscapes; so that finally he put out the light and somewhat shakily lit a candle, and was comforted by its wan, familiar glow.

He pondered long on what he had seen. His grandfather had called the lamp his 'most priceless possession'; its properties must then have been known to him. And what were its properties but an ancestral memory and a magic gift of revelation so that he who sat in its glow was enabled to see in turn the places of beauty and terror its owners had known? What Phillips had seen, he was convinced, were landscapes known to Alhazred. But how inadequate this explanation was! And how perplexed Phillips grew, the more he thought of what he had seen! He turned at last to the work he had put aside and lost himself in it, pushing back from his awareness all the fancies and alarms which clamoured for recognition.

Late next day, Phillips went out into the October sunlight, away from the city. He took the car-line to the edge of the residential district and then struck out into the country. He penetrated a terrain which took him almost a mile from any spot he had ever before trod in the course of his life, following a road which branched north and west from the Plainfield Pike and ascending a low rise which skirted Nentaconhaunt's western foot, and which commanded an utterly idyllic vista of rolling meadows, ancient stone walls, hoary groves, and distant cottage roofs to the west and south. He was less than three miles from the heart of the city, and yet basked in the primal rural New England of the first colonists.

Just before sunset, he climbed the hill by a precipitous cart-path bordering an old wood, and from the dizzy crest obtained an almost stupefying prospect of outspread countryside, gleaming rivulets, far-off forests, and mystical orange sky, with the great solar disc sinking redly amidst bars of stratus clouds. Entering the woods, he saw the actual sunset through the trees, and then turned east to cross the hill to a more familiar city-ward slope which he had always sought. Never before had he realized the great extent of Nentaconhaunt's surface. It was in reality a miniature plateau or table-land, with valleys, ridges, and summits of its own, rather than a simple hill. From some of the hidden interior meadows – remote from every sign of nearby human life – he secured truly marvellous glimpses of the remote urban skyline – a dream of enchanted pinnacles and domes half-floating in air, and with an obscure aura of mystery around them. The upper windows of some of the taller towers held the fire of the sun after he had lost it, affording a spectacle of cryptic and curious glamour. Then he saw the great round disc of the Hunter's moon floating about the belfries and mina-rets, while in the orange-glowing west Venus and Jupiter com-menced to twinkle. His route across the plateau was varied – sometimes through the interior – sometimes getting towards the wooded edge where dark valleys sloped down to the plain be-low, and huge balanced boulders on rocky heights imparted a spectral, druidic effect where they stood out against the twilight.

He came finally to better-known ground, where the grassy ridge of an old buried aqueduct gave the illusion of a vestigial Roman road, and stood once more on the familiar eastward crest which he had known ever since his earliest childhood. Before him, the outspread city was rapidly lighting up, and lay like a constellation in the deepening dusk. The moon poured down increasing floods of pale gold, and the glow of Venus and Jupiter in the fading west had grown intense. The way home lay before him down a steep hillside to the car-line which would take him back to the prosaic haunts of man.

But throughout all these halcyon hours, Phillips had not once forgotten his experience of the night before, and he could not

deny that he looked upon the coming of darkness with an increased anticipation. The vague alarm which had stirred him
had subsided in the promise of further nocturnal adventure of a
nature hitherto unknown to him.

He ate his solitary supper that night in haste so that he could
go early to his study where the rows of books that reached to the
ceiling greeted him with their bland assurance of permanence.
This night he did not even glance at the work which awaited
him, but lit the lamp of Alhazred at once. Then he sat to wait
for whatever might happen.

The soft glow of the lamp spread yellowly outward to the
shelf-girt walls. It did not flicker; the flame burned steadily,
and, as before, the first impression Phillips received was one
of comforting, lulling warmth. Then, slowly, the books and the
shelves seemed to grow dim, to fade, and gave way to the scenes
of another world and time.

For hour upon hour that night Phillips watched. And he
named the scenes and places he saw, drawing upon a hitherto
unopened vein of his imagination, stimulated by the glow from
the lamp of Alhazred. He saw a dwelling of great beauty, wrea-
thed in vapours, on a headland like that near Gloucester, and
he called it the strange high house in the midst. He saw an ancient, gambrel-roofed town, with a dark river flowing through
it, a town like to Salem, but more eldritch and uncanny, and
he called the town Arkham, and the river Miskatonic. He saw
the dark brooding sea-coast town of Innsmouth, and Devil
Reef beyond it. He saw the watery depths of R'lyeh where dead
Cthulhu lay sleeping. He looked upon the windswept Plateau
of Leng, and the dark islands of the South Seas – the places
of dream, the landscapes of other places, of outer space, the
levels of being that existed in other time continua, and were
older than earth itself, tracing back through the Ancient Ones to
Hali in the start and even beyond.

But he witnessed these scenes as through a window or a door
which seemed to beckon him invitingly to leave his own mundane world and journey into these realms of magic and wonder;
and the temptation rose ever stronger within him, he trembled

with a longing to obey, to discard that which he had become and chance that which he might be; and, as before, he darkened the lamp and welcomed the book-lined walls of his Grandfather Whipple's study.

And for the rest of that night, by candle-light, abandoning the monotonous revisions he had planned to do, he turned instead to the writing of short tales, in which he called up the scenes and beings he had seen by the light of the lamp of Alhazred.

All that night he wrote, and all the next day he slept, exhausted.

And the following night, once again he wrote, though he took time to answer letters from his correspondents, to whom he wrote of his 'dreams,' unknowing whether he had seen the visions that had passed before his eyes or whether he had dreamed them, and aware that the worlds of his fiction had been woven inextricably with those which belonged to the lamp, having blended in his mind's eye the desires and yearnings of his youth with the visions of his creative drive, absorbing alike the places of the lamp and the secret recesses of his heart, which like the lamp of Alhazred, had coursed the far reaches of the universe.

For many nights Phillips did not light the lamp.

The nights lengthened into months, the months into years.

He grew older, and his fictions found their way into print, and the myths of Cthulhu; of Hastur the Unspeakable! of Yog-Sothoth; and Shub-Niggurath, the Black Goat of the Woods with a Thousand Young; of Hypnos, the god of sleep; of the Great Old Ones and their messenger, who was Nyarlathotep – all became part of the lore of Phillips's innermost being, and of the shadow-world beyond. He brought Arkham into reality, and delineated the strange high house in the mist; he wrote of the shadow over Innsmouth and the whisperer in darkness and the fungi from Yuggoth and the horror at Dunwich; and in his prose and verse the light from the lamp of Alhazred shone brightly, even though Phillips no longer used the lamp.

Sixteen years passed in this fashion, and then one night Ward Phillips came upon the lamp where he had put it, behind a row of books on one of the lowermost shelves of his Grandfather Whipple's library. He took it out, and at once all the old enchantment and wonder were upon him, and he polished it anew and set it once more on his table. In the long years which had passed, Phillips had grown progressively weaker. He was now mortally ill, and knew that his years were numbered; and he wanted to see again the worlds of beauty and terror that lay within the glow of the lamp of Alhazred.

He lit the lamp once more and looked to the walls.

But a strange thing came to pass. Where before there had been on the walls the places and beings of Alhazred's adventures, there now came to be a magical presentation of a country intimately known to Ward Phillips – but not to his time, rather of a time gone by, a dear lost time, when he had romped through his childhood playing his imaginative games of Greek mythology along the banks of the Seekonk. For there, once again, were the glades of childhood; there were the familiar coves and inlets where he had spent his tender years; there was once more the bower he had built in homage to great Pan; and all the irresponsibility, the happy freedoms of that childhood lay upon those walls; for the lamp now gave back his own memory. And he thought eagerly that perhaps it had always given him an ancestral memory, for who could deny that perhaps in the days of his Grandfather Whipple's youth, or the youth of those who had gone before him, someone in Ward Phillips' line had seen the places illuminated by the lamp?

And once again it was as if he saw as through a door. The scene invited him, and he stumbled weakly to his feet and walked towards the walls.

He hesitated only for a moment; then he strode towards the books.

The sunlight burst suddenly all about him. He felt shorn of his shackles, and he began to run lithely along the shore of the Seekonk to where, ahead of him, the scenes of his childhood waited and he could renew himself, beginning again, living once more the halcyon time when all the world was young . . .

It was not until a curious admirer of his tales came to the city to visit him that Ward Phillips' disappearance was discovered. It was assumed that he had wandered away into the woods, and been taken ill and died there, for his solitary habits were well known in the Angell Street neighbourhood, and his steady decline in health was no secret.

Though desultory searching parties were organized and sent out to scour the vicinity of Nentaconhaunt and the shores of the Seekonk, there was no trace of Ward Phillips. The police were confident that his remains would some day be found, but nothing was discovered, and in time the unsolved mystery was lost in the police and newspaper files.

The years passed. The old house on Angell Street was torn down, the library was bought up by book shops, and the contents of the house were sold for junk – including an old-fashioned antique Arabian lamp, for which no one in the technological world past Phillips' time could devise any use.

The Fisherman of Falcon Point

Along the Massachusetts coast where he lived many things are whispered about Enoch Conger – and certain others are hinted at in lowered voices and with great caution – things of surpassing strangeness which flow up and down the coast in the words of sea-farers from the port of Innsmouth, for he lived only a few miles down the coast from that town, at Falcon Point, which was so named because it was possible to see the peregrines and merlins and even sometimes the great gyrfalcons at migration time passing by this lonely finger of land jutting into the sea. There he lived until he was seen no more, for none can say he died.

He was a powerful man, broad in the shoulders, barrel-chested, with long, muscular arms. Even in middle age he wore a beard, and long hair crowned his head. His eyes were a cold blue in colour, and set deep in his square face, and when he was clad in rainproof garments with a hat to match, he looked like someone who had stepped from an old schooner a century ago. He was a taciturn man, given to living alone in a house of stone and driftwood which he himself had constructed on the windswept point of land where he heard the voices of the gulls and terns, of wind and sea, and, in season, of migrants from far places passing by, sometimes invisibly high. It was said of him that he answered them, that he talked with the gulls and terns, with the wind and the pounding sea, and with others that could not be seen and were heard only in strange tones like the muted sounds made by great batrachian beasts unknown in the bogs and marshes of the mainland.

Conger made his living by fishing, and a spare one it was, yet it contented him. He cast his net into the sea by day and by night, and what it brought up he took into Innsmouth or Kingsport or even farther to sell. But there was one moonlight night when he brought no fish into Innsmouth, but only himself, his

eyes wide and staring, as if he had looked too long into the
sunset and been blinded. He went into the tavern on the edges
of town, where he was wont to go, and sat by himself at a table
drinking ale, until some of the curious who were accustomed to
seeing him came over to his table to join him, and, with the aid
of more liquor, set his tongue to babbling, even though he talked
as though he spoke but to himself, and his eyes did not seem to
see them.

And he said he had seen a great wonder that night. He had
brought his boat up to Devil Reef more than a mile outside
Innsmouth, and cast his net, and brought up many fishes – and
something more – something that was a woman, yet not a woman, something that spoke to him like a human being but with
the gutturals of a frog speaking to the accompaniment of fluting
music such as that piped from the swamps in the spring months,
something that had a wide slash of a mouth but soft eyes and
that wore, beneath the long hair that trailed from her head,
slits that were like gills, something that begged and pleaded for
its life and promised him his own life if ever the need came
upon him.

'A mermaid,' said one, with laughter.

'She was not a mermaid,' said Enoch Conger, 'for she had
legs, though her toes were webbed, and she had hands, though
her fingers were webbed, and the skin of her face was like that
of mine, though her body wore the colour of the sea.'

They laughed at him and made many a jest, but he heard
them not. Only one of their number did not laugh, for he had
heard strange tales of certain things known to old men and
women of Innsmouth from the days of the clipper ships and
the East India Trade, of marriages between men of Innsmouth
and sea-women of the South Pacific islands, of strange happenings in the sea near Innsmouth; he did not laugh, but only
listened, and later slunk away and held his tongue, taking no
part in the jesting of his companions. But Enoch Conger did
not notice him any more than he heard the crude baiting of his
tavern companions, going on with his tale, telling of how he
had held the creature caught in the net in his arms, describing

the feeling of her cold skin and the texture of her body, telling of how he had set her free and watched her swim away and dive out of sight off the dark mound of Devil Reef, only to reappear and raise her arms aloft to him and vanish for ever.

After that night Enoch Conger came seldom to the tavern, and if he came, sat by himself, avoiding those who would ask him about his 'mermaid' and demand to know whether he had made any proposal to her before he had set her free. He was taciturn once more, he spoke little, but drank his ale and departed. But it was known that he did not again fish at Devil Reef; he cast his net elsewhere, closer to Falcon Point, and though it was whispered that he feared to see again the thing he had caught in his net that moonlit night, he was seen often standing on the point of land looking out into the sea, as if watching for some craft to make its appearance over the horizon, or longing for that tomorrow which looms for ever but never arrives for most searchers for the future, or indeed, for most men, whatever it is they ask and expect of life.

Enoch Conger retired into himself more and more, and from coming seldom to the tavern at the edge of Innsmouth, he came not at all, preferring to bring his fish to market, and hasten home with such supplies as he might need, while the tale of his mermaid spread up and down the coast and was carried inland to Arkham and Dunwich along the Miskatonic, and even beyond, into the dark, wooded hills where lived people who were less inclined to make sport of the tale.

A year went by, and another, and yet another, and then one night the word was brought to Innsmouth that Enoch Conger had been grievously hurt at his lonely occupation, and only rescued by two other fishermen who had come by and seen him lying helpless in his boat. They had brought him to his house on Falcon Point, for that was the only place he wished to go, and had come back hastily to Innsmouth for Dr. Gilman. But when they returned to the house of Enoch Conger with Dr. Gilman, the old fisherman was nowhere to be seen.

Dr. Gilman kept his own counsel, but the two who had brought him whispered into one ear after another a singular tale, telling how they had found in the house a great moisture, a wetness clinging to the walls, to the doorknob, even to the bed to which they had lowered Enoch Conger only a short while before hastening for the doctor – and on the floor a line of wet footprints made by feet with webbed toes – a trail that led out of the house and down to the edge of the sea, and all along the way the imprints were deep, as if something heavy had been carried from the house, something as heavy as Enoch.

But though the tale was carried about, the fishermen were laughed at and scorned, for there had been only one line of footprints, and Enoch Conger was too large a man for but one other to bear him for such a distance; and besides, Dr. Gilman had said nothing save that he had known of webbed feet on the inhabitants of Innsmouth, and knew, since he had examined him, that Enoch Conger's toes were as they should have been. And those curious ones who had gone to the house on Falcon Point to see for themselves what was to be seen, came back disappointed at having seen nothing, and added their ridicule to the scorn of others for the hapless fishermen, silencing them, for there were those who suspected them of having made away with Enoch Conger, and whispered this, too, abroad.

Wherever he went, Enoch Conger did not come back to the house on Falcon Point, and the wind and the weather had their way with it, tearing away a shingle here and a board there, wearing away the bricks of the chimney, shattering a pane; and the gulls and terns and falcons flew by without hearing an answering voice; and along the coasts the whispers died away and certain dark hints took their place, displacing the suspicions of murder and some deed of darkness with something fraught with even greater wonder and terror.

For the venerable old Jedediah Harper, patriarch of the coastal fishermen, came ashore one night with his men and swore that he had seen swimming off Devil Reef a strange company of creatures, neither entirely human not entirely batrachian, amphibian creatures that passed through the water half in the manner of men and half in the manner of frogs, a company of more than two score, male and female. They had passed close to his boat, he said, and shone in the moonlight, like spectral beings risen from the depths of the Atlantic, and, going by, they had seemed to be singing a chant to Dagon, a chant of praise, and among them, he swore, he had seen Enoch Conger, swimming with the rest, naked like them, and his voice too raised in dark praise. He had shouted to him in his amazement, and Enoch had turned to look at him, and he had seen his face. Then the entire school of them – Enoch Conger as well – dived under the waves and did not come up again.

But, having said this, and got it around, the old man was silenced, it was told, by certain of the Marsh and Martin clan who were believed to be allied to strange sea-dwellers; and the Harper boat did not go out again, for afterwards he had no need of money; and the men who were with him were silent, too.

Long after, on another moonlit night, a young man who remembered Enoch Conger from his boyhood years in Innsmouth, returned to that port city and told how he had been out with his young son, rowing past Falcon Point in the moonlight, when suddenly out of the sea beyond him rose upward to his waist a naked man – so close to him he might almost have touched him with an oar – a man who stood in that water as if held aloft by others, who saw him not, but only looked towards the ruins of the house on Falcon Point with great longing in his eyes, a man who wore the face of Enoch Conger. The water ran down his long hair and beard, and glistened on his body, and was dark where beneath his ears he appeared to wear long slits in his skin. And then, as suddenly and strangely as he had come, he sank away again.

And that is why, along the Massachusetts coast near Innsmouth, many things are whispered about Enoch Conger – and certain others are hinted at in lowered voices. . . .

The Dark Brotherhood

It is probable that the facts in regard to the mysterious destruction by fire of an abandoned house on a knoll along the shore of the Seekonk in a little habited district between the Washington and Red Bridges, will never be entirely known. The police have been beset by the usual number of cranks, purporting to offer information about the matter, none more insistent than Arthur Phillips, the descendant of an old East Side family, long resident on Angell Street, a somewhat confused but earnest young man who prepared an account of certain events he alleges led to the fire. Though the police have interviewed all persons concerned and mentioned in Mr. Phillips' account, no corroboration — save for a statement from a librarian at the Athenaeum, attesting only to the fact that Mr. Phillips did once meet Miss Rose Dexter there — could be found to support Mr. Phillips' allegations. The manuscript follows.

I

The nocturnal streets of any city along the Eastern Seaboard afford the nightwalker many a glimpse of the strange and terrible, the macabre and *outré,* for darkness draws from the crevices and crannies, the attic rooms and cellar hideways of the city those human beings who, for obscure reasons lost in the past, choose to keep the day secure in their grey niches — the misshapen, the lonely, the sick, the very old, the haunted, and those lost souls who are for ever seeking their identities under cover of the night, which is beneficent for them as the cold light of day can never be. These are the hurt by life, the maimed, men and women who have never recovered from the traumas of childhood or who have willingly sought after experiences not meant for man to know, and every place where the human society has been concentrated for any considerable length of time abounds with them, though they are seen only in the dark hours, emerging like nocturnal moths to move about in their narrow environs for a few brief hours before they must escape daylight once more.

Having been a solitary child, and much left to my own devices because of the persistent ill-health which was my lot, I developed early a propensity for roaming abroad by night, at first only in the Angell Street neighbourhood where I lived during much of my childhood, and then, little by little, in a widened circle in my native Providence. By day, my health permitting, I haunted the Seekonk River from the city into the open country, or, when my energy was at its height, played with a few carefully chosen companions at a 'club-house' we had painstakingly constructed in wooded areas not far out of the city. I was also much given to reading, and spent long hours in my grandfather's extensive library, reading without discrimination and thus assimilating a vast amount of knowledge, from the Greek philosophies to the history of the English monarchy, from the secrets of ancient alchemists to the experiments of Niels Bohr, from the lore of Egyptian papyri to the regional studies of Thomas Hardy, since my grandfather was possessed of very catholic tastes in books and, spurning specialization, bought and kept only what in his mind was good, by which he meant that which involved him.

But the nocturnal city invariably drew me from all else; walking abroad was my preference above all other pursuits, and I went out and about at night all through the later years of my childhood and throughout my adolescent years, in the course of which I tended – because sporadic illness kept me from regular attendance at school – to grow ever more self-sufficient and solitary. I could not now say what it was I sought with such determination in the nighted city, what it was in the ill-lit streets that drew me, why I sought old Benefit Street and the shadowed environs of Poe Street, almost unknown in the vastness of Providence, what it was I hoped to see in the furtively glimpsed faces of other night-wanderers slipping and slinking along the dark lanes and byways of the city, unless perhaps it was to escape from the harsher realities of daylight coupled with an insatiable curiosity about the secrets of city life which only the night could disclose.

When at last my graduation from high school was an accomplished fact, it might have been assumed that I would turn to other pursuits; but it was not so, for my health was too precarious to warrant matriculation at Brown University, where I would like to have gone to continue my studies, and this deprivation served only to enhance my solitary occupations – I doubled my reading hours and increased the time I spent abroad by night, by the simple expedient of sleeping during the daylight hours. And yet I contrived to lead an otherwise normal existence; I did not abandon my widowed mother or my aunts, with whom we lived, though the companions of my youth had grown away from me, and I managed to discover Rose Dexter, a dark-eyed descendant of the first English families to come into old Providence, one singularly favoured in the proportions of her figure and in the beauty of her features, whom I persuaded to share my nocturnal pursuits.

With her I continued to explore nocturnal Providence, and with new zest, eager to show Rose all I had already discovered in my wanderings about the city. We met originally at the old Athenaeum, and we continued to meet there of evenings, and from its portals ventured forth into the night. What began light-heartedly for her soon grew into dedicated habit; she proved as eager as I to inquire into hidden byways and long disused lanes, and she was soon as much at home in the night-held city as I. She was little inclined to irrelevant chatter, and thus proved admirably complementary to my person.

We had been exploring Providence in this fashion for several months when, one night on Benefit Street, a gentleman wearing a knee-length cape over wrinkled and ill-kept clothing accosted us. He had been standing on the walk not far ahead of us when first we turned into the street, and I had observed him when we went past him; he had struck me as oddly disquieting, for I thought his moustached, dark-eyed face with the unruly hair of his hatless head strangely familiar; and, at our passing, he had set out in pursuit until, at last, catching up to us, he touched me on the shoulder and spoke.

'Sir,' he said, 'could you tell me how to reach the cemetery where once Poe walked?'

I gave him directions, and then, spurred by a sudden impulse, suggested that we accompany him to the goal he sought; almost before I understood fully what had happened, we three were walking along together. I saw almost at once with what a calculating air the fellow scrutinized my companion, and yet any resentment I might have felt was dispelled by the ready recognition that the stranger's interest was inoffensive, for it was rather more coolly critical than passionately involved. I took the opportunity, also, to examine him as carefully as I could in the occasional patches of streetlight through which we passed, and was increasingly disturbed at the gnawing certainty that I knew him or had known him.

He was dressed almost uniformly in sombre black, save for his white shirt and the flowing Windsor tie he affected. His clothing was unpressed, as if it had been worn for a long time without having been attended to, but it was not unclean, as far as I could see. His brow was high, almost dome-like; under it his dark eyes looked out hauntingly, and his face narrowed to his small, blunt chin. His hair, too, was longer than most men of my generation wore it, and yet he seemed to be of that same generation, not more than five years past my own age. His clothing, however, was definitely not of my generation; indeed, it seemed, for all that it had the appearance of being new, to have been cut to a pattern of several generations before my own.

'Are you a stranger to Providence?' I asked him presently.

'I am visiting,' he said shortly.

'You are interested in Poe?'

He nodded.

'How much do you know of him?' I asked then.

'Little,' he replied. 'Perhaps you could tell me more?'

I needed no second invitation, but immediately gave him a biographical sketch of the father of the detective story and a master of the macabre tale whose work I had long admired, elaborating only on his romance with Mrs. Sarah Helen Whitman, since it involved Providence and the visit with Mrs. Whitman to the cemetery whither we were bound. I saw that he listened with almost rapt attention, and seemed to be setting down in memory everything I said, but I could not decide from his expressionless face whether what I told him gave him pleasure or displeasure, and I could not determine what the source of his interest was.

For her part, Rose was conscious of his interest in her, but she was not embarrassed by it, perhaps sensing that his interest was other than amorous. It was not until he asked her name that I realized we had not had his. He gave it now as 'Mr. Allan,' at which Rose smiled almost imperceptibly; I caught it fleetingly as we passed under a street lamp.

Having learned our names, our companion seemed interested in nothing more, and it was in silence that we reached the cemetery at last. I had thought Mr. Allan would enter it, but such was not his intention; he had evidently meant only to discover its location, so that he could return to it by day, which was manifestly a sensible conclusion, for – though I knew it well and had walked there on occasion by night – it offered little for a stranger to view in the dark hours.

We bade him good-night at the gate and went on.

'I've seen that fellow somewhere before,' I said to Rose once we had passed beyond his hearing. 'But I can't think where it was. Perhaps in the library.'

'It must have been in the library,' answered Rose with a throaty chuckle that was typical of her. 'In a portrait on the wall.'

'Oh, come!' I cried.

'Surely you recognized the resemblance, Arthur!' she cried. 'Even to his name. He looks like Edgar Allan Poe.'

And, of course, he did. As soon as Rose had mentioned it, I recognized the strong resemblance, even to his clothing, and at once set Mr. Allan down as a harmless idolator of Poe's so obsessed with the man that he must fashion himself in his likeness, even to his out-dated clothing – another of the curious specimens of humanity thronging the night streets of the city.

'Well, that one is the oddest fellow we've met in all the while we've walked out,' I said.

Her hand tightened on my arm. 'Arthur, didn't you *feel* something – something *wrong* about him?'

'Oh, I suppose there is something "wrong" in that sense about all of us who are haunters of the dark,' I said. 'Perhaps, in a way, we prefer to make our own reality.'

But even as I answered her, I was aware of her meaning, and there was no need of the explanation she tried so earnestly to make in the spate of words that followed – there was something wrong in the sense that there was about Mr. Allan a profound note of error. It lay, now that I faced and accepted it, in a number of trivial things, but particularly in the lack of expressiveness in his features; his speech, limited though it had been, was without modulation, almost mechanical; he had not smiled, nor had he been given to any variation in facial expression whatsoever; he had spoken with a precision that suggested an icy detachment and aloofness foreign to most men. Even the manifest interest he showed in Rose was far more clinical than anything else. At the same time that my curiosity was quickened, a note of apprehension began to make itself manifest, as a result of which I turned our conversation into other channels and presently walked Rose to her home.

II

I suppose it was inevitable that I should meet Mr. Allan again, and but two nights later, this time not far from my own door. Perhaps it was absurd to think so, but I could not escape the impression that he was waiting for me, that he was as anxious to encounter me again as I was to meet him.

I greeted him jovially, as a fellow haunter of the night, and took quick notice of the fact that, though his voice simulated my own joviality, there was not a flicker of emotion on his face; it remained completely placid – 'wooden,' in the words of the romantic writers, not the hint of a smile touched his lips, not a glint shone in his dark eyes. And now that I had had it called to my attention, I saw that the resemblance to Poe was remarkable, so much so, that had Mr. Allan put forth any reasonable claim to being a descendant of Poe's, I could have been persuaded to belief.

It was, I thought, a curious coincidence, but hardly more, and Mr. Allan on this occasion made no mention of Poe or anything relating to him in Providence. He seemed, it was soon evident, more intent on listening to me; he was as singularly uncommunicative as he had been at our first meeting, and in an odd way his manner was precisely the same – as if we had not actually met before. But perhaps it was that he simply sought some common ground, for, once I mentioned that I contributed a weekly column on astronomy to the Providence *Journal*, he began to take part in our conversation; what had been for several blocks virtually a monologue on my part, became a dialogue.

It was immediately apparent to me that Mr. Allan was not a novice in astronomical matters. Anxious as he seemed to be for my views, he entertained some distinctly different views of his own, some of them highly debatable. He lost no time in setting forth his opinion that not only was interplanetary travel possible, but that countless stars – not alone some of the planets in our solar system – were inhabited.

'By human beings?' I asked incredulously.

'Need it be?' he replied. 'Life is unique – not man. Even here on this planet life takes many forms.'

I asked him then whether he had read the works of Charles Fort.

He had not. He knew nothing of him, and, at his request, I outlined some of Fort's theories, together with the facts Fort had adduced in support of those theories. I saw that from time to time, as we walked along, my companion's head moved in a curt nod, though his unemotional face betrayed no expression; it was as if he agreed. And on one occasion, he broke into words.

'Yes, it is so. What he says is so.'

I had at the moment been speaking of the sighting of unidentified flying objects near Japan during the latter half of the nineteenth century.

'How can you say so?' I cried.

He launched at once into a lengthy statement, the gist of which was that every advanced scientist in the domain of astronomy was convinced that earth was not unique in having life, and that it followed therefore that, just as it could be concluded that some heavenly bodies had lower life forms than our own, so others might well support higher forms, and, accepting that premise, it was perfectly logical that such higher forms had mastered interplanetary travel and might, after decades of observation, be thoroughly familiar with earth and its inhabitants as well as with its sister planets.

'To what purpose?' I asked. 'To make war on us? To invade us?'

'A more highly developed form of life would hardly need to use such primitive methods,' he pointed out. 'They watch us precisely as we watch the moon and listen for radio signals from the planets – we here are still in the earliest stages of interplanetary communication and, beyond that, space travel, whereas other races on remote stars have long since achieved both.'

'How can you speak with such authority?' I asked then.

'Because I am convinced of it. Surely you must have come face to face with similar conclusions.'

I admitted that I had.

'And you remain open-minded?'

I admitted this as well.

'Open-minded enough to examine certain proof if it were offered to you?'

'Certainly,' I replied, though my scepticism could hardly have gone unnoticed.

'That is good,' he said. 'Because if you will permit my brothers and me to call on you at your home on Angell Street, we may be able to convince you that there is life in space – not in the shape of men, but life, and life possessing a far greater intelligence than that of your most intelligent men.'

I was amused at the breadth of his claim and belief, but I did not betray it by any sign. His confidence made me to reflect again upon the infinite variety of characters to be found among the night-walkers of Providence; clearly Mr. Allan was a man who was obsessed by his extraordinary beliefs, and, like most of such men, eager to proselytize, to make converts.

'Whenever you like,' I said by way of invitation. 'Except that I would prefer it to be late rather than early, to give my mother time to get to bed. Anything in the way of an experiment might disturb her.'

'Shall we say next Monday night?'

'Agreed.'

My companion thereafter said no more on this matter. Indeed, he said scarcely anything on any subject, and it was left for me to do the talking. I was evidently not very entertaining, for in less than three blocks we came to an alley and there Mr. Allan abruptly bade me good night, after which he turned into the alley and was soon swallowed in its darkness.

Could his house abut upon it? I wondered. If not, he must inevitably come out the other end. Impulsively I hurried around one end of that block and stationed myself deep in the shadows of the parallel street, where I could remain well hidden from the alley entrance and yet keep it in view.

Mr. Allan came leisurely out of the alley before I had quite recovered my breath. I expected him to pursue his way through the alley, but he did not; he turned down the street, and, accelerating his pace a little, he proceeded on his way. Impelled by curiosity now, I followed, keeping myself as well hidden as possible. But Mr. Allan never once looked around; he set his face straight ahead of him and never, as far as I could determine, even glanced to left or right; he was clearly bound for a destination that could only be his home, for the hour was past midnight.

I had little difficulty following my erstwhile companion, for I knew these streets well, I had known them since my childhood. Mr. Allan was bound in the direction of the Seekonk, and he held to his course without deviation until he reached a somewhat rundown section of Providence, where he made his way up a little knoll to a long-deserted house at its crest. He let himself into it and I saw him no more. I waited a while longer, expecting a light to go up in the house, but none did, and I could only conclude that he had gone directly to bed.

Fortunately, I had kept myself in the shadows, for Mr. Allan had evidently not gone to bed. Apparently he had gone through the house and around the block, for suddenly I saw him approach the house from the direction we had come, and once more he walked on, past my place of concealment, and made his way into the house, again without turning on a light.

This time, certainly, he had remained there. I waited for five minutes or a trifle more; then turned and made my way back towards my own home on Angell Street, satisfied that I had done no more in following Mr. Allan than he had evidently done on the night of our initial meeting in following me, for I had long since concluded that our meeting tonight had not been by chance, but by design.

Many blocks from the Allan house, however, I was startled to see approaching me from the direction of Benefit Street, my erstwhile companion! Even as I wondered how he had managed to leave the house again and make his way well around me in order to enable him to come towards me, trying in vain to map the route he could have taken to accomplish this, he came up and passed me by without so much as a flicker of recognition.

Yet it was he, undeniably – the same Poesque appearance distinguished him from any other night-walker. Stifling his name on my tongue, I turned and looked after him. He never turned his head, but walked steadily on, clearly bound for the scene I had not long since quitted. I watched him out of sight, still trying – in vain – to map the route he might have taken among the lanes and byways and streets so familiar to me in order to meet me so once more, face to face.

We had met on Angell Street, walked to Benefit and north, then turned riverwards once more. Only by dint of hard running could he have cut around me and come back. And what purpose would he have had to follow such a course? It left me utterly baffled, particularly since he had given me not the slightest sign of recognition, his entire mien suggesting that we were perfect strangers!

But if I was mystified at the occurrences of the night, I was even more puzzled at my meeting with Rose at the Athenaeum the following night. She had clearly been waiting for me, and hastened to my side as soon as she caught sight of me.

'Have you seen Mr. Allan?' she asked.

'Only last night,' I answered, and would have gone on to recount the circumstances had she not spoken again.

'So did I! He walked me out from the library and home.'

I stifled my response and heard her out. Mr. Allan had been waiting for her to come out of the library. He had greeted her and asked whether he might walk with her, after having ascertained that I was not with her. They had walked for an hour with but little conversation, and this only of the most superficial – relative to the antiquities of the city, the architecture of certain houses, and similar matters, just such as one interested in the older aspects of Providence would find of interest – and then he had walked her home. She had, in short, been with Mr. Allan in one part of the city at the same time that I had been with him in another; and clearly neither of us had the slightest doubt of the identity of our companions.

'I saw him after midnight,' I said, which was part of the truth but not all the truth.

This extraordinary coincidence must have some logical explanation, though I was not disposed to discuss it with Rose, lest I unduly alarm her. Mr. Allan had spoken of his 'brothers'; it was therefore entirely likely that Mr. Allan was one of a pair of identical twins. But what explanation could there be for what was an obvious and designed deception? One of our companions was *not*, could not have been the same Mr. Allan with whom we had previously walked. But which? I was satisfied that my companion was identical with Mr. Allan met but two nights before.

In as casual a manner as I could assume in the circumstances, I asked such questions of Rose as were designed to satisfy me in regard to the identity of her companion, in the anticipation that somewhere in our dialogue she would reveal some doubt of the identity of hers. She betrayed no such doubt; she was innocently convinced that her companion was the same man who had walked with us two nights ago, for he had obviously made references to the earlier nocturnal walk, and Rose was completely convinced that he was the same man. She had no reason for doubt, however, for I held my tongue; there was some perplexing mystery here, for the brothers had some obscure reason for interesting themselves in us – certainly other than that they shared our interest in the night-walkers of the city and the hidden aspects of urban life that appeared only with the dusk and vanished once more into their seclusion with the dawn.

My companion, however, had made an assignation with me, whereas Rose said nothing to indicate that her companion had planned a further meeting with her. And why had he waited to meet her in the first place? But this line of inquiry was lost before the insistent cognizance that neither of the meetings I had had after leaving my companion at his residence last night could have been Rose's companion, for Rose lived rather too far from the place of my final meeting last night to have permitted her companion to meet me at the point we met. A disquieting sense of uneasiness began to rise in me. Perhaps there were three Allans – all identical – triplets? Or four? But no, surely the second Mr. Allan encountered on the previous night had been identical with the first, even if the third encounter could not have been the same man.

No matter how much thought I applied to it, the riddle remained insoluble. I was, therefore, in a challenging frame of mind for my Monday night appointment with Mr. Allan, now but two days away.

III

Even so, I was ill-prepared for the visit of Mr. Allan and his brothers on the following Monday night. They came at a quarter past ten o'clock; my mother had just gone upstairs to bed. I had expected, at most, three of them; there were seven – and they were as alike as peas in a pod, so much so that I could not pick from among them the Mr. Allan with whom I had twice walked the nocturnal streets of Providence, though I assumed it was he who was the spokesman for the group.

They filed into the living-room, and Mr. Allan immediately set about arranging chairs in a semi-circle with the help of his brothers, murmuring something about the 'nature of the experiment,' though, to tell the truth, I was still much too amazed and disquieted at the appearance of seven identical men, all of whom bore so strong a resemblance to Edgar Allan Poe as to startle the beholder, to assimilate what was being said. Moreover, I saw now by the light of my Welsbach gas-lamp, that all seven of them were of a pallid, waxen complexion, not of such a nature as to give me any doubt of their being flesh and bone like myself, but rather such as to suggest that one and all were afflicted with some kind of disease – anaemia, perhaps, or some kindred illness which would leave their faces colourless; and their eyes, which were very dark, seemed to stare fixedly and yet without seeing, though they suffered no lack of perception and seemed to perceive by means of some extra sense not visible to me. The sensation that rose in me was not predominantly one of fear, but one of overwhelming curiosity tinged with a spreading sense of something utterly alien not only to my experience but to my existence.

Thus far, little had passed between us, but now that the semi-circle had been completed, and my visitors had seated themselves, their spokesman beckoned me forward and indicated a chair placed within the arc of the semi-circle facing the seated men.

'Will you sit here, Mr. Phillips?" he asked.

I did as he asked, and found myself the object of all eyes, but not essentially so much their object as their focal point, for the seven men seemed to be looking not so much at me as through me.

'Our intention, Mr. Phillips,' explained their spokesman – whom I took to be the gentleman I had encountered on Benefit Street – 'is to produce for you certain impressions of extra-terrestrial life. All that is necessary for you to do is to relax and to be receptive.'

'I am ready,' I said.

I had expected that they would ask for the light to be lowered, which seems to be integral to all such seance-like sessions, but they did not do so. They waited upon silence, save for the ticking of the hall clock and the distant hum of the city, and then they began what I can only describe as singing – a low, not unpleasant, almost lulling humming, increasing in volume, and broken with sounds I assumed were words though I could not make out any of them. The song they sang and the way they sang it was indescribably foreign; the key was minor, and the tonal intervals did not resemble any terrestrial musical system with which I was familiar, though it seemed to me more Oriental than Occidental.

I had little time to consider the music, however, for I was rapidly overcome with a feeling of profound malaise, the faces of the seven men grew dim and coalesced to merge into one swimming face, and an intolerable consciousness of unrolled aeons of time swept over me. I concluded that some form of hypnosis was responsible for my condition, but I did not have any qualms about it; it did not matter, for the experience I was undergoing was utterly novel and not unpleasant, though there was inherent in it a discordant note, as of some lurking evil looming far behind the relaxing sensations that crowded upon me and swept me before them. Gradually, the lamp, the walls, and the men before me faded and vanished and, though I was still aware of being in my quarters on Angell Street, I was also cognizant that somehow I had been transported to new surroundings, and an element of alarm at the strangeness of these surroundings, together with one of repulsion and alienation began to make themselves manifest. It was as if I feared losing consciousness in an alien place without the means of returning to earth – for it was an extra-terrestrial scene that I witnessed, one of great and magnificent grandeur in its proportions, and yet one completely incomprehensible to me.

Vast vistas of space whirled before me in an alien dimension, and central in them was an aggregation of gigantic cubes, scattered along a gulf of violet and agitated radiation – and other figures moving among them – enormous, iridescent, rugose cones, rising from a base almost ten feet wide to a height of over ten feet, and composed of ridgy, scaly, semi-elastic matter, and sporting from their apexes four flexible, cylindrical members, each at least a foot thick, and of a similar substance, though more fleshlike, as that of the cones, which were presumably bodies for the crowning members, which, as I watched, had an ability to contract or expand, sometimes to lengthen to a distance equal to the height of the cone to which they adhered. Two of these members were terminated with enormous claws, while a third wore a crest of four red, trumpetlike appendages, and the fourth ended in a great yellow globe two feet in diameter, in the centre of which were three enormous eyes, darkly opalescent, which, because of their position in the elastic member, could be turned in any direction whatsoever. It was such a scene as exercised the greatest fascination upon me and yet at the same time spread in me a repellence inspired by its total alienation and the aura of fearful disclosures which alone could give it meaning and a lurking terror. Moreover, as I saw the moving figures, which seemed to be *tending* the great cubes, with greater clarity and more distinctness, I saw that their strange heads were crowned by four slender grey stalks carrying flowerlike appendages, as well as, from their nether side, eight sinuous, elastic tentacles, moss green in colour, which seemed to be constantly agitated by serpentine motion, expanding and contracting, lengthening and shortening and whipping around as if with life independent of that which animated, more sluggishly, the cones themselves. The whole scene was bathed in a wan, red glow, as from some dying sun which, failing its planet, now took second place to the violent radiation from the gulf.

The scene had an indescribable effect on me; it was as if I had been permitted a look into another world, one incredibly vaster than our own, distinguished from our own by antipodally different values and life-forms, and remote from ours in time and space, and as I gazed at this far world, I became aware – as were this intelligence being funnelled into me by some psychic means – that I looked upon a dying race which must escape its planet or perish. Spontaneously then, I seemed to recognize the burgeoning of a menacing evil, and with an urgent, violent effort, I threw off the bondage of the chant that held me in its spell, gave vent to the uprushing of fear I felt in a cry of protest, and rose to my feet, while the chair on which I sat fell backwards with a crash.

Instantly the scene before my mind's eye vanished and the room returned to focus. Across from me sat my visitors, the seven gentlemen in the likeness of Poe, impassive and silent, for the sounds they had made, the humming and the odd word-like tonal noises, had ceased.

I calmed down, my pulse began to slow.

'What you saw, Mr. Phillips, was a scene on another star, remote from here,' said Mr. Allan. 'Far out in space – indeed, in another universe. Did it convince you?'

'I've seen enough,' I cried.

I could not tell whether my visitors were amused or scornful; they remained without expression, including their spokesman, who only inclined his head slightly and said, 'We will take our leave then, with your permission.'

And silently, one by one, they all filed out into Angell Street.

I was most disagreeably shaken. I had no proof of having seen anything on another world, but I could testify that I had experienced an extraordinary hallucination, undoubtedly through hypnotic influence.

But what had been its reason for being? I pondered that as I set about to put the living-room to rights, but I could not adduce any profound reason for the demonstration I had witnessed. I was unable to deny that my visitors had shown themselves to be possessed of extraordinary faculties – but to what end? And I had to admit to myself that I was as much shaken by the appearance of no less than seven identical men as I was by the hallucinatory experience I had just passed through. Quintuplets were possible, yes – but had anyone ever heard of septuplets? Nor were multiple births of identical children usual. Yet here were seven men, all of very much the same age, identical in appearance, for whose existence there was not a scintilla of explanation.

Nor was there any graspable meaning in the scene that I had witnessed during the demonstration. Somehow I had understood that the great cubes were sentient beings for whom the violet radiation was life-giving; I had realized that the cone-creatures served them in some fashion or other, but nothing had been disclosed to show how. The whole vision was meaningless; it was just such a scene as might have been created by a highly organized imagination and telepathically conveyed to a willing subject, such as myself. That it proved the existence of extra-terrestrial life was ridiculous; it proved no more than that I had been the victim of an induced hallucination.

But, once more, I came full circle. As hallucination, it was completely without reason for being.

Yet I could not escape an insistent disquiet that troubled me long that night before I was able to sleep.

IV

Strangely enough, my uneasiness mounted during the course of the following morning. Accustomed as I was to the human curiosities, to the often incredible characters and unusual sights to be encountered on the nocturnal walks I took about Providence, the circumstances surrounding the Poesque Mr. Allan and his brothers were so *outré* that I could not get them out of mind.

Acting on impulse, I took time off from my work that afternoon and made my way to the house on the knoll along the Seekonk, determined to confront my nocturnal companion. But the house, when I came to it, wore an air of singular desertion; badly worn curtains were drawn down to the sills of the windows, in some places blinds were up; and the whole milieu was the epitome of abandonment.

Nevertheless, I knocked at the door and waited.

There was no answer. I knocked again.

No sound fell to ear from inside the house.

Powerfully impelled by curiosity now, I tried the door. It opened to my touch. I hesitated still, and looked all around me. No one was in sight, at least two of the houses in the neighbourhood were unoccupied, and if I was under surveillance it was not apparent to me.

I opened the door and stepped into the house, standing for a few moments with my back to the door to accustom my eyes to the twilight that filled the rooms. Then I moved cautiously through the small vestibule into the adjacent room, a parlour sparely occupied by horsehair furniture at least two decades old. There was no sign here of occupation by any human being, though there was evidence that someone had not long since walked here, making a path through dust visible on the uncarpeted flooring. I crossed the room and entered a small dining-room, and crossed this, too, to find myself in a kitchen, which, like the other rooms, bore little sign of having been used, for there was no food of any kind in evidence, and the table appeared not to have been used for years. Yet here, too, were footprints in substantial numbers, testifying to the habitation of the house. And the staircase revealed steady use, as well.

But it was the far side of the house that afforded the most disturbing disclosures. This side of the building consisted of but one large room, though it was instantly evident that it had been three rooms at one time, but the connecting walls had been removed without the finished repair of the junctions at the outer wall. I saw this in a fleeting glance, for what was in the centre of the room caught and held my fascinated attention. The room was bathed in violet light, a soft glowing that emanated from what appeared to be a long, glass-encased slab, which, with a second, unlit similar slab, stood surrounded by machinery the like of which I had never seen before save in dreams.

I moved cautiously into the room, alert for anyone who might prevent my intrusion. No one and nothing moved. I drew closer to the violet-lit glass case and saw that something lay within, though I did not at first encompass this because I saw what it laid upon – nothing less than a life-sized reproduction of a likeness of Edgar Allan Poe, which, like everything else, was illuminated by the same pulsing violet light, the source of which I could not determine, save that it was enclosed by the glass-like substance which made up the case. But when at last I looked upon that which lay upon the likeness of Poe, I almost cried out in fearful surprise, for it was, in miniature, a precise reproduction of one of the rugose cones I had seen only last night in the hallucination induced in my home on Angell Street! And the sinuous movement of the tentacles on its head – or what I took to be its head – was indisputable evidence that it was alive!

I backed hastily away with only enough of a glance at the other case to assure myself that it was bare and unoccupied, though connected by many metal tubes to the illuminated case parallel to it; then I fled, as noiselessly as possible, for I was convinced that the nocturnal brotherhood slept upstairs and in my confusion at this inexplicable revelation that placed my hallucination of the previous night into another perspective, I wished to meet no one. I escaped from the house undetected, though I thought I caught a brief glimpse of a Poesque face at one of the upper windows. I ran down the road and back along the streets that bridged the distance from the Seekonk to the Providence River, and ran so for many blocks before I slowed to a walk, for I was beginning to attract attention in my wild flight.

As I walked along, I strove to bring order to my chaotic thoughts. I could not adduce an explanation for what I had seen, but I knew intuitively that I had stumbled upon some menacing evil too dark and forbidding and perhaps too vast as well for my comprehension. I hunted for meaning and found none; mine had never been a scientifically-oriented mind, apart from chemistry and astronomy, so that I was not equipped to understand the use of the great machines I had seen in that house ringing that violet-lit slab where that rugose body lay in warm, life-giving radiation – indeed, I was not even able to assimilate the machinery itself, for there was only a remote resemblance to anything I had ever before seen, and that the dynamos in a power-house. They had all been connected in some way to the two slabs, and the glass cases – if the substance were glass – the one occupied, the other dark and empty, for all the tubing that tied them each to each.

But I had seen enough to be convinced that the dark-clad brotherhood who walked the streets of Providence by night in the guise of Edgar Allan Poe had a purpose other than mine in doing so; theirs was no simple curiosity about the nocturnal characters, about fellow walkers of the night. Perhaps darkness was their natural element, even as daylight was that of the majority of their fellowmen; but that their motivation was sinister, I could not now doubt. Yet at the same time I was at a loss as to what course next to follow.

I turned my steps at last towards the library, in the vague hope of grasping at something that might lead me to some clue by means of which I could approach an understanding of what I had seen.

But there was nothing. Search as I might, I found no key, no hint, though I read widely through every conceivable reference – even to those on Poe in Providence on the shelves, and I left the library late in the day as baffled as I had entered.

Perhaps it was inevitable that I would see Mr. Allan again that night. I had no way of knowing whether my visit to his home had been observed, despite the observer I thought I had glimpsed in an upper window in my flight, and I encountered him therefore in some trepidation. But this was evidently ill-founded, for when I greeted him on Benefit Street there was nothing in his manner or in his words to suggest any change in his attitude, such as I might have expected had he been aware of my intrusion. Yet I knew full well his capacity for being without expression – humour, disgust, even anger or irritation were alien to his features, which never changed from that introspective mask which was essentially that of Poe.

'I trust you have recovered from our experiment, Mr. Phillips,' he said after exchanging the customary amenities.

'Fully,' I answered, though it was not the truth. I added

something about a sudden spell of dizziness to explain my bringing the experiment to its precipitate end.

'It is but one of the worlds outside you saw, Mr. Phillips,' Mr. Allan went on. 'There are many. As many as a hundred thousand. Life is not the unique property of Earth. Nor is life in the shape of human beings. Life takes many forms on other planets and far stars, forms that would seem bizarre to humans, as human life is bizarre to other life forms.'

For once, Mr. Allan was singularly communicative, and I had little to say. Clearly, whether or not I laid what I had seen to hallucination – even in the face of my discovery in my companion's house – he himself believed implicitly in what he said. He spoke of many worlds, as if he were familiar with them. On occasion he spoke almost with reverence of certain forms of life, particularly those with the astonishing adaptability of assuming the life forms of other planets in their ceaseless quest for the conditions necessary to their existence.

'The star I looked upon,' I broke in, 'was dying.'

'Yes,' he said simply.

'You have seen it?'

'I have seen it, Mr. Phillips.'

I listened to him with relief. Since it was manifestly impossible to permit any man sight of the intimate life of outer space, what I had experienced was nothing more than the communicated hallucination of Mr. Allan and his brothers. Telepathic communication certainly, aided by a form of hypnosis I had not previously experienced. Yet I could not rid myself of the disquieting sense of evil that surrounded my nocturnal companion, nor of the uneasy feeling that the explanation which I had so eagerly accepted was unhappily glib.

As soon as I decently could, thereafter, I made excuses to Mr. Allan and took my leave of him. I hastened directly to the Athenaeum in the hope of finding Rose Dexter there, but if she had been there, she had already gone. I went then to a public telephone in the building and telephoned her home.

Rose answered, and I confess to an instantaneous feeling of gratification.

'Have you seen Mr. Allan tonight?' I asked.

'Yes,' she replied. 'But only for a few moments. I was on my way to the library.'

'So did I.'

'He asked me to his home some evening to watch an experiment,' she went on.

'Don't go,' I said at once.

There was a long moment of silence at the other end of the wire. Then, 'Why not?' Unfortunately, I failed to acknowledge the edge of truculence in her voice.

'It would be better not to go,' I said, with all the firmness I could muster.

'Don't you think, Mr. Phillips, I am the best judge of that?'

I hastened to assure her that I had no wish to dictate her actions, but meant only to suggest that it might be dangerous to go.

'Why?'

'I can't tell you over the telephone,' I answered, fully aware of how lame it sounded, and knowing even as I said it that perhaps I could not put into words at all the horrible suspicions which had begun to take shape in my mind, for they were so fantastic, so *outré*, that no one could be expected to believe in them.

'I'll think it over,' she said crisply.

'I'll try to explain when I see you,' I promised.

She bade me good-night and rang off with an intransigence that boded ill, and left me profoundly disturbed.

V

I come now to the final, apocalyptic events concerning Mr. Allan and the mystery surrounding the house on the forgotten knoll. I hesitate to set them down even now, for I recognize that the charge against me will only be broadened to include grave questions about my sanity. Yet I have no other course.

Indeed, the entire future of humanity, the whole course of what we call civilization may be affected by what I do or do not write of this matter. For the culminating events followed rapidly and naturally upon my conversation with Rose Dexter, that unsatisfactory exchange over the telephone.

After a restless, uneasy day at work, I concluded that I must make a tenable explanation to Rose. On the following evening, therefore, I went early to the library, where I was accustomed to meeting her, and took a place where I could watch the main entrance. There I waited for well over an hour before it occurred to me that she might not come to the library that night.

Once more I sought the telephone, intending to ask whether I might come over and explain my request of the previous night.

But it was her sister-in-law, not Rose, who answered my ring.

Rose had gone out. 'A gentleman called for her.'

'Did you know him?' I asked.

'No, Mr. Phillips.'

'Did you hear his name?'

She had not heard it. She had, in fact, caught only a glimpse of him as Rose hurried out to meet him, but, in answer to my insistent probing, she admitted that Rose's caller had had a moustache.

Mr. Allan! I had no further need to inquire.

For a few moments after I had hung up, I did not know what to do. Perhaps Rose and Mr. Allan were only walking the length of Benefit Street. But perhaps they had gone to that mysterious house. The very thought of it filled me with such apprehension that I lost my head.

I rushed from the library and hurried home. It was ten o'clock when I reached the house on Angell Street. Fortunately, my mother had retired; so I was able to procure my father's pistol without disturbing her. So armed, I hastened once more into night-held Providence and ran, block upon block, towards the shore of the Seekonk and the knoll upon which stood Mr. Allan's strange house, unaware in my incautious haste of the spectacle I made for other night-walkers and uncaring, for perhaps Rose's life was at stake – and beyond that, vaguely defined, loomed a far greater and hideous evil.

When I reached the house into which Mr. Allan had disappeared I was taken aback by its solitude and unlit windows. Since I was winded, I hesitated to advance upon it, and waited for a minute or so to catch my breath and quiet my pulse. Then, keeping to the shadows, I moved silently up to the house, looking for any sliver of light.

I crept from the front of the house around to the back. Not the slightest ray of light could be seen. But a low humming sound vibrated just inside the range of my hearing, like the hum of a power line responding to the weather. I crossed to the far side of the house – and there I saw the hint of light – not yellow light, as from a lamp inside, but a pale lavender radiance that seemed to glow faintly, ever so faintly, from the wall itself.

I drew back, recalling only too sharply what I had seen in that house.

But my role now could not be a passive one. I had to know whether Rose was in that darkened house – perhaps in that very room with the unknown machinery and the glass case with the monster in the violet radiance.

I slipped back to the front of the house and mounted the steps to the front door.

Once again, the door was not locked. It yielded to the pressure of my hands. Pausing only long enough to take my loaded weapon in hand, I pushed open the door and entered the vestibule. I stood for a moment to accustom my eyes to that darkness; standing there, I was even more aware of the humming sound I had heard – and of more – the same kind of chant which had put me into that hypnotic state in the course of which I had witnessed that disturbing vision purporting to be that of life in another world.

I apprehended its meaning instantly, I thought. Rose must be with Mr. Allan and his brothers, undergoing a similar experience.

Would that it had been no more!

For when I pushed my way into that large room on the far side of the house, I saw that which will be for ever indelibly imprinted on my mind. Lit by the radiance from the glass case, the room disclosed Mr. Allan and his identical brothers all prone upon the floor around the twin cases, making their chanting song. Beyond them, against the far wall, lay the discarded life-size likeness of Poe I had seen beneath that weird creature in the glass case bathed in violet radiance. But it was not Mr. Allan and his brothers that so profoundly shocked and repelled me – it was what I saw in the glass cases!

For in the one that lit the room with its violently pulsating and agitated violent radiation lay Rose Dexter, fully clothed, and certainly under hypnosis – and on top of her lay, greatly elongated and with its tentacles flailing madly, the rugose cone-like figure I had last seen shrunken on the likeness of Poe. And in the connected case adjacent to it – I can hardly bear to set it down even now – lay, identical in every detail, *a perfect duplicate of Rose!*

What happened next is confused in my memory. I know that I lost control, that I fired blindly at the glass cases, intending to shatter them. Certainly I struck one or both of them, for with the impact the radiance vanished, the room was plunged into utter darkness, cries of fear and alarm rose from Mr. Allan and his brothers, and, amid a succession of explosive sounds from the machinery, I rushed forward and picked up Rose Dexter.

Somehow I gained the street with Rose.

Looking back, I saw that flames were appearing at the windows of that accursed house, and then, without warning, the north wall of the house collapsed, and something – an object I could not identify – burst from the now burning house and vanished aloft. I fled, still carrying Rose.

Regaining her senses, Rose was hysterical, but I succeeded in calming her, and at last she fell silent and would say nothing. And in silence I took her safely home, knowing how frightening her experience must have been, and resolved to say nothing until she had fully recovered.

In the week that followed, I came to see clearly what was taking place in that house on the knoll. But the charge of arson – lodged against me in lieu of a far more serious one because of the pistol I abandoned in the burning house – has blinded the police to anything but the most mundane matters. I have tried to tell them, insisting that they see Rose Dexter when she is well enough to talk – and willing to do so. I cannot make them understand what I now understand only too well. Yet the facts are there, inescapably.

They say the charred flesh found in that house is not human, most of it. But could they have expected anything else? Seven men in the likeness of Edgar Allan Poe? Surely they must understand that whatever it was in that house came from another world, a dying world, and sought to invade and ultimately take over Earth by reproducing themselves in the shape of men! Surely they must know that it must have been only by coincidence that the model they first chose was a likeness of Poe, chosen because they had no knowledge that Poe did not represent the average among men? Surely they must know, as I came to know, that the rugose, tentacled cone in the violet radiance was the source of their material selves, that the machinery and the tubing – which they say was too much damaged by the fire to identify, as if they could have identified its functions even undamaged! – manufactured from the material simulating flesh supplied by the cone in the violet light creatures in the shape of men from the likeness of Poe!

'Mr. Allan' himself afforded me the key, though I did not know it at the time, when I asked him why mankind was the object of interplanetary scrutiny – 'To make war on us? To invade us?' – and he replied: '*A more highly developed form of life would hardly need to use such primitive methods.*' Could anything more plainly set forth the explanation for the strange occupation of the house along the Seekonk? Of course, it is evident now that what 'Mr. Allan' and his identical brothers afforded me in my own house was a glimpse of life on the planet of the cubes and rugose cones, which was their own.

And surely, finally, most damning of all – it must be evident to any unbiased observer why they wanted Rose. They meant to reproduce their kind in the guise of men and women, so that they could mingle with us, undetected, unsuspected, and slowly, over decades – perhaps centuries, while their world died, take over and prepare our Earth for those who would come after.

God alone knows how many of them may be here, among us, even now!

Later. I have been unable to see Rose until now, tonight, and I am hesitant to call for her. For something unutterably terrible has happened to me. I have fallen prey to horrible doubts. While it did not occur to me during that frightful experience in the shambles following my shots in that violet-lit room, I have now begun to wonder, and my concern has grown hour by hour until I find it now almost unbearable. How can I be sure that, in those frenzied minutes, I rescued the *real* Rose Dexter? If I did, surely she will reassure me tonight. If I did not – God knows what I may unwittingly have loosed upon Providence and the world!

From *The Providence Journal* – July 17

LOCAL GIRL SLAYS ATTACKER

Rose Dexter, the daughter of Mr. and Mrs. Elisha Dexter of 127 Benevolent Street, last night fought off and killed a young man she charged with attacking her. Miss Dexter was apprehended in an hysterical condition as she fled down Benefit Street in the vicinity of the Cathedral of St. John, near the cemetery attached to which the attack took place.

Her attacker was identified as an acquaintance, Arthur Phillips . . .

At dusk, the wild, lonely country guarding the approaches to the village of Dunwich in north central Massachusetts seems more desolate and forbidding than it ever does by day. Twilight lends the barren fields and domed hills a strangeness that sets them apart from the country around that area; it brings to everything a kind of sentient, watchful animosity – to the ancient trees, to the brier-bordered stone walls pressing close upon the dusty road, to the low marshes with their myriads of fireflies and their incessantly calling whippoorwills vying with the muttering of frogs and the shrill songs of toads, to the sinuous windings of the upper reaches of the Miskatonic flowing among the dark hills seaward, all of which seem to close in upon the traveller as if intent upon holding him fast, beyond all escape.

On his way to Dunwich, Abner Whateley felt all this again, as once in childhood he had felt it and run screaming in terror to beg his mother to take him away from Dunwich and Grandfather Luther Whateley. So many years ago! He had lost count of them. It was curious that the country should affect him so, pushing through all the years he had lived since then – the years at the Sorbonne, in Cairo, in London – pushing through all the learning he had assimilated since those early visits to grim old Grandfather Whateley in his ancient house attached to the mill along the Miskatonic, the country of his childhood, coming back now out of the mists of time as were it but yesterday that he had visited his kinfolk.

They were all gone now – Mother, Grandfather Whateley, Aunt Sarey, whom he had never seen but only knew to be living somewhere in that old house – the loathsome cousin Wilbur and his terrible twin brother few had ever known before his frightful death on top of Sentinel Hill. But Dunwich, he saw as he drove through the cavernous covered bridge, had not changed;

its main street lay under the looming mound of Round Mountain, its gambrel roofs as rotting as ever, its houses deserted, the only store still in the broken-steepled church, over everything the unmistakable aura of decay.

He turned off the main street and followed a rutted road up along the river, until he came within sight of the great old house with the mill wheel on the river-side. It was his property now, by the will of Grandfather Whateley, who had stipulated that he must settle the estate and 'take such steps as may be necessary to bring about that dissolution I myself was not able to take.' A curious proviso, Abner thought. But then, everything about Grandfather Whateley had been strange, as if the decadence of Dunwich had infected him irrevocably.

And nothing was stranger than that Abner Whateley should come back from his cosmopolitan way of life to heed his grandfather's adjurations for property which was scarcely worth the time and trouble it would take to dispose of it. He reflected ruefully that such relatives as still lived in or near Dunwich might well resent his return in their curious inward growing and isolated rustication which had kept most of the Whateleys in this immediate region, particularly since the shocking events which had overtaken the country branch of the family on Sentinel Hill.

The house appeared to be unchanged. The river-side of the house was given over to the mill, which had long ago ceased to function, as more and more of the fields around Dunwich had grown barren; except for one room above the mill-wheel – Aunt Sarey's room – the entire side of the structure bordering the Miskatonic had been abandoned even in the time of his boyhood, when Abner Whateley had last visited his grandfather, then living alone in the house except for the never seen Aunt Sarey who abode in her shuttered room with her door locked, never to move about the house under prohibition of such movement by her father, from whose domination only death at last had freed her.

A verandah, fallen in at the corner of the house, circled that part of the structure used as a dwelling; from the lattice-work

under the eaves great cobwebs hung, undisturbed by anything
save the wind for years. And dust lay over everything, inside
as well as out, as Abner discovered when he had found the
right key among the lot the lawyer had sent him. He found a
lamp and lit it, for Grandfather Whateley had scorned electricity. In the yellow glow of light, the familiarity of the old
kitchen with its nineteenth-century appointments smote him
like a blow. Its spareness, the hand-hewn table and chairs, the
century-old clock on the mantel, the worn broom — all were
tangible reminders of his fear-haunted childhood visits to this
formidable house and its even more formidable occupant, his
mother's aged father.

The lamplight disclosed something more. On the kitchen
table lay an envelope addressed to him in handwriting so crabbed that it could only be that of a very old or infirm man — his
grandfather. Without troubling to bring the rest of his things
from the car, Abner sat down to the table, blowing the dust off
the chair and sufficiently from the table to allow him a resting
place for his elbows, and opened the envelope.

The spidery script leapt out at him. The words were as severe
as he remembered his grandfather to have been. And abrupt,
with no term of endearment, not even the prosaic form of greet-
ing.

'Grandson:
'When you read this, I will be some months dead. Perhaps
more, unless they find you sooner than I believe they will. I
have left you a sum of money — all I have and die possessed of
— which is in the bank at Arkham under your name now. I do
this not alone because you are my own and only grandson but
because among all the Whateleys — we are an accursed clan, my
boy — you have gone forth into the world and gathered to yourself learning sufficient to permit you to look upon all things
with an inquiring mind ridden neither by the superstition of
ignorance nor the superstition of science. You will understand
my meaning.

'It is my wish that at least the mill section of this house be destroyed. Let it be taken apart, board by board. *If anything in it lives, I adjure you solemnly to kill it. No matter how small it may be. No matter what form it may have, for if it seems to you human it will beguile you and endanger your life and God knows how many others.*

'Heed me in this.

'If I seem to have the sound of madness, pray recall that worse than madness has spawned among the Whateleys. I have stood free of it. It has not been so of all that is mine. There is more stubborn madness in those who are unwilling to believe in what they know not of and deny that such exists, than in those of our blood who have been guilty of terrible practices, and blasphemy against God, and worse.

'Your Grandfather, Luther S. Whateley.'

How like Grandfather! thought Abner. He remembered, spurred into memory by this enigmatic, self-righteous communication, how on one occasion when his mother had mentioned her sister Sarah, and clapped her fingers across her mouth in dismay, he had run to his grandfather to ask,

'Grandpa, where's Aunt Sarey?'

The old man had looked at him out of eyes that were basilisk and answered, 'Boy, we do not speak of Sarah here.'

Aunt Sarey had offended the old man in some dreadful way – dreadful, at least, to that firm disciplinarian – for from that time beyond even Abner Whateley's memory, his aunt had been only the name of a woman, who was his mother's oldest sister, and who was locked in the big room over the mill and kept for ever invisible within those walls, behind the shutters nailed to her windows. It had been forbidden both Abner and his mother even to linger before the door of that shuttered room, though on one occasion Abner had crept up to the door and put his ear against it to listen to the snuffling and whimpering sounds that went on inside, as from some large person, and Aunt Sarey, he had decided, must be as large as a circus fat lady, for she devoured so much, judging by the great platters of food – chiefly meat, which she must have prepared herself, since so much of it was raw – carried to the room twice daily by old Luther Whateley himself, for there were no servants in that house, and had not been since the time Abner's mother had married, after Aunt Sarey had come back, strange and mazed, from a visit to distant kin in Innsmouth.

He refolded the letter and put it back into the envelope. He would think of its contents another day. His first need now was to make sure of a place to sleep. He went out and got his two remaining bags from the car and brought them to the kitchen. Then he picked up the lamp and went into the interior of the house. The old-fashioned parlour, which was always kept closed against that day when visitors came – and none save Whateleys called upon Whateleys in Dunwich – he ignored. He made his way instead to his grandfather's bedroom; it was fitting that he should occupy the old man's bed now that he, and not Luther Whateley, was master here.

The large, double bed was covered with faded copies of the *Arkham Advertiser*, carefully arranged to protect the fine cloth of the spread, which had been embossed with an armigerous design, doubtless a legitimate Whateley heritage. He set down the lamp and cleared away the newspapers. When he turned down the bed, he saw that it was clean and fresh, ready for occupation; some cousin of his grandfather's had doubtless seen to this, against his arrival, after the obsequies.

Then he got his bags and transferred them to the bedroom, which was in that corner of the house away from the village; its windows looked along the river, though they were more than the width of the mill from the bank of the stream. He opened the only one of them which had a screen across its lower half, then sat down on the edge of the bed, bemused, pondering the circumstances which had brought him back to Dunwich after all these years.

He was tired now. The heavy traffic around Boston had tired him. The contrast between the Boston region and this desolate Dunwich country depressed and troubled him. Moreover, he was conscious of an intangible uneasiness. If he had not had need of his legacy to continue his research abroad into the ancient civilizations of the South Pacific, he would never have come here. Yet family ties existed, for all that he would deny them. Grim and forbidding as old Luther Whateley had always been, he was his mother's father, and to him his grandson owed the allegiance of common blood.

Round Mountain loomed close outside the bedroom; he felt its presence as he had when a boy, sleeping in the room above. Trees, for long untended, pressed upon the house, and from one of them at this hour of deep dusk, a screech owl's bell-like notes dropped into the still summer air. He lay back for a moment, strangely lulled by the owl's pleasant song. A thousand thoughts crowded upon him, a myriad memories. He saw himself again as the little boy he was, always half-fearful of enjoying himself in these foreboding surroundings, always happy to come and happier to leave.

But he could not lie here, however relaxing it was. There was so much to be done before he could hope to take his departure that he could ill afford to indulge himself in rest and make a poor beginning of his nebulous obligation. He swung himself off the bed, picked up the lamp again, and began a tour of the house.

He went from the bedroom to the dining-room, which was situated between it and the kitchen – a room of stiff, uncomfortable furniture, also handmade – and from there across to the parlour, the door of which opened upon a world far closer in its furniture and decorations to the eighteenth century than to the nineteenth, and far removed from the twentieth. The absence of dust testified to the tightness of the doors closing the room off from the rest of the house. He went up the open stairs to the floor above, from bedroom to bedroom – all dusty, with faded curtains, and showing every sign of having remained unoccupied for many years even before old Luther Whateley died.

Then he came to the passage which led to the shuttered room – Aunt Sarey's hideaway – or prison – he could now never learn what it might have been, and, on impulse, he went down and stood before that forbidden door. No snuffling, no whimpering greeted him now – nothing at all, as he stood before it, remembering, still caught in the spell of the prohibition laid upon him by his grandfather.

But there was no longer any reason to remain under that adjuration. He pulled out the ring of keys, and patiently tried one after another in the lock, until he found the right one. He unlocked the door and pushed; it swung protestingly open. He held the lamp high.

He had expected to find a lady's boudoir, but the shuttered room was startling in its condition – bedding scattered about, pillows on the floor, the remains of food dried on a huge platter hidden behind a bureau. An odd, ichthic smell pervaded the room, rushing at him with such musty strength that he could hardly repress a gasp of disgust. The room was in a shambles; moreover, it wore the aspect of having been in such wild disorder for a long, long time.

Abner put the lamp on a bureau drawn away from the wall, crossed to the window above the mill wheel, unlocked it, and raised it. He strove to open the shutters before he remembered that they had been nailed shut. Then he stood back, raised his foot, and kicked the shutters out to let a welcome blast of fresh, damp air into the room.

He went around to the adjoining outer wall and broke away the shutters from the single window in that wall, as well. It was not until he stood back to survey his work that he noticed he had broken a small corner out of the pane of the window above the mill wheel. His quick regret was as quickly repressed in the memory of his grandfather's insistence that the mill and this room above it be torn down or otherwise destroyed. What mattered a broken pane!

He returned to take up the lamp again. As he did so, he gave the bureau a shove to push it back against the wall once more. At the same moment he heard a small, rustling sound along the baseboard, and, looking down, caught sight of a long-legged frog or toad – he could not make out which – vanishing under the bureau. He was tempted to rout the creature out, but he reflected that its presence could not matter – if it had existed in these locked quarters for so long on such cockroaches and other insects as it had managed to uncover, it merited being left alone.

He went out of the room, locked the door again, and returned to the master bedroom downstairs. He felt, obscurely, that he had made a beginning, however trivial; he had scouted the ground, so to speak. And he was twice as tired for his brief look around as he had been before. Though the hour was not late, he decided to go to bed and get an early start in the morning. There was the old mill yet to be gone through – perhaps some of the machinery could be sold, if any remained – and the mill wheel was now a curiosity, having continued to exist beyond its time.

He stood for a few minutes on the verandah, marking with surprise the welling stridulation of the crickets and katydids, and the almost overwhelming choir of the whippoorwills and frogs, which rose on all sides to assault him with a deafening insistence of such proportion as to drown out all other sounds, even such as might have risen from Dunwich. He stood there until he could tolerate the voices of the night no longer; then he retreated, locking the door, and made his way to the bedroom.

He undressed and got into bed, but he did not sleep for almost an hour, bedevilled by the chorus of natural sounds outside the house and from within himself by a rising confusion about what his grandfather had meant by the 'dissolution' he himself had not been able to make. But at last he drifted into a troubled sleep.

II

He woke with the dawn, little rested. All night he had dreamed of strange places and beings that filled him with beauty and wonder and dread – of swimming in the ocean's depths and up the Miskatonic among fish and amphibia and strange men, half batrachian in aspect – of monstrous entities that lay sleeping in an eerie stone city at the bottom of the sea – of utterly *outré* music as of flutes accompanied by weird ululations from throats far, far from human – of Grandfather Luther Whateley standing accusingly before him and thundering forth his wrath at him for having dared to enter Aunt Sarey's shuttered room.

He was troubled, but he shrugged his unease away before the necessity of walking into Dunwich for the provisions he had neglected to bring with him in his haste. The morning was bright and sunny; peewees and thrushes sang, and dew pearled on leaf and blade reflected the sunlight in a thousand jewels along the winding path that led to the main street of the village. As he went along, his spirits rose; he whistled happily, and contemplated the early fulfilment of his obligation, upon which his escape from this desolate, forgotten pocket of ingrown humanity was predicated.

But the main street of Dunwich was no more reassuring under the light of the sun than it had been in the dusk of the past evening. The village huddled between the Miskatonic and the almost vertical slope of Round Mountain, a dark and brooding settlement which seemed somehow never to have passed 1900, as if time had ground to a stop before the turn of the last century. His gay whistle faltered and died away; he averted his eyes from the buildings falling into ruin; he avoided the curiously expressionless faces of passers-by, and went directly to the old church with its general store, which he knew he would find slovenly and ill-kept, in keeping with the village itself.

A gaunt-faced storekeeper watched his advance down the aisle, searching his features for any familiar lineament.

Abner strode up to him and asked for bacon, coffee, eggs and milk.

The storekeeper peered at him. He made no move. 'Ye'll be a Whateley,' he said at last. 'I dun't expeck ye know me. I'm yer cousin Tobias. Which one uv 'em are ye?'

'I'm Abner – Luther's grandson.' He spoke reluctantly.

Tobias Whateley's face froze. 'Libby's boy – Libby, that married cousin Jeremiah. Yew folks ain't back – back at Luther's? Yew folks ain't a-goin' to start things again?'

'There's no one but me,' said Abner shortly. 'What things are you talking about?'

'If ye dun't know, taint fer me to say.'

Nor would Tobias Whateley speak again. He put together what Abner wanted, took his money sullenly, and watched him out of the store with ill-concealed animosity.

Abner was disagreeably affected. The brightness of the morning had dimmed for him, though the sun shone from the same unclouded heaven. He hastened away from the store and main street, and hurried along the lane towards the house he had but recently quitted.

He was even more disturbed to discover, standing before the house, an ancient rig drawn by an old work-horse. Beside it stood a boy, and inside it sat an old, white-bearded man, who, at sight of Abner's approach, signalled to the boy for assistance, and by the lad's aid, laboriously descended to the ground and stood to await Abner.

As Abner came up, the boy spoke, unsmiling. 'Great-grampa'll talk to yew.'

'Abner,' said the old man quaveringly, and Abner saw for the first time how very old he was.

'This here's Great-grampa Zebulon Whateley,' said the boy.

Grandfather Luther Whateley's brother – the only living Whateley of his generation. 'Come in, sir,' said Abner, offering the old man his arm.

Zebulon Whateley took it.

The three of them made slow progress towards the verandah, where the old man halted at the foot of the steps, turning his dark eyes upon Abner from under their bushy white brows, and shaking his head gently.

'Naow, if ye'll fetch me a cheer, I'll set.'

'Bring a chair from the kitchen, boy,' said Abner.

The boy sped up the steps and into the house. He was out as fast with a chair for the old man, and helped to lower him to it, and stood beside him while Zebulon Whateley caught his breath.

Presently he turned his eyes full upon Abner and contemplated him, taking in every detail of his clothes, which, unlike his own, were not made by hand.

'Why have ye come, Abner?' he asked, his voice firmer now.

Abner told him, as simply and directly as he could.

Zebulon Whateley shook his head. 'Ye know no more'n the rest, and less'n some,' he said. 'What Luther was abaout, only God knowed. Naow Luther's gone, and ye'll have it to dew. I kin tell ye, Abner, I vaow afur God, I dun't know why Luther took on so and locked hisself up and Sarey that time she come back Innsmouth – but I kin say it was suthin' turrible, turrible – and the things what happened was turrible. Ain't nobody left to say Luther was to blame, nor poor Sarey – but take care, take care, Abner.'

'I expect to follow my grandfather's wishes,' said Abner.

The old man nodded. But his eyes were troubled, and it was plain that he had little faith in Abner.

'How'd you find out I was here, Uncle Zebulon?' Abner asked.

'I had the word ye'd come. It was my bounden duty to talk to ye. The Whateleys has a curse on 'em. Thar's been them naow gone to graoun' has had to dew with the devil, and thar's some what whistled turrible things aout o' the air, and thar's some what had to dew with things that wasn't all human nor all fish but lived in the water and swum aout – way aout – to sea, and thar's some what growed in on themselves and got all mazed and queer – and that's what happened on Sentinel Hill that time – Lavinny's Wilbur – and that other one by the Sentinel Stone – Gawd, I shake when I think on it. . . .'

'Now, Grandpa – don't ye git yer dander up,' chided the boy.

'I wunt, I wun't,' said the old man tremulously. 'It's all died away naow. It's forgot – by all but me and them what took the signs daown – the signs that pointed to Dunwich, sayin, it was too turrible a place to know about. . . .' He shook his head and was silent.

'Uncle Zebulon,' said Abner. 'I never saw my Aunt Sarah.'

'No, no, boy – she was locked up that time. Afore you was borned, I think it was.'

'Why?'

'Only Luther knowed – and Gawd. Now Luther's gone, and Gawd dun't seem like He knowed Dunwich was still here.'

'What was Aunt Sarah doing in Innsmouth?'

'Visitin' kin.'

'Are there Whateleys there, too?'

'Not Whateleys. Marshes. Old Obed Marsh that was Pa's cousin. Him and his wife that he faound in the trade – at Ponape, if ye know whar that is.'

'I do.'

'Ye dew? I never knowed. They say Sarey was visitin' Marsh kin – Obed's son or grandson – I never knowed which. Never heerd. Dun't care. She was thar quite a spell. They say when she come back she was different. Flighty. Unsettled. Sassed her pa. And then, not long ofter, he locked her up in that room till she died.'

'How long after?'

'Three, four months. And Luther never said what fer. Nobody saw her again after that till the day she wuz laid aout in her coffin. Two year, might be three year ago. Thar was that time nigh on to a year after she come back from Innsmouth thar was sech goins-on here at this house – a-fightin' and a-screamin' and a-screechin' – most everyone in Dunwich heerd it, but no one went to see whut it was, and next day Luther he said it was only Sarey took with a spell. Might be it was. Might be it was suthin' else. . . .'

'What else, Uncle Zebulon?'

'Devil's work,' said the old man instantly. 'But I fergit – ye're the eddicated one. Ain't many Whateleys ever bin eddicated. Thar was Lavinny – she read them turrible books what was no good for her. And Sarey – she read some. Them as has only a little learnin' might's well have none – they ain't fit to handle life with only a little learnin', they're fitter with none a-tall.'

Abner smiled.

'Dun't ye laugh, boy!'

'I'm not laughing, Uncle Zebulon. I agree with you.'

'Then ef ye come face to face with it, ye'll know what to dew. Ye wun't stop and think – ye'll jest dew.'

'With what?'

'I wisht I knowed, Abner. I dun't. Gawd knows. Luther knowed. Luther's dead. It comes on me Sarey knowed, too. Sarey's dead. Now nobody knows whut turrible thing it was. Ef I was a prayin' man, I'd pray you dun't find aout – but if ye dew, dun't stop to figger it aout by eddication, jest dew whut ye have to dew. Yer Grandpa kep' a record – look fer it. Ye might learn whut kind a people the Marshes was – they wasn't like us – suthin' turrible happened to 'em – and might be it reached aout and tetched Sarey. . . .'

Something stood between the old man and Abner Whateley – something unvoiced, perhaps unknown; but it was something that cast a chill about Abner for all his conscious attempt to belittle what he felt.

'I'll learn what I can, Uncle Zebulon,' he promised.

The old man nodded and beckoned to the boy. He signified that he wished to rise, to return to the buggy. The boy came running.

'Ef ye need me, Abner, send word to Tobias,' said Zebulon Whateley. 'I'll come – ef I can.'

'Thank you.'

Abner and the boy helped the old man back into the buggy. Zebulon Whateley raised his forearm in a gesture of farewell, the boy whipped up the horse, and the buggy drew away.

Abner stood for a moment looking after the departing vehicle. He was both troubled and irritated – troubled at the suggestion of something dreadful which lurked beneath Zebulon Whateley's words of warning, irritated because his grandfather, despite all his adjurations, had left him so little to act upon. Yet this must have been because his grandfather evidently believed there might be nothing untoward to greet his grandson when at last Abner Whateley arrived at the old house. It could be nothing other by way of explanation.

Yet Abner was not entirely convinced. Was the matter one of such horror that Abner should not know of it unless he had to? Or had Luther Whateley laid down a key to the riddle elsewhere in the house? He doubted it. It would not be grandfather's way to seek the devious when he had always been so blunt and direct.

He went into the house with his groceries, put them away, and sat down to map out a plan of action. The very first thing to be accomplished was a survey of the mill part of the structure, to determine whether any machinery could be salvaged. Next he must find someone who would undertake to tear down the mill and the room above it. Thereafter he must dispose of the house and adjoining property, though he had a sinking feeling of futility at the conviction that he would never find anyone who would want to settle in so forlorn a corner of Massachusetts as Dunwich.

He began at once to carry out his obligations.

His search of the mill, however, disclosed that the machinery which had been in it – save for such pieces as were fixed to the running of the wheel – had been removed and presumably sold. Perhaps the increment from the sale was part of that very legacy Luther Whateley had deposited in the bank at Arkham for his grandson. Abner was thus spared the necessity of removing the machinery before beginning the planned demolition. The dust in the old mill almost suffocated him; it lay an inch thick over everything, and it rose in great gusts to cloud about him when he walked through the empty, cobwebbed rooms. Dust muffled his footsteps and he was glad to leave the mill to go around and look at the wheel.

He worked his way around the wooden ledge to the frame of the wheel, somewhat uncertain, lest the wood give way and plunge him into the water beneath; but the construction was firm, the wood did not give, and he was soon at the wheel. It appeared to be a splendid example of middle nineteenth-century work. It would be a shame to tear it apart, thought Abner. Perhaps the wheel could be removed, and a place could be found for it either in some museum or in some one of those buildings which were for ever being reconstructed by wealthy persons interested in the preservation of the American heritage.

He was about to turn away from the wheel, when his eye was caught by a series of small wet prints on the paddles. He bent closer to examine them, but, apart from ascertaining that they were already in part dried, he could not see in them more than marks left by some small animal, probably batrachian – a frog or a toad – which had apparently mounted the wheel in the early hours before the rising of the sun. His eyes, raising, followed the line of the wheel to the broken out shutters of the room above.

He stood for a moment, thinking. He recalled the batrachian creature he had glimpsed along the baseboard of the shuttered room. Perhaps it had escaped through the broken pane? Or, more likely, perhaps another of its kind had discovered its presence and gone up to it. A faint apprehension stirred in him, but he brushed it away in irritation that a man of his intelligence should have been sufficiently stirred by the aura of ignorant, superstitious mystery clinging to his grandfather's memory to respond to it.

Nevertheless, he went around and mounted the stairs to the shuttered room. He half expected, when he unlocked the door, to find some significant change in the aspect of the room as he remembered it from last night, but, apart from the unaccustomed daylight streaming into the room, there was no alteration.

He crossed to the window.

There were prints on the sill. There were two sets of them. One appeared to be leading out, the other entering. They were not the same size. The prints leading outward were tiny, only half an inch across. Those leading in were double that size. Abner bent close and stared at them in fixed fascination.

He was not a zoologist, but he was by no means ignorant of zoology. The prints on the sill were like nothing he had ever seen before, not even in dream. Save for being or seeming to be webbed, they were the perfect prints in miniature of human hands and feet.

Though he made a cursory search for the creature, he saw no sign of it, and finally, somewhat shaken, he retreated from the room and locked the door behind him, already regretting the impulse which had led him to it in the first place and which had caused him to burst open the shutters which for so long had walled the room away from the outer world.

III

He was not entirely surprised to learn that no one in Dunwich could be found to undertake the demolition of the mill. Even such carpenters as those who had not worked for a long time were reluctant to undertake the task, pleading a variety of excuses, which Abner easily recognized as a disguise for the superstitious fear of the place under which one and all laboured. He found it necessary to drive into Aylesbury, but, though he encountered no difficulty in engaging a trio of husky young men who had formed a partnership to tear down the mill, he was forced to wait upon their previous commitments and had to return to Dunwich with the promise that they would come 'in a week or ten days.'

Thereupon he set about at once to examine into all the effects of Luther Whateley which still remained in the house. There were stacks of newspapers – chiefly the *Arkham Advertiser* and the *Aylesbury Transcript* – now yellowing with age and mouldering with dust, which he set aside for burning. There were books which he determined to go over individually in order that he might not destroy anything of value. And there were letters which he would have burned at once had he not happened to glance into one of them and caught sight of the name 'Marsh,' at which he read on.

'Luther, what happened to cousin Obed is a singular thing. I do not know how to tell it to you. I do not know how to make it credible. I am not sure I have all the facts in this matter. I cannot believe but that it is a rigmarole deliberately invented to conceal something of a scandalous nature, for you know the Marshes have always been given to exaggeration and had a pronounced flair for deception. Their ways are devious. They have always been.

'But the story, as I have it from cousin Alizah, is that when he was a young man Obed and some others from Innsmouth, sailing their trading ships into the Polynesian Islands, encountered there a strange people who called themselves the "Deep Ones" and who had the ability to live either in the water or on the earth. Amphibians, they would then be. Does this sound credible to you? It does not to me. What is most astonishing is that Obed and some others married women of these people and brought them home to live with them.

'Now that is the *legend*. Here are the *facts*. Ever since that time, the Marshes have prospered mightily in the trade. Mrs. Marsh is never seen abroad, save on such occasions as she goes to certain closed affairs of the Order of Dagon Hall. "Dagon" is said to be a sea god. I know nothing of these pagan religions, and wish to know nothing. The Marsh children have *a very strange* look. I do not exaggerate, Luther, when I tell you that they have such wide mouths and such chinless faces and such large staring eyes that I swear they sometimes look more like frogs than human beings! They are not, at least as far as I can see, *gilled*. The "Deep Ones" are said to be possessed of gills, and to belong to Dagon or to some other deity of the sea whose name I cannot even pronounce, far less set down. No matter. It is such a rigmarole as the Marshes might well invent to serve their purposes, but by God, Luther, judging by the way the ships Captain Marsh has in the East India trade keep afloat without a smitchin of damage done to them by storm or wear – the brigantine *Columbia*, the barque *Sumatra Queen*, the brig *Hetty* and some others – it might also seem that he has made some sort of bargain with Neptune himself!

'Then there are all the doings off the coast where the Marshes live. Night swimming. They swim way out off Devil Reef, which, as you know, is a mile and a half out from the harbour here at Innsmouth. People keep away from the Marshes – except the Martins and some such others among them who were also in the East India trade. Now that Obed is gone – and I suppose Mrs. Marsh may be also, since she is no longer seen anywhere – the children and the grandchildren of old Captain Obed follow in his strange ways.'

The letter dwindled down to commonplaces about prices – ridiculously low figures seen from this vantage of over half a century later, for Luther Whateley must have been a young man, unmarried, at the time this letter had been written to him by Ariah, a cousin of whom Abner had never heard. What it had to say of the Marshes was nothing – or all, perhaps, if Abner had had the key to the puzzle of which, he began to believe with mounting irritation, he held only certain disassociated parts.

But if Luther Whateley had believed this rigmarole, would he, years later, have permitted his daughter to visit the Marsh cousins? Abner doubted it.

He went through other letters – bills, receipts, trivial accounts of journeys made to Boston, Newburyport, Kingsport – postcards, and came at last to another letter from Cousin Ariah, written, if a comparison of dates was sufficient evidence, immediately after the one Abner had just read. They were ten days apart, and Luther would have had time to reply to that first.

Abner opened it eagerly.

The first page was an account of certain small family matters pertinent to the marriage of another cousin, evidently a sister of Ariah's; the second a speculation about the future of the East India trade, with a paragraph about a new book by Whitman – evidently Walt; but the third was manifestly in answer to something Grandfather Whateley had evidently written concerning the Marsh branch of the family.

'Well, Luther, you may be right in this matter of race prejudice as responsible for the feeling against the Marshes. I know how people here feel about other races. It is unfortunate, perhaps, but such is their lack of education that they find much room for such prejudices. But I am not convinced that it is *all* due to race prejudice. I don't know what kind of race it is that would give the Marshes after Obed that strange *look*. The East India people – such as I have seen and recall from my early days in the trade – have features much like our own, and only a different colour to the skin – copper, I would call it. Once I did see a native who had a similar appearance, but he was evidently not typical, for he was shunned by all the workers around the ships in the harbour where I saw him. I've forgotten now where it was, but I think Ponape.

'To give them their due, the Marshes keep pretty much to themselves – or to those families living here under the same cloud. And they more or less run the town. It may be significant – it may have been accident – that one selectman who spoke out against them was found drowned soon after. I am the first to admit that coincidences more startling than this frequently occur, but you may be sure that people who disliked the Marshes made the most of this.

'But I know how your analytical mind is cold to such talk; I will spare you more of it.'

Thereafter not a word. Abner went through bundles of letters in vain. What Ariah wrote in subsequent letters dealt scrupulously with family matters of the utmost triviality. Luther Whateley had evidently made his displeasure with mere gossip clear; even as a young man, Luther must have been strictly self-disciplined. Abner found but one further reference to any mystery at Innsmouth – that was a newspaper clipping dealing in very vague terms, suggesting that the reporter who sent in the story did not really know what had taken place, with certain Federal activity in and near Innsmouth in 1928 – the attempted destruction of Devil Reef, and the blowing up of large sections of the waterfront, together with wholesale arrests of Marshes and Martins and some others. But this event was decades removed from Ariah's early letters.

Abner put the letters dealing with the Marshes into his pocket, and summarily burned the rest, taking the mass of material he had gone through out along the riverbank and setting fire to it. He stood guarding it, lest a chance wind carry a spark to surrounding grass, which was unseasonably dry. He welcomed the smell of the smoke, however, for a certain dead odour lingered along the riverbank, rising from the remains of fish upon which some animal had feasted – an otter, he thought.

As he stood beside the fire, his eyes roved over the old Whate-

ley building, and he saw, with a rueful reflection that it was
high time the mill were coming down, that several panes of
the window he had broken in the room that had been Aunt
Sarey's, together with a portion of the frame, had fallen out.
Fragments of the window were scattered on the paddles of the
mill wheel.

By the time the fire was sufficiently low to permit his leaving
it, the day was drawing to a close. He ate a meagre supper, and,
having had his fill of reading for the day, decided against at-
tempting to turn up his grandfather's 'record' of which Uncle
Zebulon Whateley had spoken, and went out to watch the dusk
and the night from the verandah, hearing again the rising chorus
of the frogs and whippoorwills.

He retired early, unwontedly weary.

Sleep, however, would not come. For one thing, the summer
night was warm; hardly a breath of air stirred. For another,
even above the ululation of the frogs and the demoniac insistence of the whippoorwills, sounds from within the house
invaded his consciousness – the creaks and groans of a many-
timbered house settling in for the night; a peculiar scuffling or
shuffling sound, half-drag, half-hop, which Abner laid to rats,
which must abound in the mill section of the structure – and
indeed, the noises were muffled, and seemed to reach him as
from some distance; and, at one time, the cracking of wood and
the tinkle of glass, which, Abner guessed, very probably came
from the window above the mill wheel. The house was virtually
falling to pieces about him; it was as if he served as a catalytic
agent to bring about the final dissolution of the old structure.

This concept amused him because it struck him that, willy-
nilly, he was carrying out his grandfather's adjuration. And, so
bemused, he fell asleep.

He was awakened early in the morning by the ringing of the
telephone, which he had had the foresight to have connected
for the duration of his visit to Dunwich. He had already taken
down the receiver from the ancient instrument attached to the
wall before he realized that the call was on a party line and not
intended for him. Nevertheless, the woman's voice that leapt

out at him, burst open his ear with such screaming insistence that he remained frozen to the telephone.

'I tell ye, Mis' Corey, I heard things las' night – the graoun' was a-talkin' agen, and along abaout midnight I heerd that scream – I never figgered a caow'd scream that way – jest like a rabbit, only deeper. That was Lutey Sawyer's cow – they faoun' her this morning – more 'n haff et by animals. . . .'

'Mis' Bishop, you dun't s'pose . . . it's come back?'

'I dun't know. I hope t' Gawd it ain't. But it's the same as the las' time.'

'Was it jest that one caow took?'

'Jes the one. I ain't heerd abaout no more. But that's how it begun the las' time, Mis' Corey.'

Quietly, Abner replaced the receiver. He smiled grimly at this evidence of the rampant superstitions of the Dunwich natives. He had never really known the depths of ignorance and superstition in which dwellers in such out-of-the-way places as Dunwich lived, and this manifestation of it was, he was convinced, but a mild sample.

He had little time, however, to dwell upon the subject, for he had to go into town for fresh milk, and he strode forth into the morning of sun and clouds with a certain feeling of relief at such brief escape from the house.

Tobias Whateley was uncommonly sullen and silent at Abner's entrance. Abner sensed not only resentment, but a certain tangible fear. He was astonished. To all Abner's comments Tobias replied in muttered monosyllables. Thinking to make conversation, he began to tell Tobias what he had overheard on the party line.

'I know it,' said Tobias, curtly, for the first time gazing at Abner's face with naked terror.

Abner was stunned into silence. Terror vied with animosity in Tobias's eyes. His feelings were plain to Abner before he dropped his gaze and took the money Abner offered in payment.

'Yew seen Zebulon?' he asked in a low voice.

'He was at the house,' said Abner.

'Yew talk to him?'

'We talked.'

It seemed as if Tobias expected that certain matters had passed between them, but there was that in his attitude that suggested he was puzzled by subsequent events, which seemed to indicate that Zebulon had not told him what Tobias had expected the old man to tell him, or else that Abner had disregarded some of his Uncle's advice. Abner began to feel completely mystified; added to the superstitious talk of the natives on the telephone, to the strange hints Uncle Zebulon had dropped, this attitude of his cousin Tobias filled him with utter perplexity. Tobias, no more than Zebulon, seemed inclined to come out frankly and put into words what lay behind his sullen features – each acted as if Abner, as a matter of course, should know.

In his bafflement, he left the store, and walked back to the Whateley house determined to hasten his tasks as much as he could so that he might get away from this forgotten hamlet with its queer, superstition-ridden people, for all that many of them were his relatives.

To that end, he returned to the task of sorting his grandfather's things as soon as he had had his breakfast, of which he ate very little, for his disagreeable visit to the store had dulled the appetite which he had felt when he had set out for the store earlier.

It was not until late afternoon that he found the record he sought – an old ledger, in which Luther Whateley had made certain entries in his crabbed hand.

IV

By the light of the lamp, Abner sat down to the kitchen table after he had had a small repast, and opened Luther Whateley's ledger. The opening pages had been torn out, but from an examination of the fragments of sheets still attached to the threads of the sewing, Abner concluded that these pages were purely of accounts, as if his grandfather had taken up an old, not completely used account book for a purpose other than keeping accounts, and had removed such sheets as had been more prosaically utilized.

From the beginning, the entries were cryptic. They were undated, except for the day of the week.

'This Saturday Ariah answered my inquiry. S. was seen sevtimes with Ralsa Marsh. Obed's great-grandson. *Swam* together by night.'

Such was the first entry, clearly pertaining to Aunt Sarey's visit to Innsmouth, about which Grandfather had plainly inquired of Ariah. Something had impelled Luther to make such inquiry. From what he knew of his grandfather's character, Abner concluded that the inquiry had been made after Sarey had returned to Dunwich.

Why?

The next entry was pasted in, and was clearly part of a typewritten letter received by Luther Whateley.

'Ralsa Marsh is probably the most repellent of all the family. He is almost *degenerate* in his looks. I know you have said that it was Libby of your daughters who was the fairest; even so, we cannot imagine how Sarah came to take up with someone who is so repulsive as Ralsa, in whom all those recessive characteristics which have been seen in the Marsh family after Obed's strange marriage to that Polynesian woman – (the Marshes have denied that Obed's wife was Polynesian, but of course, he was trading there at that time, and I don't credit those stories about that uncharted island where he was supposed to have dallied) – seem to have come to fullest fruit.

'As far as I can now ascertain – after all, it is over two months – close to four, I think – since her return to Dunwich – they were constantly together. I am surprised that Ariah did not inform you of this. None of us here had any mandate to halt Sarah's seeing Ralsa, and, after all, they are cousins and she was visiting at Marshes – not here.'

Abner judged that this letter had been written by a woman, also a cousin, who bore Luther some resentment for Sarah's not having been sent to stay with her branch of the family. Luther had evidently made enquiry of her regarding Ralsa.

The third entry was once again in Luther's hand, summarizing a letter from Ariah.

'Saturday. Ariah maintains Deep Ones a sect or quasi-religious group. Sub-human. Said to live in the sea and worship Dagon. Another God named Cthulhu. Gilled people. Resembling frogs or toads more than fish, but eyes ichthic. Claims Obed's late wife was one. Holds that Obed's children all bore the marks. Marshes gilled? How else could they swim a mile and a half to Devil Reef, and back? Marshes eat sparingly, can go without food and drink a long time, diminish or expand in size rapidly.' (To this Luther had appended four scornful exclamation marks.)

'Zadok Allen swears he saw Sarah swimming out to Devil Reef. Marshes carrying her along. All *naked*. Swears he saw Marshes with tough, warty skin. Some with *scales*, like fish! Swears he saw them chase and eat fish! Tear them apart like animals.'

The next entry was again a portion of a letter, patently a reply to one from Grandfather Whateley.

'You ask who is responsible for those *ridiculous* tales about the Marshes. Well, Luther, it would be impossible to single out any one or a dozen people over several generations. I agree that old Zadok Allen talks too much, drinks, and may be romancing. But he is only one. The fact is this legendry – or *rigmarole,* as you call it – has grown up from one generation to the next. Through three generations. You have only to look at some of the descendants of Captain Obed to understand why this could have come about. There are some Marsh offspring said to have been too horrible to look upon. Old wives' tales? Well, Dr. Rowley Marsh was too ill to attend one of the Marsh women one time; so they had to call Dr. Gilman, and Gilman always said that what he delivered was less than human. And nobody ever saw that particular Marsh, though there were people later who claimed to have seen *things moving on two legs that weren't human.*'

Following this there was but a brief but revealing entry in two words: 'Punished Sarah.'

This must then mark the date of Sarah Whateley's confinement to the room above the mill. For some time after this entry, there was no mention of his daughter in Luther's script. Instead, his jottings were not dated in any way, and, judging by the difference in the colour of the ink, were made at different times, though run together.

'Many frogs. Seem to bear in on the mill. Seem to be more than in the marshes across the Miskatonic. Sleeping difficult. Are whippoorwills on the increase, too, or is this imagination? ... Counted thirty-seven frogs at the porch steps tonight.'

There were more entries of this nature. Abner read them all, but there was no clue in them to what the old man had been getting at. Luther Whateley had thereafter kept book on frogs, fog, fish and their movements in the Miskatonic – when they rose and leaped from the water, and so on. This seemed to be unrelated data, and was not in any way connected to the problem of Sarah.

There was another hiatus after this series of notes, and then came a single, underscored entry.

'*Ariah was right!*'

But about what had Ariah been right? Abner wondered. And how had Luther Whateley learned that Ariah had been right? There was no evidence that Ariah and Luther had continued their correspondence, or even that Ariah desired to write to the crotchety Luther without a letter of direct inquiry from Luther.

There followed a section of the record to which newspaper clippings had been pasted. These were clearly unrelated, but they did establish for Abner the fact that somewhat better than a year had passed before Luther's next entry, one of the most puzzling Abner found. Indeed, the time hiatus seemed to be closer to two years.

'R. out again.'

If Luther and Sarah were the only people in the house, who was 'R.'? Could it have been Ralsa Marsh come to visit? Abner doubted it, for there was nothing to show that Ralsa Marsh harboured any affection for his distant cousin, or certainly he would have pursued her before this.

The next notation seemed to be unrelated.

'Two turtles, one dog, remains of woodchuck. Bishop's – two cows, found on the Miskatonic end of the pasture.'

A little further along, Luther had set down further such data.

'After one month a total of 17 cattle, 6 sheep. Hideous alterations; size commensurate with amt. of food. Z. over. Anxious about talk going around.'

Could Z. stand for Zebulon? Abner thought it did. Evidently then Zebulon had come in vain, for he had left him, Abner, with only vague and uncertain hints about the situation at the house when Aunt Sarey was confined to the shuttered room. Zebulon, on the evidence of such conversation as he had shared with Abner, knew less than Abner himself did after reading his grandfather's record. But he did know of Luther's record; so Luther must have told him he had set down certain facts.

These notations, however, were more in the nature of notes for something to be completed later; they were unaccountably cryptic, unless one had the key of basic knowledge which belonged to Luther Whateley. But a growing sense of urgency was clearly manifest in the old man's further entries.

'Ada Wilkerson gone. Trace of scuffle. Strong feeling in Dunwich. John Sawyer shook his fist at me – safely across the street, where I couldn't reach him.'

'Monday. Howard Willie this time. They found one shoe, with the foot still in it!'

The record was now near its end. Many pages, unfortunately, had been detached from it – some with violence – but no clue remained as to why this violence had been done to Grandfather Whateley's account. It could not have been done by anyone but Luther himself; perhaps, thought Abner, Luther felt he had told too much, and intended to destroy anything which might put a later reader on the track of the true facts regarding Aunt

Sarey's confinement for the rest of her life. He had certainly succeeded.

The next entry once again referred to the elusive 'R.'

'R. back at last.'

Then, 'Nailed the shutters to the windows of Sarah's room.'

And at last: 'Once he has lost weight, he must be kept on a careful diet and to a controllable size.'

In a way, this was the most enigmatic entry of them all. Was 'he' also 'R.'? If so, why must he be kept on a careful diet, and what did Luther Whateley mean by controlling his size? There was no ready answer to these questions in such material as Abner had read thus far, either in this record – or the fragmentary account still left in the record – or in letters previously perused.

He pushed away the record-book, resisting an impulse to burn it. He was exasperated, all the more so because he was uneasily aware of an urgent need to learn the secret embalmed within this old building.

The hour was now late; darkness had fallen some time ago, and the ever-present clamour of the frogs and the whippoorwills had begun once more, rising all around the house. Pushing from his thoughts briefly the apparently unconnected jottings he had been reading, he called from his memory the superstitions of the family, representing those prevalent in the countryside – associating frogs and the calling of whippoorwills and owls with death, and from this meditation progressed readily to the amphibian link which presented itself – the presence of the frogs brought before his mind's eye a grotesque caricature of one of the Marsh clan of Innsmouth, as described in the letters Luther Whateley had saved for so many years.

Oddly, this very thought, for all that it was so casual, startled him. The insistence of frogs and toads on singing and calling in the vicinity was truly remarkable. Yet, batrachia had always been plentiful in the Dunwich vicinity, and he had no way of knowing for how long a period before his arrival they had been calling about the old Whateley house. He discounted the suggestion that his arrival had anything at all to do with it; more than likely, the proximity of the Miskatonic and a low, swampy area immediately across the river on the edge of Dunwich, accounted for the presence of so many frogs.

His exasperation faded away; his concern about the frogs did likewise. He was weary. He got up and put the record left by Luther Whateley carefully into one of his bags, intending to carry it away with him, and to puzzle over it until some sort of meaning came out of it. Somewhere there must exist a clue. If certain horrible events had taken place in the vicinity, something more in the way of a record must exist than Luther Whateley's spare notes. It would do no good to inquire of Dunwich people; Abner knew they would maintain a close-mouthed silence before an 'outsider' like himself, for all that he was related to many of them.

It was then that he thought of the stacks of newspapers, still set aside to be burned. Despite his weariness, he began to go through packs of the *Aylesbury Transcript,* which carried, from time to time, a Dunwich department.

After an hour's hasty search, he found three vague articles, none of them in the regular Dunwich columns, which corroborated entries in Luther Whateley's ledger. The first appeared under the heading: *Wild Animal Slays Stock Near Dunwich* –

'Several cows and sheep have been slain on farms just outside Dunwich by what appears to be a wild animal of some kind. Traces left at the scenes of the slaughter suggest some large beast, but Professor Bethnall of Miskatonic University's anthropology department points out that it is not inconceivable that packs of wolves could lurk in the wild hill country around Dunwich. No beast of the size suggested by the traces reported was ever known to inhabit the eastern seaboard within the memory of man. County officials are investigating.'

Search as he might, Abner could find no follow-up story. He did, however, come upon the story of Ada Wilkerson.

'A widow-lady, Ada Wilkerson, 57, living along the Miskatonic out of Dunwich, may have been the victim of foul play three nights ago. When she failed to visit a friend by appointment in Dunwich, her home was visited. No trace of her was ꞏꞏd. However, the door of her house had been broken in, and the furniture had been wildly thrown about, as if a violent struggle had taken place. A very strong musk is said to have pervaded the entire area. Up to press time today, Mrs. Wilkerson has not been heard from.'

Two subsequent paragraphs reported briefly that authorities had not found any clue to Mrs. Wilkerson's disappearance. The account of a 'large animal' was resurrected, lamely, and Professor Bethnall's beliefs on the possible existence of a wolf-pack, but nothing further, for investigation had disclosed that the missing lady had neither money nor enemies, and no one would have had any motive for killing her.

Finally, there was the account of Howard Willie's death, headed, *Shocking Crime at Dunwich*.

'Some time during the night of the twenty-first Howard Willie, 37, a native of Dunwich, was brutally slain as he was on his way home from a fishing trip along the upper reaches of the Miskatonic. Mr. Willie was attacked about half a mile past the Luther Whateley property, as he walked through an arboured lane. He evidently put up a fierce fight, for the ground is badly torn up in all directions. The poor fellow was overcome, and must have been literally torn limb from limb, for the only physical remains of the victim consisted of his right foot, still encased in its shoe. It had evidently been cruelly torn from his leg by great force.

'Our correspondent in Dunwich advises us that people there are very sullen and in a great rage of anger and fear. They suspect many of their number of being at least partly to blame, though they stoutly deny that anyone in Dunwich murdered either Willie or Mrs. Wilkerson, who disappeared a fortnight ago, and of whom no word has since been heard.'

The account concluded with some data about Willie's family connections. Thereafter, subsequent editions of the *Transcript* were distinguished only for the lack of information about the events which had taken place in Dunwich, where authorities and reporters alike apparently ran up against blank walls in the stolid refusal of the natives to talk or even speculate about what had happened. There was, however, one insistent note which recurred in the comments of investigators, relayed to the press, and that was that such trail or track as could be seen appeared to have disappeared into the waters of the Miskatonic, suggesting that if an animal were responsible for the orgy of slaughter which had occurred at Dunwich, it may have come from and returned to the river.

Though it was now close to midnight, Abner massed the discarded newspapers together and took them out to the riverbank, where he set them on fire, having saved only torn pages relative to the occurrences at Dunwich. The air being still, he did not feel obliged to watch the fire, since he had already burned a considerable area, and the grass was not likely to catch on fire. As he started away, he heard suddenly above the ululation of the whippoorwills and frogs, now at a frenzied crescendo, the tearing and breaking sound of wood. He thought at once of the window of the shuttered room, and retraced his steps.

In the very dim light flickering towards the house from the burning newspapers, it seemed to Abner that the window gaped wider than before. Could it be that the entire mill part of the house was about to collapse? Then, out of the corner of his eye, he caught sight of a singularly formless moving shadow just beyond the mill wheel, and a moment later heard a churning sound in the water. The voices of the frogs had now risen to such a volume that he could hear nothing more.

He was inclined to dismiss the shadow as the creation of the wild flames leaping upward from the fire. The sound in the water might well have been that of the movement made by a school of fish, darting forward in concert. Nevertheless, he thought, it would do no harm to have another look at Aunt Sarey's room.

He returned to the kitchen, took the lamp, and mounted the stairs. He unlocked the door of the shuttered room, threw open the door, and was almost felled by the powerful musk which pushed hallward. The smell of the Miskatonic, of the marshes, the odour of that slimy deposit left on the stones and sunken debris when the Miskatonic receded to its low water stage, the cloying pungence of some animal lairs – all these were combined in the shuttered room.

Abner stood for a moment, wavering on the threshold. True, the odour in the room could have come in through the open window. He raised the lamp so that more of its light fell upon the wall above the mill wheel. Even from where he stood, it was possible to see that not only was all the window itself now gone, but so was the frame. Even at this distance it was manifest that the frame had been broken out *from inside*!

He fell back, slammed the door shut, locked it, and fled downstairs with the shell of his rationalizations tumbling about him.

V

Downstairs, he fought for self control. What he had seen was but one more detail added to the proliferating accumulation of seemingly unrelated data upon which he had stumbled ever since his coming to his grandfather's home. He was convinced now that however unlikely it had at first seemed to him, all these data must be related. What he needed to learn was the one basic fact or element which bound them together.

He was badly shaken, particularly because he had the uneasy conviction that he did indeed have all the facts he needed to know, that it was his scientific training which made it impossible for him to make the primary assumption, to state the premise which the facts before him would inevitably prove. The evidence of his senses told him that something laired in that room – some bestial creature; it was folly to assume that odours from outside could so permeate Aunt Sarey's old room and not be noticeable outside the kitchen and at the windows of his own bedroom.

The habit of rational thinking was strong in him. He took out Luther Whateley's final letter to him once more and read it again. That was what his grandfather had meant when he had written 'you have gone forth into the world and gathered to yourself learning sufficient to permit you to look upon all things with an inquiring mind ridden neither by the superstition of ignorance nor the superstition of science.' Was this puzzle, with all its horrible connotations, beyond rationalization?

The wild ringing of the telephone broke in upon his confused thoughts. Slipping the letter back into his pocket, he strode rapidly to the wall and took the receiver off the hook.

A man's voice screamed over the wire, amid a chaos of inquiring voices as everyone on the line picked up his receiver as if they waited, like Abner Whateley himself, for word of another tragedy. One of the voices – all were disembodied and unidentifiable for Abner – identified the caller.

'It's Luke Lang!'

'Git a posse up an' come quick,' Luke shouted hoarsely over the wire. 'It's jeest aoutside my door. Snufflin' araoun'. Tryin' the door. Feelin' at the winders.'

'Luke, what is it?' asked a woman's voice.

'Oh, Gawd! It's some unairthly thing. It's a hoppin' raoun' like it was too big to move right – like jelly. Oh, hurry, hurry, afore it's too late. It got my dog . . .'

'Git off the wire so's we can call for help,' interrupted another subscriber.

But Luke never heard in his extremity. 'It's a-pushin' at the door – it's a-bowin' the door in . . .'

'Luke! Luke! Git off'n the wire!'

'It's a-trying the winder naow.' Luke Lang's voice rose in a scream of terror. 'There goes the glass. Gawd! Gawd! Hain't yew comin'? Oh, that hand! That turr'ble arm! Gawd! That face . . .!'

Luke's voice died away in a frightful screech. There was the sound of breaking glass and rending wood – then all was still at Luke Lang's, and for a moment all was still along the wire. Then the voices burst forth again in a fury of excitement and fear.

'Git help!'

'We'll meet at Bishop's place.'

And someone put in, 'It's Abner Whateley done it!'

Sick with shock and half-paralysed with a growing aware-

ness, Abner struggled to tear the receiver from his ear, to shut
off the half-crazed bedlam on the party line. He managed it
with an effort. Confused, upset, frightened himself, he stood
for a moment with his head leaning against the wall. His
thoughts seethed around but one central point – the fact that
the Dunwich rustics considered him somehow responsible for
what was happening. And their conviction, he knew intuitively,
was based on more than the countryman's conventional distrust
of the stranger.

He did not want to think of what had happened to Luke
Lang – and to those others. Luke's frightened, agonized voice
still rang in his ears. He pulled himself away from the wall,
almost stumbling over one of the kitchen chairs. He stood for
a moment beside the table, not knowing what to do, but as his
mind cleared a little, he thought only of escape. Yet he was
caught between the desire to get away, and the obligation to
Luther Whateley he had not yet fulfilled.

But he had come, he had gone through the old man's things
– all save the books – he had made arrangements to tear down
the mill part of the house – he could manage its sale through
some agency; there was no need for him to be present. Impulsively, he hastened to the bedroom, threw such things as he had
unpacked, together with Luther Whateley's note-filled ledger,
into his bags, and carried them out to his car.

Having done this, however, he had second thoughts. Why
should he take flight? He had done nothing. No guilt of any
kind rested upon him. He returned to the house. All was still,
save for the unending chorus of frogs and whippoorwills. He
stood briefly undecided; then he sat down at the table and took
out Grandfather Whateley's final letter to read it once more.

He read it over carefully, thoughtfully. What had the old
man meant when, in referring to the madness that had spawned
among the Whateleys, he had said 'It has not been so of all that
is mine' though he himself had kept free of that madness?
Grandmother Whateley had died long before Abner's birth; his
Aunt Julia had died as a young girl; his mother had led a
blameless life. There remained Aunt Sarey. What had been

her madness then? Luther Whateley could have meant none
other. Only Sarey remained. What had she done to bring about
her imprisonment unto death?

And what had he intended to hint at when he adjured Abner
to kill anything in the mill section of the house, anything that
lived? *No matter how small it may be. No matter what form
it may have* ... Even something so small as an inoffensive toad?
A spider? A fly? Luther Whateley wrote in riddles, which in
itself was an affront to an intelligent man. Or did his grandfather think Abner a victim to the superstition of science?
Ants, spiders, flies, various kinds of bugs, millers, centipedes,
daddy long-legs – all occupied the old mill; and doubtless in
its walls were mice as well. Did Luther Whateley expect his
grandson to go about exterminating all these?

Behind him suddenly something struck the window. Glass
fragmented to the floor, together with something heavy. Abner
sprang to his feet and whirled around. From outside came the
sound of running footsteps.

A rock lay on the floor amid the shattered glass. There was
a piece of 'store paper' tied to it by common store string. Abner
picked it up, broke the string, and unfolded the paper.

Crude lettering stared up at him. 'Git out before ye git kilt!'
Store paper and string. It was not meant so much as a threat
as a well-intentioned warning. And it was clearly the work of
Tobias Whateley, thought Abner. He tossed it contemptuously
to the table.

His thoughts were still in turmoil, but he had decided that
precipitate flight was not necessary. He would stay, not only
to learn if his suspicions about Luke Lang were true – as if the
evidence of the telephone left room for doubt – but also to make
a final attempt to fathom the riddle Luther Whateley had left
behind.

He put out the light and went in darkness to the bedroom
where he stretched out fully clothed, upon the bed.

Sleep, however, would not come. He lay probing the maze
of his thoughts, trying to make sense out of the mass of data
he had accumulated, seeking always that basic fact which was

the key to all the others. He felt sure it existed; worse, he was positive that it lay before his eyes – he had but failed to interpret it or to recognize it.

He had been lying there scarcely half an hour, when he heard, rising above the pulsating choir of the frogs and whippoorwills, a splashing from the direction of the Miskatonic – an approaching sound, as if a large wave were washing up the banks on its seaward way. He sat up, listening. But even as he did so, the sound stopped and another took its place – one he was loath to identify, and yet could define as no other than that of someone trying to climb the mill wheel.

He slid off the bed and went out of the room.

From the direction of the shuttered room came a muffled, heavy falling sound – then a curious, choking whimpering that sounded, horribly, like a child at a great distance trying to call out – then all was still, and it seemed that even the noise and clamour of the frogs diminished and fell away.

He returned to the kitchen and lit the lamp.

Pooled in the yellow glow of light, Abner made his way slowly up the stairs towards the shuttered room. He walked softly, carefully to make no sound.

Arriving at the door, he listened. At first he heard nothing – then a susurration smote his ears.

Something in that room – *breathed*!

Fighting back his fear, Abner put the key in the lock and turned it. He flung open the door and held the lamp high.

Shock and horror paralysed him.

There, squatting in the midst of the tumbled bedding from that long-abandoned bed, sat a monstrous, leathery-skinned creature that was neither frog nor man, one gorged with food, with blood still slavering from its batrachian jaws and upon its webbed fingers – a monstrous entity that had strong, powerfully long arms, grown from its bestial body like those of a frog, and tapering off into a man's hands, save for the webbing between the fingers . . .

The tableau held for only a moment.

Then with a frenzied growling sound – '*Eh-ya-ya-ya-yaa-*

haah – ngh'aaa – h'yuh, h'yuh –' it rose up, towering, and launched itself at Abner.

His reaction was instantaneous, born of terrible, shattering knowledge. He flung the kerosene-filled lamp with all his might straight at the thing reaching towards him.

Fire enveloped the thing. It halted and began to tear frantically at its burning body, unmindful of the flames rising from the bedding behind it and the floor of the room, and at the same instant the calibre of its voice changed from a deep growling to a shrill, high wailing – '*Mama-mama – ma-aa-ma-aa-ma-aaah*!'

Abner pulled the door shut and fled.

Down the stairs, half falling, through the rooms below, with his heart pounding madly, and out of the house. He tumbled into the car, almost bereft of his senses, half-blinded by the perspiration of his fear, turned the key in the ignition, and roared away from that accursed place from which the smoke already poured, while spreading flames in that tinder-dry building began to cast a red glow into the sky.

He drove like one possessed – through Dunwich – through the covered bridge – his eyes half-closed, as if to shut out for ever the sight of that which he had seen, while the dark, brooding hills seemed to reach for him and the chanting whippoorwills and frogs mocked him.

But nothing could erase that final, cataclysmic knowledge seared into his mind – the key to which he had had all along and not known it – the knowledge implicit in his own memories as well as in the notes Luther Whateley had left – the chunks of raw meat he had childishly supposed were going to be prepared in Aunt Sarey's room instead of to be *eaten raw,* the reference to 'R.' who had come 'back at last' after having escaped, back to the only home 'R.' knew – the seemingly unrelated references also in his grandfather's hand to missing cows, sheep, and the remains of other animals – the hideous suggestion clearly defined now in those entries of Luther Whateley's about R.'s 'size commensurate with amt. of food,' and 'he must be kept on a careful diet and to a controllable size'

– like the Innsmouth people! – controlled to nothingness after Sarah's death, with Luther hoping that foodless confinement might shrivel the thing in the shuttered room and kill it beyond revival, despite the doubt that had led him to adjure Abner to kill 'anything in it that lives,' – *the thing Abner had unwittingly liberated when he broke the pane and kicked out the shutters, liberated to seek its own food and its hellish growth again, at first with fish from the Miskatonic, then with small animals, then cattle, and at last human beings – the thing that was half-batrachian, half human, but human enough to come back to the only home it had ever known and to cry out in terror for its Mother in the face of the fatal holocaust – the thing that had been born to the unblessed union of Sarah Whateley and Ralsa Marsh, spawn of tainted and degenerate blood, the monster that would loom for ever on the perimeter of Abner Whateley's awareness – his cousin Ralsa, doomed by his grandfather's iron will, instead of being released long ago into the sea to join the Deep Ones amongst the minions of Dagon and great Cthulhu!*

Other Panthers For Your Enjoyment

Science Fiction and Fiction

☐ **H. P. Lovecraft**   **AT THE MOUNTAINS OF MADNESS**   **25p**

A great collection of sinister and uncanny tales for connoisseurs of terror.

☐ **H. P. Lovecraft**   **THE CASE OF CHARLES DEXTER WARD**   **25p**

A short macabre novel by the 20th century's undisputed master of horror.

☐ **Keith Roberts**   **PAVANE**   **30p**

An alternative universe in which 20th century England is still under the grimly reactionary rule of the Roman Church. 'His blend of telling detail, gripping story line and pure exalted fantasy is little short of miraculous' – *Tribune*. 'Brilliant' – *SF Review*

☐ **Roger Zelazny**   **LORD OF LIGHT**   **40p**

'A triumph' said the *Magazine of Fantasy and Science Fiction*. 'A rare work of SF imagination' added the *Sunday Telegraph*. And the final accolade – the Hugo Award. In an era yet to come and a planet far distant from this one a group of way-out men and women, backed by a powerful technology that makes ours look primitive, take over the role of the ancient Hindu pantheon.

☐ **Roger Zelazny**   **THE DREAM MASTER**   **25p**

A mind-stretching story of a lonely voyager's nightmare journey in o the infinity of inner space. By a master of contemporary SF.

☐ **John Blackburn**   **CHILDREN OF THE NIGHT**   **30p**

A pothole on the Yorkshire moors and an ancient race emerging from it to once more – after eons of time – take its 'rightful' place on Earth's surface – 'rightfully' meaning that humans go to the wall. One of the eeriest thrillers published in years. John Blackburn is streets ahead of all his competitors in this field.

Science Fiction

☐ **Theodore Sturgeon**   **E PLURIBUS UNICORN**   25p

Already classic but completely modern stories by a giant of science fiction and fantasy.

☐ **D. F. Jones**   **DON'T PICK THE FLOWERS**   30p

A mohole is drilled deep through Earth's crust – and the trapped nitrogen blows. To escape the horror two men and two girls put out to sea – only to discover that seething nitrogen is the least of their terrors. It's in the classic disaster story tradition of John Wyndham.

☐ **Charles Harness**   **THE ROSE**   25p

Acclaimed by masters of SF – Brian Aldis, Arthur C. Clarke, Michael Moorcock, Judith Merril and many others – as a rare masterpiece.

☐ **Robert A. Heinlein**   **DOUBLE STAR**   25p

A fantastic double-take in deep space and time A vintage example of the unique Heinlein imagination at work. A Hugo Award winner.

☐ **Thomas M. Disch**   **ECHO ROUND HIS BONES**   25p

By the prize winning novelist whose work is *not* just for SF fans, but for all who enjoy the modern novel. A man on the moon meets his exact double who wishes to destroy him.

☐ **J. Z. Ballard**   **THE CRYSTAL WORLD**   30p

Switch off the reality around you and voyage up an African river into one of Ballard's fantastic futures. Accompanying are a couple of adulterous lovers, a manic gunman and a priest who's lost his faith in favour of a very wayout ritual indeed. But for all of them – including the reader – universal crystallisation's what's in store.

Obtainable from all booksellers and newsagents. If you have any difficulty please send purchase price plus 7p postage per book to Panther Cash Sales, P.O. Box 11, Falmouth, Cornwall.

I enclose a cheque/postal order for titles ticked above plus 7p a book to cover postage and packing.

Name...

Address...

....